BACKWARD IN HIGH HEELS

BACKWARD IN HIGH HEELS

Judith Kelman

Severn House Large Print

London & New York

This first large print edition published in Great Britain 2008 by
SEVERN HOUSE LARGE PRINT BOOKS LTD of
9-15 High Street, Sutton, Surrey, SM1 1DF.
First world regular print edition published 2006 by
Severn House Publishers, London and New York.
This first large print edition published in the USA 2008 by
SEVERN HOUSE PUBLISHERS INC., of
595 Madison Avenue, New York, NY 10022.

British Library Cataloguing in Publication Data

Kelman, Judith
  Backward in high heels. - Large print ed.
  1. Adultery - Fiction 2. Separated women - Fiction 3. Large
  type books
  I. Title
  813.5'4[F]

  ISBN-13: 978-0-7278-7658-4

Printed and bound in Great Britain by
MPG Books Ltd, Bodmin, Cornwall.

The Slashed Picture Show

At the worst of times you take your help where you find it, and today mine came in the form of a sociopathic former Mouseketeer. Born unscrupulous, Janine Bookman had pushed and shoved her way to the top of the game as a child actress on the wildly popular Mickey Mouse Club in the 1950s. She now worked down the hall from me, and had a way of showing up when I needed her most, and least.

When Janine barged into my office, I was grappling with the horrifying realization that while a split lip could be camouflaged tolerably well with snips of tape, a busted nose presented a far more daunting challenge. No matter how I nudged and prodded, one nostril flared like a little parachute while the other bunched in a claustrophobic nub. The bridge resembled a rocky outcrop, and pained consternation registered in the eyes with their sockets hopelessly askew. At least such was the case with the snapshots of my future former husband that I had shredded in a hot fit of rage.

Janine's wilting gaze bounced from the partially reconstructed Harolds to me. I was dressed in my standard camouflage: baggy black slacks, black flats, and a speak-no-evil black tunic top. 'Don't tell me you're going like that!'

At that moment, I happened upon a missing ear, asserting itself from a ragged fragment of Harold's skull. With a thrill of relief, I slid it in place beneath the outsized Panama hat that had perched like a laying hen on my husband's head after we boarded a week-long Caribbean cruise in celebration of our silver anniversary almost three years ago.

With a wistful twinge, I recalled how Harold's grin fell away when the giant bow thrusters prodded our ship, *The Island Queen*, from the St Thomas pier. As we trudged out to sea, a playful gust kicked up and the hull responded with a near imperceptible series of hiccoughs. No one else even noticed, but my beloved turned the color of steam-table string beans and lunged for the rail. He spent the rest of the voyage in a medicated stupor in the bottom-of-the-line, way-below-decks cabin he had booked to mark the occasion. The space was so tiny; there was no room for anything as extravagant as claustrophobia. Had Harold been up to the task, the narrow bunk beds would have made sex impossible, if not downright hazardous. Instead, while my husband variously moaned and lunged toward the minuscule bathroom, I slept like a babe, blissfully fatigued by long, languid swims, glorious snorkeling, tasty rum drinks and a torrid (though imaginary) flirtation

6

with the Nicolas Cage look-alike who sang with the band.

'No, of course I'm not going like this, Janine. It's twenty-three degrees out, sixteen with the wind chill. I'm going to wear a coat.'

She leaned in and puffed her exasperation, scattering the scraps I'd painstakingly assembled of a sloppy, affectionate, inebriated Harold making the champagne toast a dozen years ago at our son Brian's bar mitzvah. Peering up at our scruffy-cheeked baby, who had already soared to a gangly six-foot-two, Harold's face had gone all goofy with sentiment and Scotch. 'I am so proud right now of our little big man. I mean, our big little man. Oh, who the hell cares what I mean? Thank you all for coming to help us celebrate this wonderful day with my incredible family. I must say I'm a lucky, lucky man.'

It occurred to me that Harold was always most endearing at times like that, when he bore the least possible resemblance to himself.

Janine broke the reverie. 'Jesus, Maggie, when are you going to stop moping around and move on?'

'I'm trying.'

'Oh, you're trying all right.'

I didn't bother to defend myself, though Janine's assessment struck me as unfair. Hadn't I stopped fixing obsessively on images of Harold and Bethany copulating in all twenty-seven ergonomic positions offered by his Herman Miller Aeron chair? Hadn't I gotten past lying in bed for days on end listening to plaintive Carole King tunes and bawling in my Krispy Kremes? Why, weeks ago, I'd graduated to Alanis Morissette and merely weeping in my Ben & Jerry's. Excellent progress, if you ask me.

'I'm not you, Janine.'

'Nobody is, sweetie.'

'It's a process. You said so yourself. And I'm working through it as best I can. A little while ago, I got furious and ripped up these pictures. But then, I thought: that was childish and silly, Maggie. This is the father of your children.'

Janine rolled her outsized bitter chocolate eyes. 'This is a cock-sucking, Donald Ducking, son of a bitch.'

'Anger won't solve anything. What I need to do is get past all that and move on, as you put it. I have a little time before we meet with the lawyers, so I thought I'd put these back together and drop them off to be copied. Maybe I'll even send a set to Harold. Remind him how gracious and thoughtful I can be.' My voice broke. 'We had a good marriage, Janine. How could he just go crazy like that and throw it all away? What's wrong with him? What's wrong with me?'

'Stop.'

'Stop what?'

'Crying. Carrying on.'

'I'm not,' I said between great blubbering sobs. 'I just want to know how he could do such a thing. What could he be thinking? I don't understand.'

'Come. I'm going to dress you in something fabulous.'

'What for?'

'I haven't got all day, Maggie. Get moving.'

'I am moving.'

'No, you're not. I mean it. Now!'

I sat up, almost vertically. I was merely snuffling. Barely snuffling at all. 'Why bother, Janine? I mean, honestly, what's the point?'

'The better you look, the better you'll feel. The better you feel, the better you'll deal. Trust me.'

'I'm dealing fine.'

'Compared to what?'

'The meeting today is nothing. A stupid settlement conference.'

'Then why are you acting like it's the end of the world?'

I slumped under a fresh weight of terror-laden grief. In truth, I was scared to death. I was afraid to see Harold; terrified that I'd walk out of this meeting divorced; positive that I'd break down and crack in a million pieces in front of everyone. Above all, I was scared that this was actually happening and not just a persistent bad dream.

'Because it is the end of the world?'

'Wrong. Look at it this way. Everything you do is a scene from the Maggie movie, and you get to write, direct and star. That means you take charge. You go for the costume, make-up, lighting, special effects. The works.'

'You mean I try to look as little like my

frumpy, dumpy pathetic self as possible.'

'Exactly.'

'No one would come to this movie, Janine. The producers would lose their shirts.'

'Move!'

Janine's custom couture line, Pandora's Frocks, occupied an enormous suite three doors down from the modest office where I worked as a speech therapist with a specialty in dialect coaching. Her showroom was a jarring blend of Vegas bordello and Versailles, with flocked scarlet chairs, gilt moldings, ornate armoires and antique French settees. In the cramped, dingy workroom at the rear, five sallow, grim-faced women hunched over chunky old sewing machines. Bolts of expensive silks and woolens lined the shelves. Beside the worktables were mannequins posed in the sort of slouchy, jut-hipped poses that would drive my mother insane. Everyone, including the dress forms, seemed to stiffen at the sight of Janine.

She strutted about like a drill sergeant, barking like a child with croup. 'How's that gown coming? Where's the black two-piece? The DeLuca bitch needs it by four sharp!'

Heads nodded stiffly. Thread snapped between skittish teeth.

'Magda, where's the Denison red?'

Magda leveled a knobby finger toward the wall where dozens of dresses, suits, and gowns hung from a long sway-backed chrome rack. Janine flipped through and picked out a striking crimson number with a fitted jacket and a slim skirt with a daring side slit. Perfect for playing peek-a-boo with the varicose veins.

A copy of the order form was pinned to the padded hanger. When Janine came closer, I noticed the name and the price. Who'd have imagined a suit could cost more than the three bedroom, one-and-a-half bath starter house Harold and I had bought fully furnished in '72? The getup was destined for the wardrobe of Letitia Lane Denison, a self-styled socialite and permanent fixture on Mr Blackwell's best-dressed list.

Janine held the ensemble under my chin like a buttercup. 'It's perfect, Maggie. It's you.'

'It's a felony. You can't take Letty Denison's money for an exclusive design and let me run around wearing it.'

'Don't be ridiculous. Letty doesn't have any money. It all comes from little Dickie's trust fund which all comes courtesy of big Dick's daddy, who as rumor has it was the biggest dick of all. Anyhow, Letty's a whiny, arrogant, annoying twit who doesn't deserve all that green. She just happens to be married to someone who happened to win the sperm derby, and I only put up with her out of the incredible goodness of my heart.'

She neglected to mention the incredible goodness of the profit. 'I was just suggesting that she might not appreciate paying that kind of money for used clothing.'

'You think I care what she appreciates?

11

Besides, how would she ever find out?'

'She could accidentally see me in it. It's a small world, after all, as they say in Fantasyland.'

'Who cares? Letty Denison needs me way more than I need her. As far as I'm concerned, that bitch can go to hell in something off-the-rack!' Slamming drawers in the ornate armoire near the door, she pulled out a sapphire silk camisole and a draconian-looking undergarment in a bilious flesh tone. 'Now go put on these mother-ducking things before I get upset!'

'All right.' Saying no to Janine was not a sensible option in much the same way that you wouldn't try to reason with an oncoming train.

The body shaper slid on like a second skin and behaved far more admirably than my first one. As I left the dressing room, I caught sight of myself in the three-way gilt-framed mirror. I peered over my shoulder to get the rear view, and I couldn't help but smile. The magic under-contraption shaved many pints of Chubby Hubby from my waistline and backside, flattened my gelatinous abs, and cast a shadow on my chest that could pass, in low light, for actual cleavage.

'You see?' Janine said.

'It's amazing.'

'Of course it is. It's a genuine Janine. Now sit. We need to accessorize. I'll grab some things from costumes and have Daphne do your hair and make-up.'

'Don't. Really, this is enough.'

'Enough is never enough. Sit! Stay!' She strode off, spike heels spanking the parquet floor.

My eyes drifted to a snapshot of Janine as a gap-toothed six-year-old, looking oddly sinister in her Mickey Mouse Club shirt and black felt ears. Across the top of the white ceramic picture frame, a kick line of red letters with top hats, tap shoes and canes proclaimed: Janine!

Janine spelled her name with the exclamation point, which summed her up quite well. As she told it, the spelling was an artifact of her days on the show. At the start of each Mouse Club episode, every Mouseketeer was expected to burst forth when introduced as if the exclamation point on the announcer's teleprompter was a stick of dynamite bursting, ever so gently, in that child's precious little behind.

Cubby!

Annette!

Maureen!

Janine took the drill to heart. For years, any mention of her name launched her in a paroxysm of perilous zeal. No matter where she was, she would spring to her feet, fling out her surprisingly powerful arms, and flash the great white whale of smiles. More than once, this resulted in injury to whatever unfortunate soul happened to be in the way. During one such incident, Mrs Greevey, one of the precious few babysitters in the tri-state

New York area willing to endure Janine more than once, lost two perfectly serviceable front teeth. Of course, Janine convinced her doting, delusional parents that, despite the sitter's pained ramblings to the contrary, the teeth had actually fallen out after Mrs Greevey bit with unfortunate greed on a chicken leg. In Janine's view, if you were meant to take responsibility for your actions, God would not have invented the wonderful world of lies and all the marvelous excuses a person can make with them.

To this day, any mention of the show moved Janine to reminisce about the glorious Mouse Club season when her Q-rating soared for a heady couple of weeks over Annette's. She neglected to mention that she accomplished this by tripping Annette, so the little star fell and broke her arm. Before Annette could muster the breath to shriek, Janine 'accidentally' stomped on the twisted limb for good measure. As Janine liked to say: anything worth doing was worth overdoing (or if sufficiently messy and unpleasant – contracting out).

In minutes she returned, cradling sexy black pumps, a mock Chanel clutch, and an array of highly convincing faux jewelry in blue velvet boxes. Daphne trailed behind, toting a blow dryer, a purple plastic basket packed with hair unguents and accessories, and a large black leather make-up case on wheels. Janine's chief stylist appraised me from several angles, traded weighty frowns

14

with Janine, and set to work.

The sight of Daphne still left me speechless. Mere months ago, she had completed her sexual reassignment, shedding the scrawny, socially maladroit chrysalis of the former David Sherman Goldfarb for the sleek, buxom, doe-eyed, leggy, satin-haired and sultry Daphne Starr Gold. Janine oversaw the transformation personally, hooking Daphne up with her own first-rate preservation team: plastic surgeon, dermatologist, facialist, colorist, stylist, personal trainer and so on. The results spoke for themselves. Daphne stood as undeniable proof that, despite my mother's frequent assertions to the contrary, you *can* get perfume from an onion.

My hair was long overdue for a touch-up and a trim. Since Harold left, even the most basic personal maintenance seemed too demanding. Many mornings it took all my remaining resolve to squeeze an acceptable line of paste on to the toothbrush bristles. Often, after I'd managed to pull that off, the tube cruelly slurped the paste back in again, and I was forced to start the whole impossible project again. So forget the Herculean prospect of finding the number of my beauty salon, dialing it correctly, speaking the words required to make an appointment and then actually showing up. Even if all that didn't feel too overwhelming, I couldn't bear the thought of my colorist's disappointment at seeing how low I'd sunk. She was a nice, chipper young woman named Alyssa, who managed to look adorable and sound completely lucid despite having three kids in diapers and a husband who, by her report, spent all of his time traveling the amateur skateboard circuit and ended every sentence with 'Dude'.

Gray roots formed a dusty dirt road at my part. Daphne combed through a temporary color gel and clipped my overlong, uneven mop into an optimistic, chin-length bob. Next, she attacked my face like a long neglected room: polishing, tidying, dusting and rearranging.

'Open,' she ordered. 'Look down. Don't breathe. Blot.'

I watched in amazement as the bruise-colored troughs beneath my eyes vanished and my lips and lids lost their look of puffy bewilderment. My cheeks turned the warm pink of a desert sunset over a complexion reminiscent of warm, silken, toe-wiggling sand. By the time she finished, my skin looked clear and smooth. No crow's feet, chicken skin, spider veins or incipient turkey wattles. The entire menagerie: gone.

'What happens when I move?'

'I wouldn't.'

After Daphne swished on a final choking fog of powder, Janine posed me again in front of the three-way. 'Look at yourself, Maggie. You are a beautiful, smart, funny, youthful, revoltingly good person.'

'I know all about *youthful*, Janine. That's code for over-the-hill but deluded. Youthful is

16

my mother in a miniskirt and Jimmy Choos. Youthful is Great Aunt Rose hitting on a hot, young orderly at the home.'

'Nonsense. You could pass for thirty-five. Forty, tops. OK. Maybe forty-five.'

I gazed at this trimmer, far more attractive, and yes, more *youthful* version of myself. In truth, people used to comment all the time about how young I looked. I got rather skilled at masking my shameless pride in the dubious accomplishment, brushing off a stranger's lovely astonishment that I was old enough to have *kids*, much less *teenagers*. I swore I would never place any serious stock in such compliments, knowing they would eventually stop. But I never imagined it happening with such a jolt. Last weekend, I hauled myself up from the dregs of depression to see a movie, and the gum-snapping, teenaged ticket-seller at the AMC on Forty-Second Street presumed I was eligible for the senior citizen discount.

Janine kept pelting me with her peculiar idea of encouragement. 'You don't need that lying, ugly, boring *putz*, Maggie. You're better off without him.'

'Sure, I am. Look at all the wonderful things I have to look forward to: dinner for one, playing the fifth wheel, dying alone.'

'You are better off. Trust me.'

'Then why don't I feel better?'

'Because you've been with Harold how long?'

'Almost twenty-eight years.'

She whistled low. 'So you've spent your

whole adult life making excuses for the *zhlub*, building him into someone you could bear to wake up and go to bed with and spend time with in between. You talked yourself into thinking he was your one and only despite the putrid morning breath and ever-spreading paunch. You convinced yourself that you liked all his irritating habits, including the two idiotic jokes he repeated so many times you couldn't decide whether to shoot him or yourself.'

'How did you know about that?'

'Because all men in long marriages are exactly the same. They all fart whenever they feel like it, toss their dirty socks on the floor and leave the seat up. They all adore their infuriating mothers, whine about how much you're spending, posture for their buddies, come too fast, and snore.'

'Harold's mother died before the wedding.'

'Listen to me, Maggie. I've been married and divorced enough to know. As soon as you get past the shock, you'll see Harold for what he is. And once that happens, you're on your way, honey. More fun, fabulous adventure, better everything.'

My shoulders slumped with a fresh load of grief. 'I wouldn't know where to begin.'

'I'm going to help you, Maggie. I'm going to be your guide. You'll be amazed what can happen if you follow my advice.'

'You mean like a prison term?'

'I'm talking liberation, honey. Being the goddess mistress of your own mother-ducking fate.'

'I don't want that, Janine. I want to be under Harold's thumb, where I belong. I don't know how to be on my own. I don't want to be. Not anymore.'

'Yes you do, Maggie. You just don't know it yet.' She walked to my chalkboard and wrote in a bold, round hand. 'Here's rule number one: *You're right, he's wrong.* Now you say it.'

I felt the tears welling up again. 'Please, Janine.'

'Say it!'

'I'm right, he's wrong.'

'Excellent.'

'How about when he's right?'

'He's dead wrong, Maggie, even when he's right. Especially then. That's the key, the bedrock. You got it?'

I nodded miserably and the tears spilled over, laying grief tracks on my freshly paved face. 'Sure.'

Blamer vs Blamer

Harold had retained Randy Schlam of Schlam & Dunkelman to represent him in the divorce. 'Slam dunk', as the firm was popularly known, handled captains of industry, politics, and entertainment. These were the high profile, high stakes break-ups chronicled in the tabloids and on Page Six of the *Post.* Trump exes had passed this way, not to mention Perelmans, Welches, and Giulianis. And now they could boast of having Harold Strickland as a client, Professor of Philosophy and last year's recipient of the 'coveted' Arnold Breslow Award for contributions to the field of ethical thought. Arnold Breslow was Harold's former college roommate, longtime colleague, fellow rabid Yankee fan and duplicate bridge partner, so in ethical parlance Harold's receiving the award could be summed up in two words: *don't ask.*

Entering Slam Dunk's palm-infested Park Avenue reception area, I was grateful to find my lawyer scrunched into one of the ultramodern, beet red, glove-shaped chairs. Lena Rossini may have been a minor league, single practitioner, but she was sensible, solid and smart. She'd come highly recommended by my gay cousin Stanley from Scarsdale, who had dated her next-to-youngest brother during law school. Among her many virtues were a reasonable retainer and the fact that she was not among the dozen or so well-known divorce lawyers in New York that Harold had interviewed before choosing Slam Dunk, making it unethical for them to take me on. Lena called this 'peeing on all the fire hydrants', one of a long list of unfortunate divorce behaviors she referred to collectively as 'stupid spouse tricks'.

'Wow, do you look terrific!' she said. 'Harold's going to swallow his tongue.'

20

'Promise?'

'What's wrong, Maggie?' Lena asked at the sight of my quaking jaw.

'Tell me the truth. Do I look like a clown? Should I run home and change? Should I wash all this gunk off my face?'

'You look terrific. Try to relax. Everything's going to be fine.'

'I don't want to see Harold. Can't we do this in separate rooms?'

'It's a conference, which means we have to confer.'

'Can't you do it and let me know how it went later on?'

'It's going to be all right, I promise. Now breathe.'

'I am.'

'You're only inhaling. You have to exhale, too.'

'Sorry. I guess I'm a little nervous.'

'You are? Who would have guessed?'

I perched at the edge of a glove-shaped chair, fearful of getting trapped in its diabolical contours. I imagined dying right here in Slam Dunk's waiting room, rigor mortis setting in so I'd be doomed to scrunch for all eternity while my mother nagged me to sit up straight.

'This is *pro forma*, Maggie. We go in, we talk, and we leave. Simple stuff.'

'Not for me.'

'It will be. You'll see.'

Lena's idea, radical for a divorce lawyer, was to get things settled as quickly as possible

21

at the lowest possible cost. During our first meeting, she explained the idiotic economics of divorce. If I was to battle Harold over, say, the custody of a favorite dishtowel, by the time we got through wrangling, negotiating, and having our lawyers write up the terms of the deal, that stupid towel would cost more in legal fees than buying one of those ultra-chic linen stores on Madison Avenue. To me, this made perfect, though unsatisfying sense. Logic had nothing whatsoever to do with a break up. My grief at the shocking demise of our marriage was only surpassed by my seething desire to castrate and dismember Harold for his betrayal, which was only surpassed by an overwhelming urge to grab him like a raft in a shark-infested sea and cling for dear life. According to Lena, all these seething fear, hurt and confusion molecules tended to get displaced in the heat of things and attach themselves to things like dishtowels and barbecue tongs, which could take on a consuming, expensive emotional life of their own.

Harold huddled with Randy Schlam at the large, freeform, smoked glass table in the conference room. At the sight of him, my heart thrashed like a beached flounder. Our last encounter was the day he'd stormed out of our apartment, lugging a pair of suitcases. After he'd gone, I'd stood staring at the door for a small eternity, positive he'd reappear at any moment to shout April Fool or whatever equivalent thing one might shout on a

Tuesday in June. But he had not. I'd raced in a panic to the window in time to watch him climb into the backseat of a cab beside the slim, young, brilliant, auburn beauty he preferred, for some unfathomable reason, to me.

Glancing my way now, Harold did a cartoon double-take. I tried to convince myself that this was because, thanks to Janine, I looked far better than he expected, rather than simply bizarre.

Harold's appearance, I noted with a heart-warming and calming surge of spite, had taken a sizeable turn for the worse. He had shaved off the lush beard and moustache he'd sported since '83, and somehow, his upper lip and chin had come away in the process. Or perhaps, they'd been stunted by all those years spent cowering in the shade. His getup was unfortunate as well. The Harold I'd thought I knew favored professorial clothes: baggy corduroy pants, plaid shirts and boxy tweed jackets with suede elbow patches. This new, alien, un-Harold sported a shiny, three-button, Italian cut sports coat in a color that could best be described as pimp blue.

'You're looking well, Margaret.'

'Hello, Harold.'

Randy Schlam, trim and ferret-faced, slid a matched pair of weighty documents to our side of the table. 'I must say, this is the kind of case that makes life easy. Two capable career people. No minor kids or complex encumbrances. Everything lean, clean and

23

simple.'

Lena served up a stingy nightlight of a smile. 'Would be nice.'

'What we've written up reflects the standard fifty-fifty asset split. I suggest we go through the document here and now so we can clear up any questions on the spot and put this matter to bed.'

As Lena pored through the pages scrawling marginal notes, I was stalled on the cover sheet. Strickland vs Strickland, it said, citing me as *Defendant* and Harold, of all people, as *Plaintiff*.

He was complaining?

Wasn't I the one who'd spent three hours certain he'd been burnt to ash in that horrific fire? Wasn't I the one who'd made frantic attempts to reach him in his office and on his cell phone, while images of the hellish inferno at Hadley Hall played again and again on CNN? Wasn't it me who'd had to track everyone down and tell them what was happening, and then somehow hold myself together while they fell apart? Try dealing with my daughter Allison's impossible second-guessing – *Why did you let him go to work today, Mom? Why didn't you make him stay home and grade the damned papers?* – while at the same time trying to blunt my son Brian's hostility-induced guilt and my mother's (a) palpitations, (b) hyperventilating, (c) shrieking like a car alarm, and (d) impossible quandary over whether or not to cancel with her podiatrist, given the crippling severity of her corns.

I'll never forget the bristling shock, the scorching pain, my railing fury at the cruel fates that had lured Harold to his office on a Saturday morning to grade exams. It was our 28th anniversary, no less, and the newscast came on as I knelt on the living-room floor amid a festive clutter of gift wrap, Scotch tape, curly ribbon, greeting cards and pre-made sticky bows.

I'd splurged on the tawny glove-leather portfolio Harold had been drooling over for months in the Levenger Catalogue for Serious Readers. And as I gazed at it then, the finality of his death hit me like a truck. Harold would never be able to enjoy his gift. He would never again sit across from me at the breakfast table or lay snoring beside me at night. He would never again have the chance to be aggravated to death by his beloved Yankees or Giants or Rangers or Mets. Never again would he get to refuse a table at a restaurant or send back his food because it was under or overcooked or too hot, salty, tough, soggy, spicy, tasteless, graceless, bland or cold. My beloved would never again refuse to take a hotel room because it was too noisy, hot, cold, centrally located, isolated, oddly configured, close to the elevator or ice machine, draughty, smelly, antiseptic, poorly decorated or small. At that desperate, un-imaginable moment, all of Harold's Goldilocksian niggling struck me as precious beyond words.

I imagined the weeping eulogies at his

funeral. I pictured how sobbing colleagues, friends and relatives would describe him as a highly discerning, discriminating man of impeccable taste. How I hated myself at that moment for all the times I'd seethed in silence, thinking that Harold was being a petty, irritating, embarrassing pain in the ass. After all, those very quirks were an integral part of the man I'd loved and lived with for nearly three decades.

At that moment, I would have given anything to have him back. I begged; I prayed. I promised to cure all my hideous faults, never to drink from the milk carton again or eat a frozen Snickers bar in the middle of the night or have a snide or homicidal thought about anyone, even my mother. I was willing to become a different person altogether. Anything to have Harold back!

And then he called.

'Just finishing up, Margaret. Should be home in about half an hour.'

'Harold? My God! Where are you?'

'The office, remember? I told you, I was coming in to grade exams. My, my, aren't we a tad young to be so forgetful?'

'Your office at Hadley Hall?'

'Of course. If that was you calling, I decided to let it go. Wanted to concentrate on the papers, so I could get through sooner.'

'You heard the phone ring at your office in Hadley Hall?'

'As I said. What on earth is wrong with you, Margaret? You sound awfully peculiar.'

I stared at the television, where flames were shooting skyward like triumphal fists and a section of the roof suddenly augured in with a crushing roar. Grim, soot-streaked firefighters trained their impotent hoses on the crumpling façade. At that moment, a generic blond reporter declared that thanks to the day and the hour, the building was deserted when the fire broke out, so there had been no casualties.

Unless you counted me.

Turns out that while I, *Defendant,* was mourning her husband's horrifying demise, *Plaintiff* was in the Morningside Heights apartment of Bethany Whitmore, the graduate student who happened to be studying under him at the time, unclothed.

'Why does he get to be plaintiff?' I demanded.

Randy Schlam shrugged. 'It's meaningless. Just a matter of who files.'

'It's not meaningless to me!'

'Must we get bogged down in such minutiae?' Harold huffed.

'Not at all. We can file an amended complaint,' Lena said.

'I have no problem with that,' Schlam conceded.

'Well I do. This is typical of you, Margaret. Focusing on niggling nonsense that wastes valuable time and resources.'

'It's no big deal,' Schlam said.

Harold scowled. 'Not to you who charges five dollars and seventy-five cents a minute to do the deed.'

Lena's look dripped with meaning I couldn't decipher. 'Let's put it aside for now.'

She tried to draw my attention to certain key paragraphs. But I found it hard to focus on the numbing details: a formula for equalizing our IRAs, a proposal to minimize the tax consequences of splitting up our various accounts. For a price, Harold would allow me to have the two-bedroom eastside co-op, which we bought with the proceeds after the kids were grown and we sold the house in Connecticut. He proposed buying me out of the cottage in the Berkshires (which he'd always detested and now could not live without), and paying for my half of the frequent flyer miles on American while I absorbed half of his Continental and Delta awards and our Marriott points in exchange for the Hyatt and Starwood. We would each keep our office furnishings, ancestral possessions, and rights to our respective businesses.

My lawyer lobbed questions, and Randy Schlam volleyed them back with ease. 'You're proposing separate tax filings for this year?'

'Given the separate business entities, we see no particular financial advantage to a joint return.'

'Any disadvantage?'

'Six of one,' Schlam said, showing both sides of his fey, manicured hand. 'Not enough to justify further, unnecessary wrangling or delay.'

'Appraisal of the personality?'

28

'If you think a formal appraisal is necessary, we often use Van de Grath and Moore.'

Harold advanced to gorilla-quality table-thumping. 'That's absurd. We need nothing of the sort. More money wasted.'

Lena ignored him with such finesse, I wanted to applaud. 'Certifications?' she asked Schlam.

'I'm sure we can trust Ms Strickland's sworn word.'

'As am I.'

'And Dr Strickland's,' Harold's lawyer was quick to add.

A coy smile played on Lena's lips. Score one for my knight in shining Armani. 'Valuation of the property and businesses?'

'Normal procedure, I'd presume. Three years tax returns for the businesses. Dr Strickland is salaried and Ms Strickland's income is pretty constant on an annual basis, as I understand. Very straightforward.'

Lena stood and packed her briefcase. '*Mrs* Strickland and I will need to review this in greater detail. We'll get back to you.'

Harold sat straighter, always an ominous sign. 'I thought you agreed that we were going to resolve this amicably, Margaret.'

'Mrs Strickland would like nothing more,' Lena said. 'However, I can't allow my client to sign anything that we haven't had time to analyze and digest, Mr Strickland.'

'That's *Dr* Strickland,' he huffed.

Harold was the kind of doctor you'd go to if you had a pain in your philosophy.

'Whatever. I'm sure there's no particular rush,' Lena said.

'No. Certainly not. I just can't see a reason to prolong any of this unpleasantness,' Harold said.

As soon as we were out the door, my lawyer's slow burn flared. She held mute until we were on the elevator. 'I think we should hire a forensic accountant to check Harold's finances.'

'Why?'

'There are too many red flags in that agreement.'

'Such as?'

'The big rush to get it signed. No joint filing this year, on and on. Lord, do I hate red flags.'

'I don't know, Lena. Harold may have gone a little nuts with that graduate student, but I can't believe that he'd try to cheat me out of what's right and fair. He's an ethicist, for heaven's sake.'

'Ever hear of a crooked cop? An irreverent priest? Ever see a fat nutritionist?'

'Well sure. I suppose. But I've never known Harold to be dishonest.'

'Yes you have. That's why we're here.'

'OK, fine. I guess you could claim that cheating on your wife with a student and lying about it isn't entirely honest.'

Lena smiled. 'Ever hear of Ernie Kovacs, the old time comedian?'

'The one who invented the Nairobi trio and Percy Dovetonsils? Sure. He was my dad's absolute favorite. We watched a couple of his specials together when I was little.'

'My parents loved him, too. When I was a kid, my mom taught me an important lesson she learned from Ernie Kovacs. On one of his shows, he explained why bulls get mad when you wave a red flag in front of them. Turns out they're color-blind. Actually, it's cows who get pissed off by red flags, so when you wave one in front of a bull, he knows that you think he's a cow, and that pisses him off – big time.'

'Sorry. I'm afraid you've lost me.'

'I have a feeling Harold may think we're a cow, Maggie. So I say we follow the red flags and expose his line of bull. I know an excellent and very reasonable forensic accountant.'

'All right, if you think it's necessary.'

'I do.'

'I'm sure he's not going to find anything. Harold isn't like that, Lena. I know him.'

'You want to *really* know someone, divorce him. Believe me. I've seen it a thousand times.'

The Past and the Curious

When I consider the mess that started next, I have to admit the carrot was to blame. New Yorkers are notoriously nonchalant. We barely blink at the sight of the cowboy clad in nothing but a ten gallon hat, boots and jockey shorts as he strums his guitar and poses with giggling, ogling tourists in Times Square. We are utterly unfazed by the lizard lady, who dresses to match the twin Gila monsters sprawled across her shoulders and sports two dozen salamanders on her arm. Ditto the gloss-haired, mustachioed tango dancer whose partner, a sultry scarlet-lipped brunette in flamenco garb, happens to be stuffed.

But even in this town, the sight of a seven-foot-tall carrot, strolling across Park Avenue on slim green stems as if it hadn't a care in the world, was not something you happened upon every day. From what I could tell, the outsized root vegetable wasn't advertising anything, wasn't doing some weirdo performance piece, wasn't lobbying for carrot-friendly legislation or research money for a tragic orphan carrot disease. The alpha specimen of beta carotene was simply minding its business, having a nice, midday stroll.

Unsurprisingly, this distracted me. For a blessed instant, I ceased obsessing about Harold and the divorce. The carrot drove away the bleak thoughts I'd been having about the future, where I pictured myself as a homeless, toothless lady with filthy nails or a twirly-eyed mental patient who, after years of electric shock therapy, remembered nothing except being dumped for a brilliant, beautiful graduate student. The carrot commanded my complete attention, causing me to collide at oomph-speed with an on-coming pedestrian. His cell phone went flying as did my draft separation agreement. As I scurried to retrieve the papers, a capricious wind kicked up and propelled them beyond my reach.

The man I'd body-checked recovered and pitched in to help. He rescued several pages as they were about to hurl themselves into the rush of oncoming traffic. Then he crouched to retrieve a few others that had slipped through the wrought iron fence in front of an elegant brownstone. As he handed them over, it struck me that he seemed familiar, not to mention handsome, with generous lips, chiseled features, and dark, soulful, adopt-this-puppy eyes.

'Sorry for bunking into you,' I blithered.

He chuckled. 'Did you say *bunking*? I haven't heard that since junior high.'

'I probably haven't said it since junior high.'

'My Lord. Maggie Evantoff? Is that really you?'

'Well, yes. I mean, sort of – in a way.'

'I can't believe it. It's been what? Forty years?'

I struggled to subtract the dash of salt in his dense, wavy hair, add flesh to the chiseled cheekbones and delete some from the body that had aged so admirably well. 'Tony Carlucci?'

'That I haven't heard since high school. My dad died soon after we moved, and my Mom remarried a few years later. My stepfather adopted me, so my name changed to Sinclair. From the time I started college, I've been pretty much known as Anthony. Hearing Tony Carlucci does take me back.'

'Eighth grade homeroom, right?'

'Right. Remember what a misery Mrs Crawshaw was?'

'Do I ever? Old bag sentenced me to so much detention; I bet I still owe a couple of years.'

'Same here. Kids used to tease that she was in love with me, wanted me to stay behind so she and I could be alone.'

'You think that's bad? The kids used to say she wanted *me* to stay after because she thought I'd make a tasty snack.'

He shook his head. 'What a bunch of characters. Remember how they used to call me Tony Spumoni?'

'Actually, as I recall they mostly called you Wop.' I also recalled, with a sudden flush of embarrassment, the mammoth crush I had on this guy until he shattered my firm pubescent plans for our future – marriage and five

34

children (three boys, two girls) – by moving to Tenafly, New Jersey.

'True, and didn't they call you Magpie?'

'That was Maggie Hutchins. Me they called Crisco, as in fat in the can.'

His eyes boldly toured my terrain. 'Well there's no way anyone would call you that now.'

I averted my gaze. 'This is not how I really look.'

'Sorry?'

'Forget it. Listen, I'm the one who's sorry. I feel terrible. Is your cell phone OK?'

'No way. Stupid thing drives me crazy. If it's broken, I'll be eternally grateful to you.'

'I was distracted by the carrot.'

'What?'

'Didn't you see it? An enormous carrot was crossing the street. It had the most extraordinary posture.'

His brow furrowed. 'Are you OK, Maggie? Did you hit your head?'

'Really. It turned in up there, near the Asia Society.'

He checked his watch. 'Damn. I've got to run. Any chance we could get together some time and catch up?'

'That'd be nice.'

'You have a card?'

'Not on me. I'm listed though, under Margaret Strickland.'

'Wonderful. Here's my card, I'll give you a call.'

The Good, the Bad, the Snugli

My daughter Allison and her husband Jon
live two blocks from Lincoln Center on the
penultimate floor of a glass-faced, chandelier-
infested high rise. Their 'modern classic' six-
room co-op, replete with ornate, non-work-
ing fireplaces and reproduction antique
moldings, resembled a cluster of model
rooms with the velvet ropes implied. There
was no mess, no chaos, not a hint that the
place was occupied, much less lived in.

From birth, Ali has been one of those
intimidating souls who kept every aspect of
their lives ordered without fail. I'd always
suspected she studied child development *in
utero* and came into the world with her first
five-year plan in place. My daughter was born
precocious, socially adept, flawlessly stylish
and preternaturally neat. Aside from the
breathtaking sense of inadequacy she'd
inspired, the biggest difficulty I'd had rearing
her was the persistent, nagging conviction
that I had somehow brought the wrong infant
home from Lenox Hill Hospital.

She hung up my coat in the guest closet,
which otherwise held nothing but an obedi-
ent line of initialed wooden hangers. People

36

in New York City do not have empty closets. I believe it's against the law.

'Something to drink, Mom?'

I had a yen for a nice, refreshing cyanide and soda. 'Wine. If you have any open.'

'Champagne OK? I have a nice Grande Dame on ice.'

As did her old man. 'Sounds fine.'

'You look amazing. Love the suit.'

'Thanks. Janine lent it to me.'

'Nice to see you looking stylish for a change. Normally, you dress like such a frump.'

'Leave it to you, Ali. I don't know whether to thank you for the compliment or shoot myself.'

'Seriously, looking attractive is more important than you seem to realize. Especially now.'

'Shoot myself. Definitely.'

'Come on, Mom. Lighten up. I just meant that it's a good idea to do something with yourself; look like you're trying, at least.'

'Oh. You were being constructive. Silly me.'

'So, you ready for the big surprise?'

'No, I'm not. But I don't suppose that'll stop you from springing it on me.'

She handed me a gleaming Baccarat flute and filled it precisely. 'Prepare to be completely blown away.'

'Please, Ali. You're scaring me.'

'Don't be silly. You're going to love this. You'll see. Close your eyes.'

'How am I supposed to see with my eyes closed?'

'Don't give me a hard time, Mom.'

37

'Is this necessary? It's been a rough day.'

'It's about to get way better. Eyes closed.' She went to the door, practically skipping with delight, a sight that deepened my terror exponentially. Gleeful and silly were not Ali's style. While other little girls were playing with their Barbie dolls and dreaming of marriage to a prince, my seven-year-old daughter announced that she had decided on a career in finance. Growing up, she read the business section of *The Times* and *The Wall Street Journal*. Early on, she'd opened a Schwab account where she'd invested her birthday money and later, her babysitting earnings in stocks she selected herself. By age twelve, she'd known all about 30-day moving averages, price/earnings/growth ratios, triple witching, EBITDA, and puts and calls. After Yale, she'd gone to the Harvard Business School and then become a venture capitalist, which meant she invested obscene amounts of other people's money for a pornographic salary. Jon, her equally goal-oriented and mature spouse, was doing just as well managing something called a fund-of-funds for Merrill Lynch. I suspected that shorting stocks was Ali and Jon's idea of guilty pleasure. Perhaps, when they were really feeling down-and-dirty, they did so in business casual.

Eyes shut, I imagined the worst: hail, locusts, a rain of frogs, some biblical horror of Haroldian proportions. Then a greater terror struck me. What if it was Harold himself? The

38

thought of facing him without the buffer of lawyers and a large conference table was more than I could bear.

I knew Ali was capable of engineering such a disaster. She viewed our separation as a temporary aberration, one of those petty emotional annoyances best ignored and bound to clear up on its own, like a zit. She turned a deaf ear and blind eye to the altered order of things, especially any mention of her father's new life and nubile love. In my daughter's unshakable view, parents did not have sex, they had estate plans.

In a rush, I was embraced by strong, lanky arms, hauled off my aching feet and twirled in a dizzying circle. I opened my eyes to my son's beaming face.

'Brian!'

'Hey, gorgeous. Get a look at you!'

'Oh, honey. What are you doing here? Why didn't you tell me? How long are you staying? Are you staying with me?'

'All in due time, my lovely. Ready for the surprise?'

'Aren't you it?'

'As they say on the game shows, "And there's more!"' Brian beat a silent drum roll on the air. 'And heeeere it comes!'

Ali opened the door again. A young woman in a plump white down coat stood in the hallway. She had wide pale eyes, a strawberry milkshake complexion and the kind of soft-edged features that told you exactly how she'd looked at age three.

Brian looped his arm around her back. 'Mom, meet Valerie, my wife.'

'Your what?'

'We got married a month ago. Maui sunset in the background. Gorgeous surf. Pretty amazing, huh?'

Amazing indeed. Even for Brian, who had always been as full of whiplash-inducing surprises as Allison was predictable.

'But I spoke to you a bunch of times. You didn't say a thing.'

'I wanted to wait and tell you in person. This was too big for the phone.'

Valerie approached with outstretched arms. I took in her puffy softness and sugary scent. 'I'm so glad to meet you, Mom!'

Mom? I detected a trace of vintage thirties Kansas in her voice: shades of Dorothy on the road to Oz. When she hugged me, I felt odd squirming. Startled, I recoiled.

A grand flurry kicked up beneath her coat.

'Look who's up!' Valerie crooned. She unbuttoned to expose the complex navy blue rigging strapped to her chest. A halo of lemon blonde ringlets poked out from the top. Dangling below were chubby little legs encased in red tights. At the sides, tiny dimpled hands protruded from the arms of a pink hooded jacket. Brian liberated Valerie from the coat and plucked out the baby.

'Hey, Wooble dee boo,' he crooned. 'Hey, Wumpky bumpky.'

I had seen Brian through many phases. He had at various times proclaimed himself a

40

river rafting guide, a rock drummer, a stand-up comedian, an ovo-lacto-cocoa-gummy bear vegetarian, a Buddhist, a Vinyasa yoga instructor, a pre-school teacher, and a screen-writer. He had worn his hair almost waist length, shaved it to the scalp, clumped it in a Mohawk, and dyed it bread-mold blue. For a time, he was into fire-walking, and he'd spent an entire summer leading a line of donkeys into the Grand Canyon with actual paying customers astride. Still, for the first time, it occurred to me that the son I adored might be simply and seriously deranged.

He set the child down on Allison's antique Aubusson rug. She wobbled like a three-legged stool and then dropped on her well-padded rump. Her cheeks were bubble-gum pink; her eyes the startling hue of full-strength Windex. She had aged beyond the toothless, wisp-haired stage, but had not yet acquired a neck. I estimated fifteen to eighteen months.

'Mom, this is Delia, our baby girl.'

'Your—?'

'Valerie had Delia on her own. Turkey baster, you know. I'm in the process of adopting her.'

Valerie knelt in front of the child. 'What do you say, sweetie?'

'Coo-kee?'

'In a minute. First, remember who we said you were going to meet?'

'Ew-mo?'

Allison giggled with manic delight, as if

there had just been a giant surge in the Dow. 'Delia just loves Elmo. Isn't she too much?'

I was tempted to remind my daughter that she had no use, whatsoever, for children, never did, not even when she was one, or at least, could physically pass. But the world had gone insane. 'Too much. Definitely.'

The child trundled over to me and pointed. 'Gammy.'

'Yes!' Brian exulted. 'Did you hear that, Mom? She called you Granny. We've been practicing. Good little Beeble Weeble.'

'Gammy,' she declared again, chortling with delight at her own extravagant cleverness.

Valerie swept the baby up and planted her astride an ample hip. 'I hope Granny's OK with you, Mom. Bri and I just love it. But, of course, you're welcome to choose something else if you'd prefer.'

'Nanny's cute, too,' Allison opined. 'That's what Jon's niece calls his mom.'

'Or Nana,' Brian offered. 'Can you say Nana, Doobie doobs?'

'Nah-nah.' This emerged on a bungee cord of drool.

'Or that Jewish thing,' Valerie snapped her plump fingers, trying to summon the word.

'Bubbeh,' Brian said.

'Right. Booby. Maybe you'd like Delia to call you that. Can you say Booby, cutes?'

'Boo bee coots,' she chirped.

Brian handed the baby an oatmeal cookie and offered one to me.

'No, thanks. I'm on a strict ice cream and

alcohol diet.'

'You have to taste one, Mom. Valerie happens to be *the* Valerie, founder and CEO of Valerie's Sweet Treats. She started five years ago in her own kitchen and the rest, as they say, is history. In fact, we've outgrown our Midwest plant, so we've decided to shift our base of operations to Queens.'

'We?'

'Partners all the way. Until we can ramp up the staff, I'm the go-to-guy for Ops, as well as VP of Sales and Marketing. Amazing expansion possibilities in the northeast. We've got a series of key meetings lined up in the next few weeks. Keep your fingers crossed.'

'You? In business?'

'You bet. Nothing like growing a company. Exploring new opportunities in the space.'

The walls had begun to waver. 'I see.'

'We'll be living right here in Manhattan. In fact we've rented a little place a few blocks from your apartment for the time being.'

'Can you believe it, Mom?' Ali squealed. 'Isn't this the best?'

'Now that you ask, I don't know if I can believe it.' I would wake up. This would all go away as I brushed my teeth, washed my face, and popped a couple of thorazine.

'Granny is definitely the winner. Don't you think, Mom?'

'Let Mom decide for herself, Bri honey,' Valerie urged.

Delia toddled about, gnawing on the cookie as she took inventory. She touched Valerie's

43

leg. 'Hi, Mama.' Then Brian's. 'Hi, Dah-dee.'

'Can you say "Hi Auntie Allison?"' Valerie prompted.

'Hi, Annie Ow-thin.'

'Ohmigod, she's so cute! I could just eat her with a spoon,' Ali gushed.

'Really?' I asked in all sincerity. 'Did a proper baby eating spoon come with the Grand Baroque?'

My daughter's look was stern.

Delia stalled in front of me, mashing saliva-soaked cookie crumbs into Letty Denison's zillion dollar suit. 'Hi, boo bee gammy nah-nah.'

All of them burst into hysterics. I did my utmost to keep from joining in.

'You have to decide, Mom,' Valerie said. 'What do you want her to call you?'

I felt the familiar sting of rising tears. This was all too much, too overwhelming. All I wanted anyone to call me at that moment was a cab.

Some Like It Not

When I opened my door to retrieve the morning paper, I discovered a paper bag. At my touch it burped the aroma of singed bran muffins, still oven warm.

Mrs Feder strikes again.

My 86-year-old next door neighbor viewed Harold's leaving as a disaster that was somehow punishable by relentless gifts of food. Most every day she left something unwelcome on my welcome mat. More often than not, it was a burnt offering: scorched banana bread, overcooked chicken in a pot, or an immolated dirt-brown substance that I took to be the specialty meatloaf she often bragged about, though I lacked the courage to ask. No matter how I protested, she continued to besiege me with unsolicited nourishment: navel oranges, honey in a perky plastic bear, greasy hot pastrami, pickled herring, hard candies, brisling sardines, and no end of chocolate-covered, chalk-flavored halvah.

The phone rang the instant I closed the door. Of course, it was Mrs Feder, checking to make sure her muffins had not been filched by a roving band of pastry thieves. I caught the hospital hush in her voice. 'How are you feeling, sweetheart?'

'Fine, Mrs Feder. Thanks for the muffins, but you shouldn't have, *really*.'

'I'm brewing you a nice pot of chamomile tea, Maggie. I'm going to bring it over with a nice lavender sachet. You put it under the pillow. Excellent for the nerves.'

'That's sweet of you. But not necessary. I've told you, I'm fine.'

'You don't have to put on such a brave face, darling. You think I forget how it was when my Morty left me? Impossible. Unbearable. The worst.'

Morty Feder had died of a massive coronary in 1962, while racing to catch the crosstown bus on the way to his accounting office at the frenzied height of a grueling tax season. But in my neighbor's view, a betrayal was a betrayal. Another woman, pine box. Same thing.

'Men,' she said, transforming the word into a strident feminist rant. 'I'm telling you, Maggie, Harold must be going through a midlife crisis.'

'Could be.' I didn't bother to point out that for this to qualify as Harold's midlife, he would have to live to be a hundred and four.

'Male menopause, they call it. Did you know?'

'I've heard the term, but I don't think it's been established as scientific fact.'

'Trust me, it happens. I'm ashamed to even admit this, but when my Morty was that age, he bought a Pontiac Impala.'

'Oh, my.'

'A convertible, no less. In blue.'

'No!'

'Not even navy or even royal, mind you. More like – ' her voice dipped to a pained whisper – 'Robin's egg.'

'Ouch.'

'Men. Do you need me to come zip you up or anything, sweetheart? I must say that's one of the things I miss most, having someone to zip me.'

'No, thanks. I'm all set. I was just heading to the office, in fact. So please, don't bother with the tea.'

'All right, dear. It's good you have something to keep you busy.'

'True.'

'Pity Harold didn't leave you better off, though, so you wouldn't have to work.'

'I like my work. Really, Mrs Feder. You don't have to worry about me.'

'Sure I do. What are neighbors for? I'll bring you some nice pot roast later. You'll be home?'

'Actually, I won't. I'm going out.'

'You found someone? That's marvelous! Wonderful! I'm so glad to hear it! Though if you don't mind my saying, it is a little soon.'

'I haven't found anyone. I'm having dinner with friends.'

She spewed air. 'That's good, Maggie. Take your time. Believe me. Play the field.'

'I don't think there is a field.'

'Sure there is. Just don't hide your light under a bushel, darling. It's like my mother always said, Prince Charming is not going to find you if you sit home in your robe and slippers like a bump on a log.'

I headed to the office by way of the nearest Starbucks. I'd had to boost my caffeine intake to compensate for all the endless nights of tossing angst. This had triggered a guilty addiction to double frappuccinos with an extra espresso shot, which was basically a panic attack in convenient liquid form. I would revel in the jolt, and then spend the rest of the morning wallowing in jittery regret. So naturally the next day I repeated the moronic routine. Why go to the trouble of making new mistakes when the old ones were so comforting and familiar?

Entering the coffee shop, I spotted Ellie Matthias on the order line, a friend I hadn't seen in months. I'd called her a couple of times since Harold left, but my timing had been off. I'd always managed to catch her in a meeting or on the verge of being late for a reservation at some ultra-trendy restaurant.

Ellie worked as Managing Editor at one of those mammoth agglomerated publishing houses (I think it's now called something like Random Tandem Tripleday Delaware) and as best I could tell, one of her key responsibilities was lunch.

Seeing her now, I felt an irrational swell of affection. Ellie was one of those stunningly neurotic people who never ceased to amaze you with the sheer range and originality of their off-the-wall ideas. Playfully, I tapped her bony shoulder and gave her my best Humphrey Bogart. 'Of all the java joints in the world, you had to walk into mine.'

'Oh, Maggie. Hey listen. Gotta run. See you. Bye.'

I trailed her outside and watched her dart like a ferret into Bed, Bath, & Beyond. After an exhaustive search of linens, housewares, cleaning supplies, gadgets and gifts, I found her in interior lighting, trying to hide behind a pole lamp. Ellie was nearly skinny enough to pull it off, but the riot of chestnut frizz gave her away.

'What's going on, Ellie?'

'Nothing. I just needed, I just—'

'Is something wrong?

'Of course not.'

'Are you angry with me?'

'Why would I be angry?' Her eyes bugged, and the choking lie raised her voice by nearly an octave.

'Please, if I've done something to offend you, tell me. I realize I haven't exactly been myself. Preoccupied with the divorce and all. Not that I have to tell you.' Ellie had been divorced twelve years ago, when her son was only three. I couldn't count the hours she'd spent regaling me with horror stories about her ex-mate, disastrous dates, and the virtual Mardi Gras of crushing craziness that was her life as a single mother in New York.

The frizzy head reared back, and she struck like a cobra. 'Don't you dare compare yourself to me!'

'Huh?'

'Let's not go there, Maggie. I just don't want to get involved.'

'Involved in what?'

'First Harold. Now you. I mean, come on!'

'Harold called you? Why would he do a thing like that?' Harold had no use for my sane friends, much less Ellie.

'I haven't the slightest idea, and I frankly don't care. I don't have room in my life for needy people, Maggie. Just lose my number, OK?'

Star Chores

For the first time, I recognized a striking similarity between me and Amelia Burkart, the gorgeous, sexy film star. Both of us had been tragically miscast. I was in no way equipped to play the dumped divorcee and Amelia should never have been signed for the plum role of Princess Di in the forthcoming Farlow Brothers biopic. True, she more than looked the part, but her voice was barely suitable for talkies, much less British royalty. Amelia sounded like a chipmunk from the South Bronx who'd been struck in the throat by a Frisbee. This was not a problem in the parts she typically played, which were heavy on bounce and jiggle and light on lines. Her usual scripts read more or less as follows:

Amelia: (running from slavering beast, mobster, serial killer or hair-do-threatening storm.) *Ooh!*
Slavering beast, or whatever: (catching up) *Mmmmmmmm. Live girl!*
Amelia: (breathing hard to exaggerate the jiggle and bounce) *Heeeeeelp! Ooh!!!!*

Needless to say, the Princess Diana role

qualified as what was known in the biz as a 'departure', which in this case suggested that the casting director, the director and the producer had suffered a simultaneous psychotic break.

'Oy can't do it, Maggie.'

'Yes you can.' I demonstrated for her in the mirror, trying to ignore the way her magnificence made me look precisely like a troll. From the corner of my eye, I caught sight of the new rule Janine had written on my chalkboard in screaming neon pink: *Screw living well. Revenge is the best revenge.*

I trained my focus on Amelia. 'I simply can't abide Charles's betrayal any longer, your Majesty,' I intoned.

'Oy simply can't aboyd Chawls buhtrayal any lawnguh, yaw mahjusty.'

'Better.'

'Don't be gentle with me, Maggie. It's OK to tell me oy suck.'

'You're sucking a little less. Watch my mouth. I simply can't abide Charles's betrayal any longer, your Majesty. Think wide and exaggerated. Open your mouth fully. Relax your jaw. Bring the sound lower down in your chest. "I cahnt..."'

'Oyyyy cannnnt.'

'Better.'

'Yaw so wonduhful, Maggie. I wish I could be as togethuh and confuhdent as you.'

'Oh you are, Amelia. Believe me, you are.'

51

The Wild Lunch

My mother waited in women's purses at Macy's, tapping one of the size 10 feet that sprawled beneath her squat, ferocious form like pontoons. Mom had a rabid fetish for promptness, which she fed by setting her watch several time zones ahead. Years ago, I gave up trying to mollify her with simple logic or showing up early or the unassailable verdict of neutral clocks. My mother really enjoyed being annoyed with me, and who was I to rob an elderly sadist of one of her few remaining pleasures?

'Noon is noon, Maggie,' she informed me.

'Excellent point.'

'My God, look at those bags under your eyes.'

'Actually, I'd rather not.'

'So you want to go to the coffee shop?'

'Where else?'

We always met at noon in women's purses at Macy's and then went to the highly forgettable coffee shop down the street, where my mother always ordered the tasteless tuna on dry rye toast with a side of crappy coleslaw and the bitter black sludge they called coffee and I, like it or not, had the same. Once, years ago, in a moment of weakness, I'd agreed to this and that was that. In addition to tardiness, my mother had zero tolerance, or less than that, for change.

She leaned down and met the sandwich millimeters from the plate, as if it might otherwise flee. And well it might, given the terrifying speed and ferocity with which the woman sucked down food. Naturally, she expected you to match her, bite for breathless bite. Otherwise, when you least expected it, your plate vanished. A five-course Thanksgiving at my mother's house was once clocked at a world-record-beating eleven minutes, flat. And that included time out for the traditional holiday snipe-fest with her sister.

To keep up the punishing pace, she chewed while she talked, putting a fresh, revolting spin on the concept of multi-tasking. 'So how are things?' she mumbled around a scenic mouthful of masticated tuna, toast and slaw.

'OK.'

Her brow shot up. 'Yeah? So Harold's back?'

'Harold's not coming back, Mom. I told you.'

'Don't be silly.'

'He wants a divorce.' I forced the word past the grief plug wedged deep in my throat.

'Who cares what he wants? You don't want to be single, Maggie. Not at your age.'

'I told you, Mom. He's found someone else. That's how it is.'

She scowled. 'Nonsense. What does he

know?'

'He knows he wants a divorce.'

'We don't divorce in our family.'

'What about cousin Rudy? What about Louise and cousin Jim?'

'That's your father's side. I'm talking Evantoffs.'

'What about Aunt Frieda? She divorced twice.'

'Frieda's crazy. She doesn't count.'

'What about cousin Ruthie then? You'd never say a bad word about her.'

'That wasn't a marriage. It was playing house. Besides, it was mixed.'

'Right. He was Catholic. She was shrewish.'

'Don't be fresh. And don't argue.'

Some people looked to their mothers for support. Mine was more the type you could rely on for a peptic ulcer. 'Fine. Believe me. I'd rather not talk about it at all.'

In one giant bite, she dispatched the remains of her lunch. 'Harold's thinking with his *shmekel*. Men do that. He'll come to his senses. You'll see.'

What I saw was that I needed to change the subject or give my mother a tuna facial now. 'I have big news about Brian, Mom. Believe it or not, he showed up with a wife.'

'Your Brian?'

'And your grandson. Yes.'

'Jewish?'

'I don't know. Her name's Valerie. She has a cookie business. And a baby girl.'

'This coffee is cold. Waiter! I ordered hot,

not iced.'

'So this makes you a great-grandmother. What do you think of that?'

'Valerie doesn't sound like a Jewish name. Waiter! Some hot!'

'I asked what you think of being Great-grandma Pearl.'

She flapped away the question. 'You know I'm not one for all that nonsense. What did I always tell you?'

'Not to walk like a duck.'

'Not that.'

'That the boys won't like me if I let them know I'm smart.'

'Not that either.'

'That I should learn to type in case – God forbid – anything should ever happen to my husband.'

'So you see?'

I did, through the sting of welling tears. 'Sure. You were right. What I regret most is not having better typing skills.'

'Don't be fresh. I always told you I don't knit and I don't sit. That whole grandmother business is a bunch of *mishigas*. Foolishness invented by kids who expect their parents to do their job.'

'Believe it or not, some people love spending time with their grandkids.'

'Some people love tripe, too. And beef jerky.'

'And church every Sunday,' I said to bait her. 'And a nice glass of milk with their ham and cheese.'

'*Feh.* Just goes to prove my point. There's no accounting for some people's taste.'

She dipped into the plastic dispenser on the table and slipped a dozen packets of artificial sweetener into her purse. My mother had enough purloined Sweet'N Lo and Equal to turn the Atlantic Ocean cloyingly sweet with a dreadful aftertaste.

'I ask you, did I ever once take care of Allison or Brian?'

'Nope. Not once.'

'You see?'

'Not even the time when Harold was out of town and I had that terrible case of food poisoning.'

'So? Was it my idea you should eat bad Chinese? What was I supposed to do? Disappoint my whole Canasta group?'

'Of course not. First things first.'

She set a hand over her coffee cup when the waiter moved to top it off. 'Bring me fresh. Her, too.'

'Please,' I said on her rude behalf. 'And thank you.'

'The way I see it, I brought you up, and that's more than plenty.'

'So you've said, many times.' Just when I thought I couldn't feel any crappier, leave it to my mother to prove me wrong.

'You get to a certain age; it's time to look after number one.'

'And what age was that for you exactly?'

'Don't be snide. It just so happens I'm not the maternal type. Never was. Never will be.'

'Now there's a news flash.'

Have I mentioned that I was an accident? Lest I should ever forget this, my mother regularly reminds me, and anyone else who'll listen, that I came to be despite her firm desire to remain blissfully childless for life. Over the years, I've heard many versions of how the unthinkable travesty of my existence occurred.

In one account, my father, who was the sweetest, dearest, most loving and giving soul imaginable, somehow tricked her into becoming pregnant. Once, in an unusually impertinent and suicidal mood, I asked if Pop used his magic wand, and she slapped me.

In another version, my mother was a bit under the weather at the time, i.e. drunk, after consuming an excess of spiked punch at Aunt Harriet and Uncle Stanley's wedding, where, as my mother tells it, they served inedible food (and in such small portions!).

Yet another scenario had her agreeing to the tragic folly of my conception under extreme duress after her own mother was diagnosed with a mysterious stomach ailment and expressed her tearful desire to have a grandchild before she died. When I was a bun in the oven, so to speak, the old lady had the unmitigated gall to kick off. My mother's resentment of this was eerily similar to Mrs Feder's feelings about her Morty's myocardial infarction. Both women seemed to believe that accidental death and lethal illness were unforgivable acts of willful spite.

'Take Harold back, Maggie. Believe me. Men like that don't grow on trees.'

My eyes went liquid again. 'Why can't you listen, Mom? He doesn't want me. He wants Bethany. He wants a divorce.'

She waved her fork with menace. 'You're not getting any younger, you know.'

'Is that so? Never occurred to me.'

'I read that a woman your age has a better chance of getting abducted by aliens than finding a man.'

'Male aliens or female?'

'Don't be fresh. And for heaven's sake, keep that grandchild nonsense to yourself. There's nothing sexy about being a grandmother. In fact it's the exact opposite of sexy.'

'I thought the opposite of sexy was hemorrhoids.'

'I mean it, Maggie. Don't be a horse's ass. Brian will be done with this wife and baby craziness in about three minutes. Remember how he was with the fish?'

I did, though I wouldn't give my mother the satisfaction of admitting it. The notion that this might be a passing fancy had crossed my mind. Brian's attention span for pets was no more lasting than his passion for careers. Time and again, I fell for his ardent pleas and promises, only to have him lose interest in a matter of days. The tropical fish, along with their elaborate, expensive aquarium, went to our neighbors down the street. The petting zoo took the bunnies. The kittens were adopt-

58

ed by a mystery bookshop. Tweety and Sylvester, the parakeets, went on the lam when Brian got it in his head to take them for a ride on the handlebars of his ten-speed bike. Huey and Dewey, the golden retrievers, naturally fell to me.

'That baby isn't your grandchild. Not legally. Anyhow, men don't like their women old.'

'Or smart,' I reminded her. 'Or duck-like.'

'Old is worse.'

'Then how do you explain the fact that you always have a gentleman suitor or two?'

'Because old is an attitude, not a number. The number doesn't matter one bit.'

'No? Then how old are you?'

'None of your business. You want a man? Don't ask, don't tell. Especially about grandchildren you don't even have. Now drink before that coffee gets cold.'

A Beautiful Find

Janine was snooping shamelessly in my office when she happened on Wop's business card. 'You know him, Maggie? You actually *know* Anthony Sinclair?'

'I wouldn't go that far. We were in homeroom together in junior high, and I haven't seen him since. I ran into him after I left the lawyers.'

'Do you realize who this is, Maggie? Do you have even the vaguest, Jiminy Fricking idea?'

'Yes I do, actually. Sinclair is his stepfather's name. He's the former Tony Carlucci, also known as Tony Spumoni or simply Wop, who sat two seats in front of me two or three hundred years ago in Mrs Crawshaw's eighth grade homeroom at Southside Junior High.'

'Wop, my Alice in Wonderland. This happens to be *the* Anthony Sinclair, Chairman and CEO of Luxury Brands International. He's got about a zillion dollars, corporate villa and private jet at his disposal, the works. If you weren't my close and pathetically depressed friend, I'd steal him so fast you'd get windburn.'

'He's not mine to steal.'

'When are you seeing him? I'm calling Daphne. I'm setting up a war room. We have to start getting you in fighting trim right away.'

'Slow down. This was just an accidental meeting. I'll probably never hear from him again.'

'Then he'll hear from you. That's the amazing thing about phones, sweetie. They work both ways.'

'I wouldn't call him. I could never do that. Not in a million years.'

'Of course you can. And you will. You simply do not let a prize catch like Anthony Sinclair spit the hook.'

'He's not on the hook. We ran into each other. Or rather, I ran into him. That's all.'

'That's not all. That's only the beginning, the kickoff. And now you pick up the ball and run with it like the blazes until you get to goal.'

'I'm not interested in meeting anyone right now. To be honest, I don't know if I ever will be. I'd be terrified of getting hurt again. That's the truth.' I ordered myself not to cry, but my eyes refused to obey. In seconds, I was reduced to a heaving, drip-nosed sob.

'Stop that!' Janine frowned in a way that could only be described as blood-chilling. 'You are going to listen to me on this, Maggie. And that's final. First, we're going to look up Anthony Sinclair's bio and compensation package at LBI, so you get the whole, juicy picture, and then we're going to plan a very careful, foolproof campaign to reel the guy in.'

'Hear me, Janine. I'm not ready, not interested. Not.'

She sat at my computer and went online. Why wasn't I in the least surprised that she knew my ultra-secure, top secret, well-guarded password? In seconds, I was looking at the staggering sum Anthony Sinclair earned last year in salary, bonuses and stock options.

'So Wop's done well. Good for him.'

'And good for you, honey. As my mother always says: rich or poor, it's great to have lots and lots of money.'

'Even if I was interested, which I'm not, what would someone like that want with someone like me? I'm old; I'm overweight and pathetically depressed, like you said. I'm such a great big loser; I'm not even good enough for Harold.'

'Hush. I can *not* listen to such crap in the presence of all this yummy power and wealth.'

Janine pulled up Anthony Sinclair's CV, which sketched his meteoric rise from UCLA undergrad to Stanford business school to the corporate stratosphere.

My eye dipped to the giant loophole at the bottom of the page. 'So much for your big plans. He's married. Three grown kids.'

Her finger popped up like a turkey timer. 'But you don't know *how* married, do you? It may be hardly at all.'

'There aren't degrees of marriage. It's like being pregnant. You are or you aren't.'

'Nonsense. How married are you?'

'That's different. Harold and I are getting a divorce.'

'So who says filthy rich, fabulous Anthony Sinclair isn't getting a divorce, too?'

'Who says he is?'

'Logic. The man is married for the love of Christ. *Married* is precisely the same as *pre-divorced*.'

'I'm not going after a married man, Janine. I know what it feels like to be on the losing end of that equation.'

She beamed her approval. 'That's right, sweetie. And that's the point. You lost one, and now it's your turn to get one even better in return. You need this, Maggie. Need it, deserve it. And I'm going to see that you get it.'

'He's taken. End of story.'

'Wrong. I'll bet you anything Anthony Sinclair has a wretched home life. I'll bet he's been looking for someone like you for years. Think of it, Maggie. You were together in junior high and now fate has brought you together again.'

'Not fate, Janine. It was a giant carrot.'

'Fate *sent* that giant carrot, and you don't duck around with fate. You know why the divorce rate in this country is over fifty per cent?'

'Why?'

'Because fate's favorite game in the whole world is musical chairs. If fate didn't want people to break up and move on, there wouldn't be office Christmas parties or class reunions or e-mail or dating services or personal ads or all the zillions of other things specially designed to encourage extramarital fooling around.'

I didn't respond. From long experience, I'd learned that there was no percentage, whatsoever, in arguing with Janine. When she was right, she was right, and when she wasn't, she was equally, if not doubly sure of herself. Still, I happened to know she was dead wrong about this one. Fate's favorite game, hands down, was Pin the Tail on the Donkey. Fate simply loved to see you get it in the end.

Body Trouble

Dr Millhauser, one of those rare, perfect doctors who never asked me to step on a scale, had stopped taking my insurance. This left me without a primary care physician, which relegated me to a frightening purgatory in the eyes of my insurance company. If something should happen to me – say I had a stroke or got attacked by rabid fans who mistook me for Kim Bassinger – I'd have to do some mighty fast talking to get treated at all. Were I comatose and unable to threaten a lawsuit, they might well leave me where I'd fallen, paralyzed, foaming at the mouth, and/or hemorrhaging, until city sanitation workers came and carted me away.

With this in mind, I'd scanned my carrier's online physician directory, cross-hatched the doctors' academic credentials, sub-specialties, years of experience and board-certifications with current lists of best physicians, and then chosen the doctor that offered what was to me the most medically significant: convenience.

Dr Melanie Borker's office was half a block from mine. She had an opening right away, which I was willing to overlook this once. If she proved unacceptable for some reason – she kept live chickens in the office, for example, or only spoke in clicks – I could always change later on. The important thing was to get the required name on my insurance card. I would be Dr Borker's patient, not a blank.

Entering the office suite that she shared with a cozy group of other Dr Borkers named Ellen, Jay and Jessica, I was pleased to find a neat, clean, well-lighted waiting room where a comforting assemblage of patients sat on brightly hued banquettes, poring through magazines. The receptionist greeted me with a smile and passed me a shiny Lucite clipboard capped by forms.

Crossing to a vacant seat, my stride was light. I so enjoyed checking off the entire *no* column when I was asked whether or not I'd ever had any of an exhaustive list of diseases. So far, I remained blessedly free of thyroid conditions, heart attacks, psoriasis, dry mouth, night sweats and urinary incontinence. As yet, I hadn't developed vertigo or unstable angina or high blood pressure (aside from the acute form I experienced when anyone so much as mentioned the H word). But Harold aside, on paper I remained in impeccable health. I'd never had major surgery or anything beyond the most trivial hallucinations. I'd never been hospitalized, except to have children. I didn't take any prescription medications, though I will admit, that's because cabernet sauvignon and Ben and

65

Jerry's could be purchased over the counter. Health had a pecking order just like everything else, and though the rules of etiquette prohibited gloating, you took your ego strokes where they came. As I claimed a vacant seat, I imagined walking the runway at the Ms Perfect Vital Signs pageant, bedecked with the queen's crown and a sash depicting my drop-dead gorgeous EKG.

After I'd settled in, I realized that the woman beside me was moaning. It was a low, rhythmic plaint, barely audible, but unquestionably a moan. 'Are you OK?' I asked.

She glanced at me and nodded her head tightly, claiming to be OK, while demonstrating that she was anything but.

I tried to catch the receptionist's eye, but she had turned her smiling attentions to the latest arrival, a pimpled teenager thumbing madly at his Gameboy. As a receptionist, her job, after all, was to receive.

My neighbor moaned on. I gazed at her furtively; trying not to breathe, hoping against hope that whatever she had was not contagious and/or lethal. With any luck, she was suffering from something innocent: her spleen had exploded or she'd accidentally swallowed a glass of paint thinner or a sixteen-wheeler had run over her foot. If I caught bubonic plague or the ebola virus from her, they'd surely strip me of my perfect-health crown, which reminded me that I still hadn't filled out the form.

I did so in a neat, careful hand. I entered my

name, address, day and evening phone numbers. I supplied my date of birth and social security number. I indicated that I was self-employed. And then I hit the wall.

The words looked innocent enough: *marital status*. The question was the simplest kind: multiple-choice. I could be single, married, widowed, separated or divorced. Up to me. All I had to do was circle the correct answer.

I urged myself along. *Come on, Maggie. You can do this*. But deep inside, I felt the first tremor of an impending quake. My temples thumped in sickening opposition to the jackhammer thwacking in my chest. Clammy sweat erupted, and I felt a major compulsion to belch.

I drew a deep, deliberate breath, and then another. This was no big deal, I told myself. No big deal.

I squared my shoulders and stared at the offending form again. Harold and I were technically still married. We had to be. *Single* was a word for confident women whose cell phones chirped while they sashayed down the street on four-inch heels. *Widow* would work but unfortunately, that's not what I was. If Harold had shown any consideration at all, he would have died a sudden, tragic, sympathy-inspiring death in the fire at Hadley Hall. But no.

I swallowed hard and poised my pencil for action. Separated seemed to sum up the way I felt. My life and I had been walking along, minding our own business, and somehow, we'd lost track of each other in the crowd. I'd searched and searched, growing ever more lost, desperate and disoriented. *Where was I? Who was I? When was this going to stop?*

Suddenly, hands were prodding me, helping me up. Soft voices coaxed. 'That's right. Take it easy. Come along.'

I found myself on an examining table bathed by the glare of fluorescent lights. Anxious faces loomed above me. I recognized the receptionist and my seatmate, the moaner. Imagine sinking so low that a plague victim had to come to your aid.

One of the strangers held a vial of something vile-smelling under my nose. Stinging vapors shot up my nostrils, and my brain snapped to military alert. I snapped up behind it, and firm hands settled me back down.

'I'm Dr Borker, Ms Strickland,' said the taller of the two strangers, an attractive woman with a riot of shoulder-length dark curls, an assertive nose, and steel-blue eyes. 'Can you tell me today's date?'

'I will if you tell me what just happened?'

She smiled. 'That's what I'm trying to find out. Are you in any pain?'

'That depends on your definition of pain.'

'Do you know where you are?'

'Sure I do. I'm in your office, making a fool of myself. Are you Dr Melanie Borker?'

'Jessica.' She listened to my lungs, checked my blood pressure, and then the nurse wheeled in a portable electro-cardiogram machine.

They hooked me up and ran a strip, which looked nothing like the pattern I'd pictured on my pageant sash. There were jerky spikes, terrifying pauses and precipitous dips, as if someone had replaced the orderly workings of my heart with a stunt plane.

'What's wrong with me? Is it serious?'

'I'd like to run a few more tests, but I'm pretty sure what you had was a panic attack. Have you been under any unusual stress lately?'

'Stress?' I cringed at the high-pitched squeal of my voice. I sounded like a hamster on speed.

'Yes. Have you been dealing with a major life change, perhaps? Even positive change can seem overwhelming.'

'I'm going through a divorce. That's all.'

'That's plenty. Take your time, Ms Strickland. When you're ready, come see me in my office and we'll talk.'

Her office was homey and reassuring. The desk was littered with photographs of smiling people doing the things smiling people do: celebrating birthdays, taking vacations, learning to ride two-wheelers, winning awards, getting diplomas, showing off large dead fish.

Dr Borker folded her hands. 'Has this happened before?'

'No. I've only been married once.'

'I meant the panic attack.'

'Definitely not. I've never been nearly that crazy before, at least, not in public.'

'This has nothing to do with being crazy.

It's a kind of overload. You need a way to alleviate the pressure.'

'Great idea. How?'

She pulled out a prescription pad. 'Are you allergic to any medications?'

'I'm not allergic to anything,' I said, still clinging to my perfect theoretical health. I was pretty sure they didn't ask you on intake forms about whether or not you'd ever made a screaming, gasping fool of yourself in a medical office waiting room.

'This is a mild tranquilizer. Should take the edge off.'

I read the form. The prescription was for Ativan, which would have suited me far better if it was called *Atta girl!*

'Have you seen your gynecologist lately?'

'I'm due. Make that overdue.'

She frowned.

'You're right. I'll call as soon as I get home.'

'Good. But I think it's important that you get supportive counseling as well.'

'You do think I'm crazy.'

'No I don't. I think you're a normal woman who's going through a rough patch and needs a place to discuss what's going on. I believe in psychotherapy. All of us can benefit by learning more about ourselves. There's never a shortage of important things to understand. Better ways to cope. I think we should all strive to be happier and more at peace with ourselves.'

The wistful sorrow in her expression was a vivid contrast to the smiling pictures on her desk. My guess was that she had a lot going on, too. True happiness took far more than birthday cake or vacations. Sometimes even a big dead fish was not enough.

Along Came a Schneider

I was passing the Midtown Synagogue when my feet somehow ferried me inside. I hadn't seen Rabbi Charles Kleinberg in a long time, but years back when Brian was going through some of his more unsettling phases, I could always rely on Rabbi Charlie, as he liked to be called, to talk me in from the ledge. Without him, I may well have wound up in a padded room, if only to catch a break from my darling son's terrifying shenanigans. Thinking of my performance in Dr Borker's office, I had to agree that I could use some of his wise counsel now.

Turned out I'd need to go to Fort Lauderdale to get it. Rabbi Charlie had retired, the stylish, pewter-haired woman at the desk informed me, but Rabbi Schneider was available if I'd like.

'Maybe not.'

She leaned closer. 'Take my word. Rabbi Schneider is wonderful. Different from Kleinberg, but every bit as good. Go see for yourself.'

'Well, since I'm here. Maybe I'll just say hello.'

'Do that. You won't be sorry.'

I found a kid sitting at Rabbi Charlie's desk behind a crystal bowl crammed with jelly beans. She had glossy chin-length hair, soulful soft brown eyes and fine features. A navy dress with a Peter Pan collar draped her boyish form. She wore no jewelry. No make-up. Nothing to betray her indeterminate age. I was thinking it must be take-your-daughter-to-work day when she came around the desk, gripped my hand warmly, and smiled. 'Welcome. I'm Rabbi Schneider.'

'You're the rabbi?'

'Yes. Call me Jennifer, please. And you're?'

A monkey's uncle.

How could this be? Rabbis were supposed to be stocky, avuncular men who reminded me of my dad. This one reminded me of how far I've traveled on that inexorable journey toward a pine box. When did I get to be older than all the authority figures? The city's Mayor was younger than me, as was the Governor and several past Presidents of the United States. So were all the most successful athletes, actors, rock stars and the vast majority of interesting felons. Some of the doctors I'd seen struck me as so young I pictured them performing surgery in footie pajamas, using toy plastic instruments, taking time out between harrowing cases for nap-time and snack.

'I'm Maggie Strickland,' I told her. 'I used

to come here from time to time to talk to Rabbi Charlie.'

'Wonderful man. And very hard shoes to fill. Sit, please.'

'No, that's OK. Since he's not here, I just thought I'd drop by for a second and say hello.'

'You know, Maggie, if you have a few minutes, you could do me a big favor.'

'Sure. I guess.'

She waved me toward a plump, gray armchair. 'Can I get you something? A soda? Hot tea?'

'Thanks, I'm fine. What would you like me to do?'

'Tell me what you wanted to talk to Rabbi Charlie about.'

'It's complicated.'

'What isn't?' Her smile was smooth and inviting, like a bright, cool, freshly laundered sheet.

'You're awfully young.'

'I'll get over that in time.' She eyed me steadily. 'So what's going on?'

'Well, for one thing, I've just become a grandmother.'

'*Mazel tov!* You must be so thrilled.'

'I know. I must be. That's the rule. But what if I'm not?'

The smile evaporated. 'People feel what they feel.'

'I don't know what I feel. This was sprung on me along with a bunch of other things. Suddenly, my son has a wife with a child and

73

my husband has a life with a child. Suddenly, black is white and green is purple, and I feel like I can't count on anything anymore.' I felt the odd, dissonant pulses starting up again. My breath came in sharp, shallow puffs. 'Just in case I should happen to pass out or start screaming, it's nothing, OK?'

'Are you sick?'

I shook my head and focused on my breathing. I tried for the kind of long, deep cleansing breaths that had proven useless when I gave birth. But now, the exercise seemed to help. The awful feeling eased its grip and backed away. 'I'm OK. Better now.'

'You sure?'

'Lately, this is about as good as it gets.'

'Sounds like you're going through an awful lot, Maggie.'

'It's just so impossible to get my head around. I thought Harold and I had a perfectly good marriage. I thought we were no more annoying to each other or incompatible than any other couple. I thought we'd go on just as we'd been doing until I died.'

'Why you?'

I shrugged. 'That's the way I always pictured things. It seemed only natural that I'd be the one pushing up daisies while Harold hung around to entertain the brisket brigade.'

'The what?'

'Brisket brigade refers to all the widowed and divorced women who descend on a man the minute his wife dies or even looks a little ill. They bring hot meals, hoping to snag the guy before he's goes on the open market. As I understand it, brisket is the covered casserole of choice.'

'I see. And what about your son? You said he's suddenly married with a child?'

'Brian's wonderful, but he never sticks with anything for long. My mother, who's the world's leading expert in most everything, is sure he'll get over the wife and baby thing the way he gave up the idea of running an alpaca llama ranch or importing something from Australia called kookooroo juice that's supposed to grow hair in all the right places.'

'He sounds interesting.'

'That he is.'

'And you sound realistic, and sensible.'

I shrugged. 'I know these aren't serious catastrophes. I mean nobody's sick or dying or anything. It's just life.'

'It is. That's true. And very wise.'

'And neurotic. Don't forget that. Credit where credit is due.'

Her smile returned. 'And bright and funny. All very useful in dealing with "just life" when it happens to throw you a curve ball or two.'

'You think?'

She waxed serious. 'I do. But talk is useful, too. It's good to have a place you can come to let loose and get things off your chest.'

I didn't know how to answer the expectant look on her baby face. In a way, this felt like trying to have a serious heart-to-heart with Delia.

'Something tells me you spend way too

much time taking care of everyone else and not nearly enough taking care of Maggie.'

'You're telling me to look out for number one? Sounds like my mother.'

'Not *only* for number one. Certainly not. But Maggie deserves your respect and attention. She's having a hard time right now, and she needs a little TLC.'

'I can't argue about the hard time part. I'm ashamed to admit this, but I never saw it coming. People always say you know if your husband is fooling around, but I honestly couldn't imagine Harold leaving me for anything less than really fabulous play-off tickets. A graduate student of all things. A gorgeous, brilliant young woman who has everything: younger, firmer, better and more promising than me. Why on earth would he leave me for that?' I let the tears spill over, too weary to fight them anymore.

'Sounds like you need a *lot* of TLC, Maggie. And that's perfectly OK.'

'You're pretty perceptive for a kid playing dress-up.'

'Come again soon then, if you like. Ask Isabel to block some time for us to sit and talk. Or if I don't seem right for you, I'd be glad to recommend someone else.'

'No, you do seem right. What will we talk about?'

'Anything you like. Although I must admit I'm eager to hear more about your mother.'

'Oh, Isabel would have to block lots and lots of time for that.'

My Best Friends' Vetting

Dish towels were far from the only things that got distributed in a divorce. People were divided up as well. As soon as we separated, certain friends had encamped on Harold's side, while others dug in and sided with me. Katie and Roger Miller, the couple that had been closest to us since we met on our mutual honeymoons in Bermuda, had elected to take the highest and most torturous road. They were determined to remain in both my life and Harold's. This made perfect, unassailable sense, though at the same time it struck me as unforgivable and absurd. How could true friends of mine have anything to do with Bethany, the slut Lolita of PhD candidates, or Harold, the Humbert Humbert of amoral ethicists, with no chin?

We met at Canaletto, our favorite neighborhood Italian restaurant. Roger had secured our regular corner table in the rear, the only one in the place that came close to meeting Harold's exasperating standards.

'What are we drinking?' Katie said, by way of her standard greeting.

'Anything in excess will do me fine.'

'Martini?'

'Not that much excess. I'm pretty fried. Tough day.'

Her patrician features registered concern. 'Talk, Mags. Get it off your little chest.'

'That's what we're here for,' Roger said. Rog is a total sweetheart, kind of a high-brow Episcopalian knockoff of my dad.

'I ran into Ellie Mathias this morning. She treated me like a leper.'

'The hell with her,' Katie said. 'Ellie is nothing but a mousy, pathetic, anorexic annoyance with hideous hair.'

'Maybe so. But I really hate being a pariah. It's all so seventeenth-century Salem.'

'Not to mention flat-chested with crooked teeth,' Katie went on. 'And that *kid* of hers. Poor thing looks like Gumby.'

'You don't deserve it, sweetie.' Roger set his broad, comforting hand over mine. 'The sad truth is that at times like this, you find out who your real friends are.'

Katie cupped my other hand as if she was trying to trap a mouse. 'The truth is most people stink.'

'Well I'm lucky to have you guys. That's for sure.'

Roger shut both eyes when he tried to wink. Like my son Brian, he could be so adorably inept. 'Back at you, Mags. How did it go with the lawyers?'

'It went.' I strived to respect their determination to remain neutral by sparing the gory details. Of course, I was not always entirely successful. 'Harold has signed on with the

Visigoths and the Huns. Very amicable.'

Roger sighed. 'You're angry. He's angry. It'll pass.'

'He's angry? What the hell does he have to be angry about?'

Roger flinched, as if I'd smacked him.

Katie preferred to snipe, 'You know what they say, Mags. There are two sides to every story. Three if you count the truth.'

'Let's change the subject, shall we? Tell us all about Brian's new bride and the baby,' Roger said.

'Valerie bakes cookies, and Delia's daddy was a kitchen gadget. And Katie, what you said was really hurtful and unfair.'

Her baby blues grew suspiciously moist. 'I'm sorry. You're right. But look, all this hasn't been easy on us either. We love both of you. You and Harold are family. Better than family. With you, we got to choose.' A tear slid majestically down her proud-boned cheek.

I was stunned. Katie and Roger were at least ninetieth generation Americans: whale-wearing, martini-swilling, mayonnaise-adoring, stoical WASPs. I suspected their forebears arrived here early enough to order up Plymouth Rock from a tony British catalogue and have it shipped over so the Pilgrims would have somewhere nice and dry to disembark, slip on their Lily Pulitzers, and sip their welcome cocktails.

The Millers were wonderful, loyal friends. They'd seen us through my father's death, Harold's mock melanoma and Brian's hyperactivity, learning disabilities, and various, charming, little adolescent run-ins with the law. They took us in during a ten-day, ice-storm-induced power outage while we were still living in Connecticut and let us shower with them for almost two months after Harold tried to fix our leaky plumbing to save money and caused so much damage, our house was pretty much condemned.

Of course, we'd returned the favor whenever we could. We'd whined for them when their glacial, genetic stoicism kept them from doing it themselves. We'd looked after their well-behaved kids while they went off on photo safaris in chicest Africa or golf outings in Palm Beach. And we had bravely served as the token Jews at their Norman Rockwell holiday celebrations, where we'd allowed ourselves to be surrounded by solemn women with pleated lips and pearl chokers and humorless, inebriated men in plaid. Once, I'd even cracked a tooth in a valiant attempt to actually taste Katie's annual Christmas fruitcake. I'd considered that chip a proud badge of friendship that I regretted having to cap.

Still, while Roger had a mutant warm fuzzy side, Katie had always been impeccably reserved. Until now, I had never seen her shed anything messier than gardening clogs or a Burberry barbecue apron.

'I didn't ask for this,' I told her, matching her tears and raising her several. 'Didn't want it, and don't get it at all. Bethany is younger than Allison, for God's sake. What does Harold think he's doing? What do they find to talk about? Besides Kant and Schopenhauer, I mean.'

Katie dabbed her face with an embroidered lace hanky and perked up like a rain-soaked plant. 'It's hard, Mags. I know. And we feel for you. Now, let's please change the subject. Rog and I want to make a party for Brian and Valerie, so she can meet everyone. Let's look at our calendars and pencil something in.'

Cutie and the Feast

7:45 a.m.
Tabrik, the night doorman, called on the house phone: 'Someone here to see you, Mrs Strickland.'

Me: Who?

He: (inaudible)

Me: Tabrik, who is it?

He: (giggling in a mildly demented fashion) It's a Ms Dee Duh.

Me: Who?

He: (trying unsuccessfully to get a grip) And a Ms Valerie. Wait. She wants to talk to you.

Valerie: Hi, Mom. Delia and I are out having a little walk before Nanny Grace comes and Delia thought maybe Granny would like to join us.

Me: (*Are you nuts? Do you have any idea what time it is. I haven't even had any coffee yet.*) A walk?

Delia: (alarmed) No Gate, Mommy. No Gate!

Valerie: No, honey. Nanny Grace comes later. This is Granny's house. You wanted to see her – remember?

Delia: Wan Gammy! See Gammy. Now!

Valerie: I know, sweetie. But I'm not sure Granny can come. It's really early.

Delia: Deduh wan GAMMY now!

Me: Be right down.

Valerie sported her Pillsbury Doughboy down coat and Sasquatch mukluks. The cold had polished her cheeks to a fetching hypertensive pink. Delia rode in a plaid stroller. She wore a rabbit motif pink snowsuit complete with floppy ears. Her limbs stuck straight out, so she looked like a cute little Playboy bunny scarecrow.

Before we left the lobby, Valerie draped the stroller with contoured plastic sheeting. Think full baby condom. She snapped, clipped and battened everything down so not a single stray outside molecule could sneak through.

Delia looked resigned, and I suffered a bit of sympathetic claustrophobia. Imagine being incarcerated like that, doomed to inhale your own bottle breath, baby farts, and quite possibly worse.

'I really like Delia to get some nice, fresh

morning air,' Valerie said without a hint of irony.

We headed up First Avenue, passing a striking number of other infants in similar biohazard gear.

'I know I should have called first, Mom. But Delia insisted.'

Calling first is good. Mom is questionable. So is taking orders from a two-foot-tall, twenty-five-pound baby girl. 'It's fine.' We passed Starbucks, where I was lured by the siren song of a double frappuccino with an espresso shot, but recalling my ugly run-in with Ellie Mathias, I slogged on.

'You must have been the most amazing mother. Raising Ali and Brian. Such great people,' Valerie said.

'Thanks, but I was far from amazing.'

'Bet you were, too. I have to admit, sometimes I just feel so gosh darned inadequate.'

Gosh darned? 'We all do sometimes.'

'You? Can't imagine. To listen to Bri, you positively walk on water.'

'Only if it's very, very shallow.'

'See? You're funny, too. Just like Bri always says.'

'He means funny in the head, not funny ha ha.'

'No he does not.' Her look went grave. 'Mind if I ask you something sort of personal?'

'What?'

'Bri told me what's going on with you and his dad. Are you OK, Mom? Is there any way

83

I can help?'

'There's nothing,' I said, looking at my son's heartland milkmaid through a fresh new lens. 'It's sweet of you to ask though, Valerie. Thanks.'

'Not at all. That's what family is for.'

'You obviously haven't met my family,' I told her.

'If there's ever anything I can do, Mom, you just let me know.'

'Sure.'

'Anything at all. Be my pleasure.'

'Back at you.'

We walked over to Second Avenue and headed south. Outside a store called Hot Jumbo Bagel, Valerie stalled. 'Mind stopping here for a sec? Bri says Delia and I just have to try some of your famous New York bagels. He says they're nothing at all like what we get back home.'

'Probably not.'

'Ever try Lenders? They're not bad.'

She was absolutely right. They didn't rise to that level.

Hot Jumbo tied for my favorite bagel place with a store on First Avenue called Tal. Years ago, Harold and I determined this in a series of rigorous, double-blind, placebo-controlled taste tests involving specimens from the six bagel emporia within reasonable walking distance of our apartment. Occasional follow-ups had confirmed the dead heat. I remained partial to the well-baked sesame variety. Apparently, Harold's breakfast preference had shifted to graduate students, over easy.

While Valerie busted the baby out of solitary, I greeted Toby, the counterwoman, in her native Thai. The grill man got his standard good morning in Albanian.

'Wow, Mom. How many languages do you know?'

'A few words of Korean greengrocer, a smattering of Turkish doorman, a little Russian saleslady, some taxicab Farsi, the basics of Thai bagel counterperson, Margarita and quesadilla Spanish, bistro French, pasta Italian, and just enough Albanian to get my coffee with a smile.'

'Could I please have a bagel with lox?' Valerie spoke with great deliberation, as if Toby were hard of hearing, backward, or both, rather than simply foreign born.

Toby rolled her eyes. 'You can pay. You can have. What kind bagel you want?'

Mild panic registered on Valerie's round pink face as she scanned the list of choices. 'How about blueberry? Doesn't blueberry sound delish, Delia?'

'Boo-bwee!' the baby chortled with glee.

'Great. I'll have a blueberry bagel with cream cheese and lox.'

Toby averted her gaze and gave that taut shake of her head she used to inform good customers that the tuna salad was questionable or that they should pass on the cheese Danish.

'Blueberry really doesn't go with lox, Valerie,' I explained, trying not to retch.

'Hey, sorry. What do I know? You're the expert, Mom. You order, please.'

Toby anointed a perfect sesame specimen with glistening, paper-thin slices of smoked salmon and the hefty layer of cream cheese locally known as a *shmear*. 'Why she call you Mom? That not you daughter,' she rasped. 'She big size fatso. You daughter like rail.'

'Valerie is Brian's wife.'

'Brian have wife and baby?' She whistled low, no doubt recalling the glory days when Brian was in his 'Hey, Mon', dreadlock-sporting Rasta phase and fancied himself a graffiti artist to boot. That naturally led to the probation and community-service phase. 'Live long enough. See everything,' Toby opined.

We sat at a tiny table at the rear.

'Bay-goo,' Delia said, munching on the fragment she'd been handed.

'Yes, cutie. Isn't it delish like Daddy said? A regular feast.'

'Boo-bwee bay-goo?'

'Sesame,' I told her firmly. 'With a *shmear.*'

Driving Miss Crazy

Dr Graybower, my bearish white-haired gynecologist, commented on my long absence with a harsh downward thrust of his brow. He did so when I was in what is medically known as the upended turtle position. My feet were perched on elevated stirrups covered with crocheted lavender sleeves. Crinkly white paper swaddled the rest of me like a Parisian baguette. A capricious current fanned my exposed nether regions, and I couldn't help imagining my privates limp and feverish with a cold.

'So how are you, Margaret? Feeling well?'

'More or less.'

'Which is it? More? Or less?'

'I'm OK.'

'When was your last period?'

'Not in a while. I have a comma every so often, though, plus plenty of run-on sentences.'

'All age-appropriate. Skootch forward please. More. That's good. This will be a little cold. Relax.'

The cavity search came next. Graybower invaded me with a gadget that looked like salad tongs and felt like the frozen jaws of life. This was followed by the scratch of a vulture's claw at my cervix. Very relaxing.

Next, he worked my breasts like Lawrence Kasden in tenth grade, who I imagine practiced his petting technique by squeezing a bicycle horn. Graybower prodded my squishy abdomen, covered me up again, and nodded. 'Good. You can get dressed now. I'll see you in the office.'

I found him at his desk, scribbling notes. Outsized plastic models of female body parts perched on the bookshelves behind him. My diabolical mind planted a turkey baster in the cross-section of a vaginal canal capped by a nice roomy uterus with a snoozing, tow-haired fetus inside. The whole concept of self-insemination with such an implement struck me as unwise. What about contamination by pan juices? Plus, didn't you risk producing a baby who bore a distressing resemblance to Frank Purdue?

'Everything looks fine, Margaret. Any problems? Concerns?'

'Only that I'm going through a divorce. But, I guess that's not technically gynecological.'

He doffed his gold-rimmed glasses, exposing world weary, ash-toned eyes. 'Sorry to hear it. Anything I can do?'

'Is there a medical treatment?'

'Tincture of time, mostly. I was divorced a dozen years ago, and it wasn't any fun. But looking back, I must tell you, I'd do it again in a heartbeat.'

'Harold left me.' As usual, this emerged on

88

a tidal flood of tears.

He passed me the Kleenex box. 'So did my wife. For our tax attorney. Took me a while to realize I was way better off without her, and him. New man got me double the refund.'

'Harold left me for a twenty-three-year-old graduate assistant.'

'Sorry. I'm sure it's been tough.'

'At least he could have had the decency to make it a laughable bimbo. But no. This one has brains, substance. Does that strike you as even the least bit reasonable?'

'It all turns out for the best. Believe me. I met someone wonderful. Never been happier in my life.'

'Nice to hear. But you're a man. At my age, a woman has about as much chance of ever finding someone as being abducted by a band of all-female aliens.'

'That statistic doesn't make much sense if you consider that half of every heterosexual couple involved in a remarriage is female.'

I dried my eyes. 'That makes sense, and I'd like to believe you. Only that would mean my mother is wrong. And my mother has never been wrong. Not once, not even a little.'

The grin wiped a decade off his face. 'Other than the irregular periods, how are you doing with menopausal symptoms?'

'No hot flushes or anything yet.'

'You may dodge that bullet. Many women do.'

'And if not?'

'Let's just see how it goes.'

'I'd like to schedule my menopause for a couple of years from now, OK? This is not the right time.'

'I'll see what I can do.' He studied my chart. 'You're due for a mammogram, a pelvic ultrasound and bone-density studies. Otherwise, you're looking great, Margaret. See you in six months.'

I was halfway back to the office when I happened to gaze at the papers he gave me. Seeing the diagnosis, I went limp. This couldn't be happening. Not to me. Not now.

Dr Oh!

I paged Dr Darlys Brewer at New York Presbyterian Hospital. Darlys, a world-renowned fertility expert, had been a dear friend and near sister since we roomed together as sophomores at Cornell. I was soothed at once by her honeyed southern drawl. 'Hi, Sweetie. What's up?'

'Sorry to bother you, but I just got back from Graybower's.'

'And?'

'And what does it mean when you have *atrophic vaginitis*?'

'Graybower said that?'

'No, he wrote it as the diagnosis on my insurance form. What does it mean?'

'Means your insurance will cover the visit.'

'You sure? It sounds terrible.'

'Believe me, it's nothing. A little thinning of the tissues. Bit less lubrication. All perfectly normal.'

'Rotting away and drying up is normal? Come on, Darlys. I'm not an autumn leaf.'

Her laugh reminded me of the wind chimes on her parents' broad veranda in Charleston. 'It's nothing like that. Just means down there is getting on like the rest of us, Maggie. Showing a bit of wear and tear.'

'No fair. Mine hasn't gotten any of that in ages.'

'Well now, that won't do. You know what they say, sweetheart: use it or lose it.'

'How am I supposed to do that, pray tell? I don't think Avis has a rent-a-stud division.'

'What do you do when there's no attendant at the gas station?'

'I look around for a place with full service.'

'Nothing wrong with pumping your own.'

'You're telling me you do this?'

'You bet. Gary travels and so do I. Sometimes we're apart for weeks at a time. Way too much drought for this girl.'

'You're recommending self-service? This is a *medical* recommendation?'

'I'll write you a prescription if you like. It's normal, natural, and fun. Plus, it'll keep that equipment of yours fit and ready for action.'

'With the way things are going, I may as well have it drained and mounted on blocks.'

'You know, sweetie. It's the damnedest

thing, but just when a person starts to talk that way – all hangdog down and defeated – things have an amazing way of turning themselves around.'

The Slutty Professor

I was doing a bit of online research when Janine padded up behind me. For a large-mouthed, devoutly obnoxious attention-seeker, she had a remarkable facility for stealth.

'Well, and what have we here?'

Desperately, I went for the browser's Back button, but in my typical clumsy way with the keyboard, I misfired and hit Reload by mistake. Up slithered the site I'd been perusing: 'Sex Toy Central – your one-stop shopping place for devilish delights at diabolically discounted prices'.

'Don't know how that came up,' I blurted through a haze of humiliation.

Janine leaned in and clicked on the link marked *good vibrations*. 'Came up. Interesting choice of words. Well look at you. Didn't know you were so – shall we say – inclined.'

'I'm not.' I stabbed the power button, and the computer ground to a stunned, whining halt. 'So happens it's a health issue.'

'You won't get an argument from me.'

'Seriously. It is. I went to see my gynecologist today.'

'And he found you have what? An impacted orgasm?' Honing in with her incredible snoop radar, she plucked Graybower's insurance form from the sprawl of papers on my desk. *Atrophic vaginitis?* My God, Maggie! You poor thing. Ick. Gross.' She backed away. 'It better not be catching.'

'It's not. It's nothing serious at all, just a normal part of aging.'

'Having your bottom shrivel up and fall off is normal? I don't think so.'

'It's not like that, Janine. Just a little thinning of the tissues, some dryness.'

She pointed at the blank computer screen. 'And that's the therapy?'

Humiliation set fire to my cheeks. 'No. Of course not. It's more about preservation. Use it or lose it. You know.'

'I do indeed. Plus, yum, while we're on the subject. So what did you order?'

'Nothing. I'm just doing a little research, studying my options.'

'Studying? This is not exactly rocket science.'

'Looking around, then.'

'As well you should. It happens to be an important quality-of-life issue. Frankly, I'm more attached than I care to admit to Old Sparky. Can't imagine what I'll do if he ever conks out. Magic Wanda is OK for a change, but she's no Sparky. You?'

I flushed harder. 'I've never owned a vibrator.'

'You're kidding me.'

'I've been married forever, Janine.'

'So just because you own a stove, you don't eat out? You don't order in? You never get hungry and scarf down a quick sandwich on the run?'

'Harold's very straight-laced. He would never have put up with a thing like that.'

'Straight-laced? Son of a witch is *shtupping* a student, for Chrissakes. Drilling her with his hard, hot, throbbing PhD.'

'Please.'

'OK, sorry. But it's true.'

'Look. I thought Harold was straight-laced. He certainly acted that way. He was opposed to erotic movies and appalled by bad language and completely aghast during most of the Sixties and Seventies. He wouldn't even listen to a Beatles album. Said it was all about sex and sin.'

'Well, duh.'

'Yes, but it honestly upset him. Brian liked that group, Pearl Jam. So Harold listened once, trying to fake a bit of tolerance, I guess. And he managed to stand the music for almost a whole minute. Then Bri told him what the group's name meant, and Harold all but took to bed with the vapors.'

'Speaking of bed. How lousy was he in the sack?'

'He was OK.'

'Come on. On a scale of one to ten, where ten is the worst you can imagine.'

I thought awhile, weighing my words, still

94

determined to be fair. 'About a twelve.'

'So I thought. What was it? Tiny dick? Limp dick? Premature ejaculation?'

'Well, he did get off quickly, but he had to so he wouldn't miss any of *The Tonight Show*. After all, the commercial breaks only last a couple of minutes.'

'And let me guess, he didn't know the territory. Couldn't find your juicy bits if his life depended on it.'

'I can't believe I'm discussing this. The last time I talked openly about sex was with Brian and Ali when they were little kids. I still remember this one time when Bri was about four and wanted to know where babies come from. It was seven in the morning and we were all sitting around the breakfast table eating French toast. Harold flushed beet red, said he had to catch a train, and raced out as if the house was about to explode. I've always wondered how long it took before he remembered he was on vacation.'

'Come on. Spill. He couldn't find your on-button with both hands and a road map, right?'

'You're presuming he ever tried.'

Janine shook her head. 'Doesn't matter. He wouldn't have known what to do with it if he tripped on it by mistake.'

'True. I would say he had the finesse of a hippo, but that would be unfair to hippos.' Nastiness was an intoxicating drug. I was literally getting drunk on it. 'I can't tell you how many times I explained to him: Softer,

Harold. That's it, right there. Nope, you lost it. Higher. A little to the left. Ah well, maybe next time.'

'While he got his socks off, rocks off, and goodbye,' Janine said.

'He didn't take his socks off. Undershirt either.' I didn't mention that he wore his glasses, for safety's sake, not – Lord knows – to watch. Once, he raced back to the living room to catch Leno before the next guest came on, only to find he'd forgotten his specs, and that was that.

'You poor, deprived, dopey girl. You know what you need, Maggie?'

'No, what?'

'Anthony Sinclair, that's what. So happens money equals power and power equals fabulous in bed.'

'That makes no sense whatsoever.'

'It doesn't have to make sense, honey. All it has to do is make you have a nice rosy complexion and a big old smile on your satisfied face. And that's what the fabulous Anthony Sinclair is going to deliver.'

'I told you I'm not interested. The man is taken.'

'All that means is you have to make sure he's doubly taken with you.' She strode to the chalkboard, erased it, and printed a new rule for the day: *A bitch in time does fine.* 'Now grab your coat. You're coming with me.'

'I can't. I have an appointment out of the office.'

'Afterwards then. I'll meet you here at six.'

96

The Fling and I

Janine was barely out the door when my phone rang. 'Maggie? Glad I caught you. It's Anthony Sinclair.'

'Oh, hi,' I croaked like the toad of honor when all his frog friends leaped out and yelled *Surprise!*

'I was hoping you might be free for dinner Wednesday night.'

'Let me check,' I said, trying to impersonate a person with a life. 'Would your *wife* be joining us?'

'Stephanie's in London. She's pretty much burnt out on traveling with me. To be honest, Maggie, I think she's pretty much burnt out on me in general.'

I bit back an unseemly smile. 'That's too bad.'

'Old marriage,' he offered by way of explanation.

'Tell me about it.'

'Sorry. I'm afraid I jumped to conclusions because I didn't see a ring. Of course, I'd love it if you and your *husband* would join me for dinner.'

'Thanks, but he can't. Bethany won't allow it.'

'Who?'

97

'Bethany Whitmore. She's the graduate student he dumped me for.'

'A table for two it is, then. Great.'

'I'd like to, Anthony. But it's probably not a good idea.'

'Why not?'

'Lots of reasons.'

'Name one.'

'Stephanie.'

'I told you, we're really not together anymore.'

'Me, then. I'm really not together anymore myself.'

'Who is?'

'Seriously. I've been in a hideous blue funk since Harold took off. I'd be lousy company.'

'If all I wanted was to be entertained, I'd buy show tickets.'

'What do you want?'

'Dinner with an old friend. A nice meal with a side of nostalgia. That's all, Maggie. Scout's honor.'

'Oh really? What kind of scout are you?'

'The fine, upstanding kind. So what do you say?'

'Well – OK, I suppose,' I blurted even as the sage little voice inside me issued several sound objections. After all, I told myself, it was only an innocent dinner. I needed the diversion. He was alone. I was alone. What harm could it do?

'Terrific! I'm really looking forward to it, Maggie. Pick you up at seven.'

As I dimly recalled, that's what happened

on an actual date. 'Why don't I just meet you at the restaurant?'

'The place is a little hard to get to. It'll work out better if you let me take you there.'

Sage of Innocence

Rabbi Jennifer wore a plaid pleated skirt and a white cabled crewneck that made her look like a cute little cheerleader for God.

'How are things going?' she asked.

'Strangely.'

'In what way?'

A large box of Kleenex perched beside the jelly bean bowl on her desk. Sensing the impending need, I helped myself to one of each. 'Can I ask you a hypothetical question?'

'Hypothetical or otherwise, sure.'

'Don't you think it's ridiculous for people of a certain age to worry about love and romance?'

'What do you think?'

'That I'm ridiculous.'

'Because you worry about love and romance?'

I shrugged. 'I'm forty-nine, not fifteen.'

'Everyone wants love and affection, Maggie. That has nothing to do with age.'

'Do you honestly believe people still have crushes and romantic fantasies when they're ninety? You think hundred-year-olds worry about looking their best to attract members of the opposite sex?'

'I think as long as people are alive and well, their desire for love and companionship is every bit as real and powerful as the need for warmth, shelter or food.'

'Seriously?'

'Seriously. My grandparents were a perfect example. They were married for fifty-six years, and they really loved each other. Then Grandpa died a few years ago after a long bout with Alzheimer's. At first, Grandma was completely lost, but over time she pulled herself together and got back to living. She has a terrific man in her life now. Uncle Bill we call him. And I swear, when they're together, she's like a kid.'

'And you don't think that's ridiculous?'

'I think it's wonderful.'

I took another jelly bean, punishing myself with my least favorite: grape. 'But you wouldn't think it was wonderful if her romantic interest was inappropriate, would you? I mean suppose instead of Uncle George, your grandmother was fixated on Liam Neeson.'

She smiled. 'I could relate to that.'

'But suppose Liam was in a serious relationship with someone else, engaged maybe. Or even married?'

'He is, but there's nothing in the marriage contract that prohibits a little innocent fantasy.'

I set the edge of my hand on the desk, trying to establish a proper border between the tissue box and the jellybean bowl. 'So where do you draw the line? I mean, would it be OK for Grandma to write Liam a fan letter?'

'Admiring his work? I can't see any particular harm in that.'

'What about finding out where he ate lunch and hanging out there in the hopes of meeting him?'

She frowned. 'That's a tough one. Hanging out at a stage door hoping for an autograph is acceptable behavior. Hanging out to watch a star have lunch seems a bit intrusive, creepy even. But that has nothing to do with Liam's marital status.'

I filled my chest. 'OK. Then suppose you are an old friend of Liam's, maybe from junior high school, and he happens to be filming on location where you live. Would it be OK to call and invite him out to dinner?'

She popped a mango jellybean. 'That would depend.'

'On what?'

'Why is this hypothetical person inviting him out? Is she just being nice to an old friend, offering to keep him company, or is she hoping to get involved?'

'Nothing like that. Just an innocent dinner. Catching up.'

'I don't have any problem with that, and I don't think Liam's wife would either.'

'No?'

'Not unless she's really insecure.'

'Can I ask you another hypothetical question?'

'Feel free.'

I felt anything but. 'Do you think...?'

'Do I think what?'

My throat went creaky again, and I coughed to dislodge the static. 'Do you think Grandma and Uncle Bill...?'

She smiled with bemusement. 'I haven't given it much thought. But why not? God wouldn't have given us the capacity for pleasure if we weren't supposed to enjoy it.'

'I don't know if I buy that. After all, God gives us the capacity for plenty of things we're not supposed to enjoy.' I ticked off several on my fingers. 'What about hatred, selfishness, cruelty, jealousy, bigotry, and arrogance? What about dishonesty and disloyalty? What about sneaking around behind your wife's back with a twenty-three-year-old?'

'Excellent point, Maggie. The truth is God gave us the capacity for good, not-so-good, and flat-out bad behavior. So it's a lucky thing he also gave us the capacity to tell which is which.'

Slutty Professor Two

When I got back to the office building, I found Janine pacing out front. 'It's about time, Maggie. You said six.'

'So it's two minutes past. You sound like my mother, for heaven's sake.' I spotted the Town Car from her favorite limo service idling at the curb, and I stopped cold. 'Where are you taking me?'

'You'll see. Get in.'

'I'm tired, Janine. All I want to do is go home.'

'In!'

'No. Not unless you tell me where.'

She planted her fists on her hips. 'I thought we agreed you were going to listen to me.'

'You agreed.'

'Right. Now cut the crap and get in!'

My stomach squirmed as I slid on to the buttery beige bank of glove-leather seats. The last time I went along on one of Janine's mystery outings, she'd ordered the driver to stop at a dry cleaners. She ran in and filched two large boxes of laundered shirts. The owner raced out after her as we sped away, screaming his head off in some Asian tongue I couldn't place. According to Janine, he had ruined a blouse of hers and refused to pay what she thought she deserved as restitution. Janine's warped brand of justice was to steal another customer's shirts, toss them in the East River and leave Mr Wu to deal with the consequences. For days, I jumped whenever I heard a police siren. The scent of a steam iron still leaves me feeling a bit queasy and insecure.

'Lighten up,' she snapped. 'Have a drink.'

'I don't want a drink. I need to have my wits about me when I go on one of your little adventures.'

'Nonsense. This is going to be fun.' She checked out the bar. 'Vodka, gin, Scotch, champagne or something mixed? Plus, there's a decent California cabernet.'

'Nothing, thanks.'

'Gin and tonic it is, then. But hold the tonic. You handle it, would you, Maggie? You don't want to be around me if I break a nail.'

The driver took us to Rivington Street on the Lower East Side and stopped in front of a shop called Toys in Babeland. The window featured a row of giant red foam hands with accusatory index fingers and a sultry-looking mannequin in a long, slinky, lace-trimmed gown.

'Forget it, Janine. There's no way I'm going into a sex shop.'

She chuckled. 'They don't sell sex, sweetie. They sell sexual toys and aids.'

'Not to me they don't.'

'Don't give me a hard time, Maggie. I'm

serious.'

'So am I. You go in if you want to. I'll wait in the car.' I opened the door to do that, but Janine caught me by the sleeve and whipped me around to face her.

'Here's your choice, Maggie. Either you go into the store with me, or I pick whatever I think you need and have everything delivered to your home and/or office, piece by piece, wrapped in clear plastic.'

'You wouldn't.'

She would.

'That's blackmail.'

Janine grinned. 'So it is.'

I skulked in behind her, seeking a neutral place to rest my gaze. My eyes skittered from the edible panties to the bondage paraphernalia and then drifted against my will to the astonishing display of penis impersonators. They came in every imaginable size, color and shape, though I noticed that nothing approached a Harold model. That would have to be one with an outsized attitude for its modest stature, smallish cranium, and slightly bowed spine. There were silicone, glass and rubber models that ranged from lifelike to surreal. I spotted a small blue nun, a purple porpoise, and a grinning hermit crab in soft, sea-foam green. Some were so enormous; they evoked presidential monuments or ancient Egyptian tombs. Others had odd appendages and tentacles whose functions I couldn't begin to imagine, and would rather not. There was a two-headed model, several globular creations, and a few that swayed like palm trees in a tropical breeze.

'I'm leaving, Janine,' I rasped. 'I can't do this.'

She clamped my wrist. 'My friend is a total newbie,' she announced with malicious glee to an androgynous blond clerk clad in a newsboy hat, black leather vest and jodhpurs. 'We need to get her fixed up.'

'Sure thing.'

Janine tugged me along like a pull toy as the clerk showed her around. Instruction videos and manuals landed in her shopping basket: *Good Vibrations*, *G Spot Run*. *How to be a Master Bater*. Janine tossed in embarrassments in liquid and gel form, tubes and tins, lubricants, sensitizers, libido enhancers, come-ons, scents.

'Stop, Janine. Please. I need to leave.'

'And you will, sweetie, as soon as we get you equipped.'

'But what if someone sees me here?'

'Then they'd be here, too, now wouldn't they?'

The clerk paused before an astonishing collection of vibrators, some of them designed to stimulate body parts I barely knew I had and others I was sure were far better left to their own devices. 'Battery-operated gives you more flexibility, but, of course, the corded models have more staying power.'

Janine nodded. 'I say she needs both.'

'It's purely a gut thing. What appeals to you?' The clerk wanted to know.

All that appealed to me was running out the door. 'I need to think it over. At home.'

Janine puffed her lips. 'Don't make me have to choose for you, Maggie, because personally, I'm drawn to that arterial-blood-red number in the *oooh baby* triple-extra large.'

Three young girls wearing mock fur coats over tourniquet tops and skirts the size of wrist bands bumped through the door without a hint of shyness. 'Is there still space in the Mindfuck workshop? We want to sign up.'

'Have to check. Be right with you,' the clerk said.

'I mean it, Maggie. Choose, or I'll do it for you,' Janine warned again, gazing pointedly at a gargantuan fuchsia apparatus with what appeared to be a full set of teeth.

I tipped my head toward the slim, innocent-looking maiden's-blush pink wand at the far end of the case. I told myself it looked sort of sweet – the sex toy equivalent of a princess phone. 'OK. That. Now please, let's go.'

'Not so fast. We need to fix you up with condoms, naughty undies, and a good class or two wouldn't hurt either. They have all kinds of lessons here, like that Mindfuck seminar, which I happened to take myself.'

'I'd think you could teach it.'

'You always pick up a little something useful in these classes.'

'No lessons, Janine. Hear me. Absolutely not.'

'Great. Let's take a look at the catalog and get you on the list before they fill up. You'll need some extra special tricks if you're going to nab Anthony Sinclair.'

'I'm not going to nab anyone. It's just a casual dinner with an old friend.' The words slipped out before my brain had a chance to kick in. Furiously, I tried to backpedal. 'I mean, just an accidental run-in.'

'Dinner with him? Fabulous! When? Come on. Cough it up.'

'Night after tomorrow, but it's just a casual little get-together. No big deal.'

'Yes big deal. We have work to do, kiddo. Lacy lovelies to buy, and then on to make-up, hair and wardrobe. Grab another basket. Hop to.'

'No more. Enough. I have to get home.'

'Jeesh, Maggie. Lighten up. Won't kill you to live a little.'

'Really, I have to go. I have an appointment. Anyway, there are other customers waiting.'

'All right. But Daphne and I are doing you up, right.'

'We'll see.'

'No, you will.'

I placed my purchase next to the register and peeled off the cash. I didn't want the clerks at MasterCard to know I'd bought such things, much less American Express. After all, I'd been a fine, upstanding card member since '79.

Lon with the Twins

Every six months, as regular as my cousin Ilona's bipolar mood swings, Lon Thrasher came in for a booster session. When I first worked with him, Lon was a gawky twelve-year-old with a severe and socially debilitating stutter. He'd had a variety of therapists and therapies starting at age four, but nothing had helped. Somehow, with me things clicked. I'd taught him to stretch his syllables to the point of fluency and then shrink the pauses until they were undetectable.

Within weeks, he'd no longer sounded like a loose shutter flapping in gale-force winds. The superstitious ticks he'd developed to help squeeze out the words disappeared as well. At the beginning of our work together, he'd stared at his fingernails or peered up at an excruciating angle as if he was trying to have a look at his brain. He'd also dipped his head like an oil crane when faced with his demon consonants, especially N and T. But all that had soon faded to a bad memory. Best of all, the other kids had ceased tormenting him and calling him la-la-la-Lon.

That same year, he'd grown almost a foot and his features had undergone a marvel of downsizing and restructuring that had morphed him from a funny-looking pre-pubescent kid to a ruggedly handsome young man.

Now, he was an on-air reporter, not a surprising turn for someone who'd come to revere fluent speech. He stood in for the lead anchor, Paul Curtis, on the nightly news and was poised to take the helm in a few years when Curtis retired. Lon had Walter Cronkite's reassuring solemnity. If countries were threatening to bomb each other into extinction, global markets were in terrifying freefall, or there was a sudden pandemic of a new and monstrous incurable disease, you simply felt better hearing it from Lon. He also had Barbara Walters' legendary way with an interview subject. When a skittish star or a reticent felon finally agreed to talk on-camera, Lon was the one you wanted to watch ripping off the protective privacy bandages and picking the emotional scabs.

'Enough about me. How are things with you, Maggie?'

'Fine.'

He fixed me in the crosshairs of his copper-shot eyes. 'You don't seem fine.'

'Just a lot going on.'

'Such as?'

'Nothing worth talking about. How's Janice? The twins? They must be what now? Three?'

'What kind of nothing? We go way back, remember?'

110

'I'm *your* therapist, remember?'

'*Quid pro quo*, Clarisse.'

His Anthony Hopkins as Hannibal Lecter was amazing. Some people had the ear, and he was one of them. Lon also had the piercing, laser gaze. My defenses began to smolder and melt away.

'Harold left me for a gorgeous, young PhD candidate. An aspiring ethicist, no less.'

'Left *you*? The guy must be an absolute idiot.'

'Thanks. All contributions to my bleeding ego fund are gratefully accepted.'

'It's the truth. I'm sure you know I had a near fatal crush on you for years.'

'Standard speech therapist transference. Happens most often with the lispers.'

'Joke all you want. The fact is you're an incredible woman, and if Harold doesn't get that, it's his loss.'

'You're a sweetheart.'

He was also pissed off. 'You don't deserve to be hurt like that.'

The tears welled up. 'I agree completely.'

'What can I do? How can I help?'

Angrily, I blotted my eyes. I was sick of crying, tired of feeling crappy. I forced an unconvincing little smile. 'There's nothing, Lon. I just need to get used to the new order of things. Being alone. Talking to myself. I was thinking that if I carry a dummy cell phone, no one will even notice.'

'That's not how it's going to be, Maggie. Believe me. When it gets out that you're on the loose, they'll be lining up, taking numbers.'

'Sure thing.'

'You'll see.'

'Doesn't matter. One way or another, I'll be fine.'

'I'm sure you will. Still, I'd give anything to be able to pay you back, even a little, for all you've done for me.'

'Well, if you insist, I wouldn't mind some good news for a change. World peace would be nice. Global prosperity. Maybe a nice early spring.'

'For you, anything.'

Janine popped in after stalking Lon to the elevator. Her young hunk radar never failed.

'Jiminy Christ, Maggie, have you noticed the buns on that guy? Enough to make me drool.'

'Our relationship is strictly professional, Janine. I focus on his vocal apparatus.'

'Lips, tongue. Absolutely. That, too. Plus teeth can be *very* good, used correctly. Introduce me.'

'Sorry to bust your bubble. But Lon has a wife and twins.'

'So?'

'If you don't want me screwing with your clients, don't screw with mine.'

She nodded in crisp approval. 'You're learning, Maggie. You're watching me and taking it in. That's good!'

Tight Panic

Breakfast was a multivitamin, an anti-anxiety pill, a cup of black coffee and a pint of Chunky Monkey stirred to the exact soft, lumpy consistency of my thighs. Staring with guilty remorse at the empty container, I tried to sell myself on the notion that ice cream for breakfast made sound nutritional sense. After all, it was high in calcium, rich in Vitamin D and packed with lots and lots of energy-boosting sugar. Plus, it was one of the few things in my life since Harold left that gave me anything resembling a boost.

The bathroom scale did not. When I made the tragic mistake of confronting the facts, I discovered that I'd gained 12 pounds since we separated. I supposed one could argue that I'd lost 187 pounds of husband for a net reduction of a 175, but try selling that to my mirror. Everything either bulged, drooped or both. Parts of me jiggled that used to stay mercifully still. Plus, none of my clothes fit. Even my most understanding slacks refused to button at the waist. The zipper struggled halfway to the summit before sliding in shameful defeat back to base camp. Buying a bigger size was not acceptable. That would mean I was resigned to keep gorging and growing until I resembled something suitable for hovering over sporting events. Janine's magical body briefer was a tempting, but illusory, solution. I had to get back in control.

Hearing footfalls outside, I opened the door to stop Mrs Feder before she could deposit a loaf of banana bread on my doorstep. 'Don't, please. It's very sweet of you, but I need to lose weight.'

'You? Ridiculous! You're skin and bones.'

'I'm too much of both, plus other things. I have to cut back.'

'Come on. A little banana bread never hurt anyone.'

From the look of hers, a blackened brick shrouded in gobs of seasick green plastic wrap, I suspected this might well be the rule-proving exception.

'Anyway, I baked it special.'

'OK, fine. Thank you, Mrs Feder. But after this, no more, please.'

She plucked a jar of strawberry preserves from the pocket of her housecoat. 'Try it with this. My Alice makes it herself.'

I wrestled into a leotard, covered up with the largest T-shirt I could find, and headed for the gym. I used to go three times a week, but since Harold's departure, I'd been far too busy mewling and cowering.

The Sportsclub LA Eastside New York branch crouched in the shadows of the famed 59th Street Bridge. I'd joined over Harold's strident objections when the health club opened several years ago. Jogging was free, he'd often reminded me, as were sit-ups and push-ups on the living-room rug. Why on earth would anyone spend hard cash to pant, grunt and sweat? Why, indeed, when one could do those things for free in the arms of one's graduate student!

Harold's carping had always left me feeling self-indulgent and guilty, like my mother did when I failed to clean my plate of her signature sawdust chicken and she invoked the starving children in Africa. But today, I was on a single-minded quest to shape up. I had never taken advantage of the two free personal training sessions everyone got for joining the club. Mustering my courage, I strode to the fitness desk and asked if any of the trainers had the hour free.

In moments, a young muscle-head appeared, wielding a clipboard. He had dark eyes, close-cropped hair, and a body that would make Janine wheeze: perfect pecs, massive shoulders, landing-strip abs and a bulge in his Spandex gym shorts that would be largely impossible for a sighted person to ignore. His name, according to the button clipped to his black personal trainer T-shirt was Dallas.

'Maggie,' I said.

'Hey, Maggie. What can I do for you?'

'Give me Halle Berry's body. She's had it long enough.'

'What's wrong with yours?'

'Only two things. There's too much of it. And not enough.'

He looked me over. 'I wouldn't say that, though everyone can do with a little tightening and toning. You run?'

'Not unless someone's chasing me.'

'What's your program then?'

'*Desperate Housewives*. So I thought I could use something a little more active to round it out.'

'You're on. Let's get to it.'

He led me from machine to machine: prodding, urging, instructing, correcting and, of course, counting. Counting was to a personal trainer as the scalpel was to the surgeon: crucial tool of the trade. If you couldn't count to at least 20 – backward and forward – personal training was not the profession for you.

'Eight more. That's it. Two ... three ... four ... five... '

For some odd reason, I found this motivating. I wanted to give him two more. I wanted to push past the limits of my burning, quivering, *kvetching* muscles. I wanted three days of crippling Charlie Horse. I did.

Footsie

Janine had done it again. The teal blue pant-suit she'd shoehorned me into transformed my body from a ragtag pack of derelict parts into a top-notch unit in perfect fighting trim. My boobs peered over the ridge of an ivory silk camisole like eager scouts. My butt rode high, proud and parade-ready.

'This can't be, Janine. It violates the laws of physics. My body doesn't look anything like this.'

'It's my own simple fashion formula, sweet-ie,' Janine explained through the supercilious smirk. 'The angle of the dangle is inversely proportional to the size of the prospect's bank account.'

'It's not simple anything.'

'So you like?'

I forced a look of stern neutrality. 'It's a lovely suit. But that still doesn't make this anything more than a casual dinner with an old friend.'

Janine motioned to Daphne, who was poised to descend with her giant make-up case and buckets of hair paraphernalia. 'Give it your best, Daph. Pull out all the stops.'

'You got it, boss.'

'Nothing extreme, Daphne. Please,' I urged.

'Close,' Daphne ordered. 'Open. Look up. Blot. Excellent. Ooooh, Maggie. Those peach and buff tones are so totally you!'

Janine squinted at me, frowning. 'You're on the right track, Daph, but not quite there yet. I want her prettier, sexier, younger and generally more kick-ass. You know what I mean?'

Fear sparked in Daphne's eyes. 'Got you, boss. Open, Maggie. Chin down! Close now! Don't move. Blot!'

Anthony Sinclair showed up exactly on time, and lucky thing. I'd spent almost three hours trying not to crease the suit, skin or make-up, and several body parts I relied on rather heavily were going numb.

He kissed my cheek, and I caught a whiff of no-fair cologne. 'Ready?'

'Don't I look ready?'

'You look great.'

'You sure? I could change. Only take a minute.'

'Don't change,' he said. 'I like you exactly as is.'

Anthony squired me out past Nerim, the evening doorman, to a chauffeured black Rolls-Royce. Nerim was impressed, which I cleverly surmised from the way he wolf-whistled and then exclaimed, 'Hoo-hah!'

The car whisked us uptown to Spanish Harlem and stopped in front of the legendary Rao's. By reputation, this venerable Italian restaurant was so exclusive that no one could ever get in. You couldn't call for reservations, not even years in advance. There were only a handful of tables – all assigned in perpetuity – and no one sane or breathing ever gave one up. Even after a recent homicide on the premises, not a single customer bolted from a coveted seat except the dead man, and he had an impeccable excuse. People like Wop, who were someone and knew someone, were sometimes offered a friend or client's table for the evening, and then, if they were so inclined, they could bring along a nobody like me.

I had imagined that such a place would have an air of arrogant restraint, but inside, a party atmosphere prevailed. Dark-paneled walls glinted with year round Christmas lights. Regulars, many pistol-packing mobsters from the neighborhood, congregated noisily at the bar. I grabbed a matchbook to show Janine, but then thought better of it. She was homicidal enough under ordinary circumstances. Restaurant envy might well push her over the edge.

The walls were lined with autographed pictures of some of the many famous people who had dined here. Wop and I were installed in a cozy booth under the warm, approving smiles of Hillary Clinton, Wilt 'the stilt' Chamberlain, and Mary Tyler Moore.

Three couples occupied the adjacent booth. Peering their way, I caught a buxom young blonde staring at Wop. Staring and mooning.

She caught me catching her and shot me with a poison eye dart. This was the first time in memory I'd been on the receiving end of sexual jealousy. And I must say it was an awful lot of fun.

Wop studied the wine list. 'Champagne OK to start?'

'Sure.'

He summoned our waiter, a human bulldog in a Hawaiian motif vest. 'The Dom Perignon,' Wop told him. 'And then we'll have the Barolo.'

'And then the hangover,' I added.

Wop smiled. 'We don't have to finish it.'

'Of course we do. Think of the starving children in Africa.'

The bulldog pulled up a chair and straddled it backward. 'You been here before?'

'Not in many years,' Anthony said.

'Me neither,' I said.

'OK, then. You gotta start with a nice antipasto, plus the fried calamari and *caprese* salad. Then, you gotta have the meatballs and spaghetti.'

'And then?' Wop wanted to know.

'Tonight, I'm gonna recommend the chicken piccata and the veal fra diavolo. You'll share.'

'No fish?'

'Why not? We got a beautiful whole sea bass.'

'Great. I'm always up for a nice piece of bass.' Wop was unreasonably cute when he leered.

'I think that should hold us, Anthony,' I said.

The waiter agreed. 'You gotta leave room for dessert.'

'Absolutely,' I said. 'Put me down for the stomach pump.'

After we consumed an absurd amount of food and drink, Wop stared me hard in the eye. His baby browns had gone vague above the crooked grin. 'I'm so glad you called, Maggie. I was hoping you would.'

'I called?'

'Amazing timing. When I got the message, I was just thinking about you, wondering when the best was time to reach you.'

'But I didn't call.'

'No? I got a message. Maggie Strickland is your married name, right?'

And Janine's name was mud. 'Yes, but it wasn't me.'

He shrugged. 'All's well that ends well.'

I tuned out for a minute, wondering if it made more sense to strangle Janine or shoot her. Rat poison struck me as the most appropriate, but as Valerie might say, poison was so gosh-darned impersonal.

'Ever see any of the old crowd from junior high?' Anthony asked.

'Once in a while. I ran into Wesley Kramer a couple of months ago.'

'The genius?'

'Exactly. He's a hot-shot cardiologist now. World famous arrhythmia specialist.'

'Predictable. I saw Ronny Unterman at a

Broadway show. Remember him?'

'Sure. Does he still look like a lowland gorilla?'

'Very much so. Acts like one, too. I asked him what he's been doing, and he told me eight to fifteen at Greenhaven. Just got out on parole last month. He was in for grand larceny, obstruction of justice and witness tampering.'

'His mother must be so proud.'

'Tell me what you've been up to all these years, Maggie.'

'Until Harold left, the usual: marriage, kids, work. I'm a speech therapist and dialogue coach. Not very exciting.'

'Not true. Sounds fascinating. How did you get into dialect coaching?'

'One of those things. I was working with a young deaf child. Turned out her uncle was an actor. He was so impressed with what I did with little Betty-Ann, he thought I could surely help him learn how to sound South African for his next film. I told him I had no idea how to go about it, but he insisted I try. And it worked out well. He referred me to his friends, and they referred me, and the next thing I knew, I was at it almost full time.'

'How do you learn the accents?'

'It's simple. Every language has a kind of melody. All you need to do is master that and then learn the few distinctive sounds. Once you understand the basics, you can imitate almost anyone.'

'Simple for you. Can't tell you how many

times I've tried to do Brando. Closest I come is sounding like a talking Italian horse with laryngitis.'

'That I've got to hear.'

He set his jaw and repeated the monologue about how he could have been a contender in lieu of the bum he'd become. He eyed me expectantly. 'So?'

'Great speech. One of my all-time movie favorites.'

'Mine too. And the accent?'

'Great speech.'

'Show me how to do it right.'

I closed my eyes and conjured Marlon as Terry Malloy in *On the Waterfront*. I imagined his swagger and truculent gaze. I gave it the best I could.

'That's amazing, Maggie. You sound just like him.'

'It has to come from the gut. Like this.' Demonstrating, I sounded like a lifetime of strong whiskey, cheap cigars and serious career disappointments.

He tried again. He didn't sound exactly like a contender, but he came closer to the freeway that led to the ballpark.

'See? That's better.'

'Better maybe. But still hopeless.'

'No it's not. I've been doing this forever. For a beginner, mastering an accent can take weeks or even months of intensive work.'

'OK. Sign me up.'

'Why would you want to go to all that trouble?'

I felt something suspiciously like his stocking foot against my calf. 'I just like the idea of doing months of intensive work with you.'

My neck heated as I pulled my leg away.

'I believe in going after what I want.' His toes honed in again, burrowing like a mole under the cuff of my miracle pantsuit. 'Whatever it takes.'

This time I moved my legs out of reach by the side of the chair. 'Can I be totally frank with you, Anthony?'

'You bet.'

'That was the most incredible meal, and by far the biggest meatball I've ever seen.'

Good Will Blunting

6:45 a.m.

When the phone rang, I thought disaster.

And it was!

'Margaret. It's Harold.'

'My God! What happened? Did somebody die?'

'Of course not.'

'Is someone sick then? Hurt?'

'My word. Must you be so histrionic?'

'Of course not. The next time I get a call in the middle of the night, I'll presume it's the MacArthur people telling me I've won the genius award.'

He snorted. 'That would most certainly be a wrong number.'

'What do you want, Harold?'

'I called early because I knew I'd be sure to catch you. I'd like to arrange a meeting, soonest. We have to talk.'

'About?'

'About working out the particulars of the divorce quickly and cleanly, without further unnecessary expense.'

'Without lawyers you mean?' I was seeing giant red flags. And a great mooing herd of pissed-off cows.

'We're two honest, intelligent people. It's absurd to be squandering hundreds of dollars an hour to have someone else help us divide by two.'

'I'm not signing anything without a lawyer.'

'Typical.' He slurped his coffee with a sound like a sucking chest wound. 'Must you always be so difficult?'

'*I'm* difficult?'

'Indeed. And irrational. You think every problem can be solved by throwing money at it.'

'Whoa. Wait a minute. Are you saying it can't?'

'You can attempt to retreat into levity all you like, Margaret. I don't find any of this in the least amusing.'

'Really? I thought your little student friend was keeping you highly amused.'

'My word. Must you be so puerile?'

'You have some goddamned nerve calling

me puerile, Harold, whatever it means.'

'How like you, Margaret. You have always taken unthinkable delight in parading your ignorance.'

'Not as much as you delight in walking your pompous intellect around like a championship poodle at Westminster.' I was getting furious, which felt way better than sad, scared, humiliated, overwhelmed and lost.

'I must say, Margaret, I do not understand you at all.'

'Of course you don't. We're different species. It's like that book. Maggie is from Venus; Harold is from Penis.'

I heard the vacuum suck of air between his teeth. 'I would sincerely appreciate it if you kept this discussion out of the gutter.'

'You're the one who couldn't keep your pants zipped, Mr Prim. You're the one who's drilling a student with your hard, hot, throbbing PhD.'

'There is no reason to stoop to such vulgarity. That is unnecessary and uncalled for.'

'You're one hundred per cent right, Harold. Forgive me. I should have said drilling her with your wishy-washy, lukewarm PhD.'

'Anyone of normal intelligence can express herself without stooping to such mindless obscenity.'

'There's nothing mindless about it. Anyway, I will fucking say whatever I cock-sucking please, you hypocritical, dick-brained son of a bitch.'

'I'm willing to let that go, given that you're obviously distraught.' He slurped again, hard. 'How does Thursday after work look for you? We can meet for a drink someplace quiet and talk things out.'

'No, we can't.'

'All right, then, if Thursday is not convenient, how about over the weekend? In the interest of expedience, I am willing to adjust my schedule to accommodate yours.'

'You want to talk settlement, have your lawyer call my lawyer.'

'At five dollars per minute? That's absurd.'

'Then have your lawyer's paralegal's secretary's assistant call my lawyer's paralegal's secretary's assistant.'

'That hardly sounds like a pragmatic approach.'

'How about having carnal relations with yourself, Harold? Is that pragmatic enough for you?'

'Please, Margaret. Take a deep breath and calm down.'

'I will not calm down. I don't want to calm down. This is the most fun I've had in months!'

'That's quite enough. I can tell you're in one of your states. I'll call back after you've had time to consider this rationally.'

'Consider this rationally, Harold.' I slammed the receiver as hard as I could and settled back in bed.

Least of Eden

Rabbi Jennifer wanted to hear more about Harold. Typical kid. She just loved those hair-raising horror stories.

'Where shall I begin?'

'How about the beginning? Where did you two meet?'

'In college. At one of those awful freshman mixers that are exactly like cattle auctions except the livestock wear mascara and heels. Harold was off in a corner, sniffing and contemptuous of the whole thing, which I found very appealing. Of course, that was before I realized that he's always sniffing and contemptuous.'

'So you dated all through college?'

'On and off. He was ambivalent and unpredictable, which somehow made me all the more interested in him. He'd go from mad about me to mad at me for no apparent reason. Or we'd see each other all the time for a month and then I wouldn't hear a word from him for weeks. It was the perfect relationship if you were aspiring to become a paranoid schizophrenic.'

'When did it turn serious?'

I leaned back in the comfy gray chair and

took that in. *Serious* was one of those words that lost its gravity when you thought about it too hard. 'I'm starting to wonder if it ever did – at least for Harold. Then I'm not sure he's capable of feeling anything except miffed.'

'He sounds difficult.'

'Not at all; he's impossible. Harold is picky, testy, arrogant, huffy, humorless, self-important and unreasonable. And those are his good qualities.' As I said this, I realized I was not entirely joking.

'And yet you stuck with him for twenty-eight years?'

I chewed on that awhile, chasing it back with a handful of jelly beans. I thought of the remarkable way Harold had of filling up the entire house so the rest of us were pretty much reduced to wallpaper. In Westport we'd owned four television sets, but Harold had considered it perfectly reasonable for all four to be tuned to whatever he cared to watch. And so it was: Monday night football in blaring quadraphonic sound, a quartet of MacNeils and Lehrers, dueling Leno clones. Harold had laid claim to the living room, the bedrooms, the kitchen and all the space between. The man was an overcrowded family unto himself.

So why on earth had I put up with that for so many years? And why did I feel so devastated by not having to put up with it any longer? Rabbi Jennifer sat with an expectant, mildly troubled look on her face, like a child awaiting her turn on Santa's lap.

129

'I guess it's like breathing,' I said. 'You simply do it, day after day, and almost never give it a thought. If there's bad pollution, you may notice it from time to time, but you don't give up breathing because the air happens to be less than pristine. You figure air is air, and rather than having none at all, you'll take what you can get.'

'But marriage isn't air, Maggie. You can live without it.'

'You're sure of that?'

'I am.'

'But you're married, right?'

'Yes, but I wouldn't be if it was like breathing noxious air all the time.'

'You'd rather do without air altogether?'

'It doesn't mean you have to do without. Air is there for the taking. Anyway, a wonderful fresh breeze can come along any time.'

I thought of Wop and the giant carrot and the capricious winds of serendipity that buffet us from here to there. 'How can you be sure it's fresh and wonderful? If you've spent thirty years believing that Harold was the only man for you, the one you loved and wanted to be with the rest of your life, how can you be sure you won't come up with another one just like him?'

'The trick is to be open to things, Maggie. To embrace the possibilities, but use your brains and instincts as well. You were very young when you and Harold got together. You've learned an enormous amount since then, and you'll use that wisdom to guide you when the time comes.'

'You think?'

'I do.'

'I mean you think the time will come? You don't think I'll be alone forever?'

'You're not alone now, Maggie. Not by a long shot.'

She was right, technically speaking. I was blessed with wonderful kids, caring friends and neighbors, great clients, and even a mother of sorts. 'Then why do I feel so alone?'

'Good question.'

'It feels so weird not to be part of a pair. What use is a single sock, or one glove?'

'In most cases, not much, but think of a single star or a solitary beacon in the darkness. Plenty of wonderful things function beautifully on their own.'

War and Cheese

Valerie and Delia wore matching gingham aprons over prim white blouses and flared skirts, all of which positively screamed homemade by someone who got a C-minus, maximum, in sewing class. They were bustling about the tiny kitchen in their furnished sublet, Mom and mini-mom, fixing supper for the folks.

'Who is she kidding with that getup?' my mother sniped.

'Hush, Mom. Be nice.'

'She looks like that nun from *The Sound of Music*. You know – the *shiksa* with the good voice. Julia something.'

'Julie Andrews,' Allison said. 'Now would you please stop! She's not deaf.'

'That I don't know. But I can tell you she's definitely not Jewish.'

'Please, Mom.'

'No way. No how. Not even half. Did you see those teeth? They never heard of orthodontia where she comes from?'

'Grandma,' Allison's husband Jon rebuked.

My mother's expression reeked of mock innocence. 'It's only talk, darling. We're here to get to know the girl. Isn't that right?'

Allison and Jon nodded in unison. 'Exactly.'

'So where is she from again?' my mother asked.

'Madison, Wisconsin,' I told her for at least the hundredth time.

'People wear curtains and tablecloths in Madison, Wisconsin? How interesting!'

'Stop!' I demanded, as if there was a snowball's chance in Miami Beach that my mother might listen or care.

Brian returned from the bathroom, sporting his proud, new, demented grin. 'Need any help, my honeys?'

'No, Bri. We're doing real good. Aren't we, Delia?'

'Doin' dood,' Delia confirmed. Her inflec-

132

tion was vintage valley girl beneath the grass-fed heartland twang.

'Dinner will be ready in five minutes,' Valerie said. 'Hope everybody likes rarebit.'

My mother made a face that would curdle milk. 'We're supposed to eat bunny? *Feh.*'

'Rarebit is cheese, Grandma,' Brian said. 'Valerie's a fabulous vegetarian cook.'

'Cheese is supposed to be dinner? What? She thinks we're mice?'

I glared my hardest. 'Stop, Mom. I mean it.'

'I can't have an opinion?'

'You can if you keep it to yourself.'

'So if she served bananas for dinner, I'm supposed to pretend I'm a happy chimpanzee?'

Hearing that, Valerie stopped short. 'I'm sorry, Granny Pearl. I should've asked what you like to eat. I'd be glad to make you something else. How about a nice veggie omelet or a soy burger? Tastes exactly like the real thing.'

'Don't bother. After rabbits and cheese, you think I still have an appetite?'

Valerie looked dejected. Delia's little Gerber face fell in a similar mask of tragedy. Brian, who normally dealt with my mother and most everything with unfailing good humor, wrapped Valerie in a protective hug and scowled at Pearl. 'What did I tell you about my grandmother, sweetheart?'

Valerie giggled behind her soft pink hand. 'OK, Bri. Now hush.'

'No. She needs to hear. I told her not to pay

any attention to you, Grandma. I told her you never have a good word to say about anything or anybody, except yourself. I told her you're a mean, old woman, nasty as they come, but you're family, so we're stuck with you.'

Delia, cowed by Brian's rare show of ire, clung to Valerie's pale, chunky leg. 'Carry you, Mommy.'

'Carry me,' Valerie corrected gently. She disengaged from Brian's arms and scooped up the baby.

'Carry you me,' Delia said.

My mother scowled. 'You may not talk to me like that, Brian Strickland. I am *not* old.'

'Valerie worked all day on this dinner and you are going to act polite and appreciative, whether you like it or not.'

'Don't be fresh,' my mother said. 'And don't try to tell me what to do, you little *pishekeh*.'

Valerie looked perplexed. 'Did she just call you a pea shaker?'

'*Pishekeh* is Yiddish for someone who pees in his pants like a little kid.'

'Brian does no such thing, Granny Pearl. You take that back!'

'Her rarebit is delicious,' Brian ranted on. 'So happens Valerie's the best cook I know.'

Delia matched the emphatic nodding of his head. 'Vow-ree cook!'

'I'm sure. Plus she sets such a lovely table,' my mother grumbled. 'Look. Genuine doilies. And napkins in the finest paper!'

Brian's hands balled in bloodless fists. 'If

you can't be nice, maybe you should leave.'

Valerie set Delia in the high chair and patted Brian's back. 'That's not necessary, hon. It's OK. Some people are just cranky and unpleasant that way. I bet she can't help herself.'

My mother sat speechless for a welcome change, as Valerie basked in the warmth of our admiring smiles. The tension in the room evaporated, as if someone had popped the noxious bubble with a pin. Valerie hummed a bright little tune as she slipped on long flowered oven mitts and pulled several heavenly-scented casseroles from the oven.

Everything tasted as wonderful as it smelled. 'It's fabulous,' I said.

'Ohmigod,' Ali gushed. 'You must give me your recipes. Not that I could ever make anything nearly as good as this.'

'You make excellent reservations, hon,' Jon had the remarkable courage to joke.

'I hear you, hon. You're asking to sleep on the couch. And I say – yes, you may.'

Valerie passed the basket she had refilled with warm, delectable rolls. 'Glad you're enjoying it.'

'Same time next week?' Jon said.

'Any time. I love being around family. Mine's so small we could fit in a phone booth. Plus, they're so far away.'

My mother had sucked every morsel from her plate and heaped it with seconds. 'OK, so you're right. She cooks OK for a *shiksa*. I bet she makes the best cheese bunny dinner in all

135

of Madison. All of Wisconsin maybe. And she looks perfectly charming in her curtains. And if she wants to hate me, fine.'

Valerie smiled. 'I don't hate you, Granny Pearl. You remind me of how Delia gets sometimes when she needs a nap. Actually, I think you're kind of cute.'

'*Oy.*'

'How about a nice, big hug sandwich, Granny? You, me, Bri and Delia.'

'Cut the Granny shit! Call me Pearl!'

'Cut Gammy thit!' Delia commanded.

Valerie cupped her mouth. 'Have to watch the language. Little pitchers have big ears.'

'And big pitchers have big other things,' my mother said with a pointed sneer.

'OK, Granny Pearl. Let's have that hug sandwich before you get any crankier.'

'Hug dam-idge,' Delia chortled, bobbing manically in the highchair.

Cringing, my mother allowed herself to be embraced. 'OK. Now, let's finish eating before everything gets cold.'

Brian watched her gobble, lanky arms folded on his chest. 'See, Grandma? I told you her cooking was delicious.'

'OK. I'm eating. I'm enjoying. Now, would you shut up and leave me alone?'

Bored of the Rings

Brian still couldn't use chopsticks. The sushi skittered away when he tried to grasp it and dropped before he could get it to his mouth. He tried again, but the rice broke in raggedy clumps that plopped on his plate. Murky soy puddles dotted the table around him and spread like garish freckles on his shirt. He chuckled dryly at his own clumsiness.

Watching him struggle reminded me of all the things he'd found hard to do. As a little boy, he couldn't whistle or snap his fingers. He couldn't tie his shoes without one of my borrowed fingers, and he'd wet the bed until he was almost ten. It took four years of remedial reading to bring him up to grade level and forget spelling, which he'd always approached in a way Ali had dubbed the frenetic method. He'd simply spewed the first few letters that come to mind, and hoped for the best.

Nevertheless, you had to love Brian. And most everyone did. Teachers had never failed him, no matter how richly he'd deserved to repeat a class. He'd always had a million friends, all ages, sizes, and species. Even the cops, who'd felt duty-bound to arrest him for some of the more idiotic stunts he pulled as a teenager, liked him. Brian was an unassailably good person, a total love. He was every bit as genuine, candid and vulnerable as Allison was calculated, calculating and titanium-clad.

'So how are you doing with the divorce thing, Mom?'

'Fine.'

'Really?'

'Coming along. Better. Really.'

'You're not wearing your rings anymore.'

'I took them off a week ago. Figured it was time.' Their absence still felt odd and twitchy like a phantom limb, but some limbs had to go.

'I saw Dad,' Brian said. 'Man does *he* look different.'

'That he does.'

'If he hadn't been critical of everything, I don't think I would have recognized him.'

'He is who he is, Brian.'

Anger hardened his boyish features. 'That's for sure. He treating you OK?'

I made a T for technical foul. 'You weren't in the marriage so you don't get to be in the divorce.'

'I'm in the family, Mom.'

'That's different. Kids are not cut out to referee for their parents.'

'I'm not a kid anymore.'

'Are to me, and always will be. No matter how old you get.'

'Some things are just wrong. What he did

was wrong.'

Tempted though I was, I bit my lip to keep from piling on. Yes, what Harold did was wrong. Taking up with Bethany, and taking off with her was outrageous, dishonest, demoralizing and selfish, and that was just for starters. But here was the joke that had been running through my mind lately: How many psychiatric patients does it take to change a light bulb? Answer: One, but she really has to want to change. When I looked the situation hard in the eye, I understood that Bethany had been a symptom of advanced disease, not the germ that caused it. The demise of our marriage had taken years of hurts, omissions, missteps and collected resentments on both our parts. Neither of us had really wanted to change. At least, we hadn't wanted to badly enough to do the long, hard, gut-wrenching work. Or maybe, we hadn't been capable of changing enough to meet each other any-where near the reasonable center of our damaging disagreements. Either way, we'd both had a hand in the death of our union. It took two to create that level of wedded blitz. 'Nothing's that simple,' I said aloud.

He looked surprised, then troubled, then annoyed, then troubled, then annoyed again. 'It was wrong. Period.'

I smiled at my son, thinking back to the heady days when, like him and Ali, I knew it all. 'More importantly, how are *you*, kiddo? Lots and lots going on.'

'True. Hope it was OK to spring Valerie and

Delia on you like that. Ali thought it would be fun.'

'It was – ' I searched for a neutral word – 'a surprise.'

'So what you think of my bride?'

I looked him hard in the hazel eyes. I'd picked Harold, so who was I to judge? 'All that matters is what you think of her.'

'Valerie's the best. She makes me feel ten feet tall, Mom. As if I can do anything.'

I saw the love in his expression, the warmth and hope and joy. And it struck me as wonderful and terrible and terrifying. I'd learned the hard way how fragile all that can be, not to mention misplaced. 'You sound happy.'

'I am. With Valerie and the baby. What a cutie.'

'She certainly is.'

His smile fell away. 'Dad thinks it's a crock. He said he'd bet anything I can't make it last six months.'

The hurt in his eyes made me ache. Harold had never been able to deal with Brian. Our son was not a good student, never cared much for watching professional sports, and had a highly developed creative side. In other words, he was nothing at all like his dad.

Brian tried to trap another piece of sushi, which slipped away and dove into his lap. He sniffed. 'He's right. You are a screw-up, Strickland. Doesn't take a genius to see that.'

'Don't you dare talk about my son like that. You're a fabulous, delicious, incredible person, Brian, and I'm a lucky lady to have you

140

for a kid.'

'Thanks.' He peered at me from under his dense fringe of dark lashes, and I remembered precisely how he'd convinced me to buy all those pets. 'So you like Valerie?'

'I don't know her very well yet, Bri. But she seems like a sweetheart.'

'She is.'

'Anyway, if she's good to you, she's a hundred per cent fine with me.'

'She is good to me.'

'I'm glad,' I said. 'She'd better be. Or else.'

Pulp Diction

Amelia Burkart needed me on the set. 'It's an uh-moy-gin-cee, Maggie,' she wailed on the phone between great, blubbering sobs.

'OK. Calm down. I'll be there as soon as I can.'

I took a cab to the Silvercup Studios in Queens, a former bread factory that still held the faint smell of yeast. When I arrived, Amelia looked distraught in her breathtakingly glorious way. 'Thank gawd yaw heah.'

'What's going on?'

The famed director, Marty Colossi, was in a sputtering fury, flailing his thick, hairy arms. 'I don't care how big a box office draw she is. She can't talk her way out of a paper

141

bag. We're blowing the budget and running way behind schedule because of her. Either you drum the damned accent into her head, or she's out.'

'Don't threttin me, you monstah. I happen to have an eye-in clad contract.'

'Which happens to say that you agree to play Princess Diana. This is not *Debbie does Flatbush*, Amelia. If you can't cut it, we cut you.'

'Let me have her lines for today,' I said evenly, though I ached to wring his squat, bulging neck. Amelia was absurd for the part when they hired her. If you bought a giraffe, you had no right to complain that it wasn't a kangaroo.

'I'll give you one hour. Either she gets it, or she goes.'

'She'll get it,' I said with a great deal more conviction than I felt. Confidence building was a crucial piece of what I did. The little trolley could climb that mountain because it thought it could. The realities of engine power, incline, thrust and propulsion were no match for a truly determined fictional machine. 'Piece of cake.'

We went to her dressing room, a lavish space replete with mirrors and sadistically accurate lighting. As soon as the door closed, Amelia burst into giant sobs again.

'Stop,' I urged. 'There's no time for that.'

'But what am oy going to do? If I lose this part, oy'm ovuh. This is moy chance, Maggie. Awl oy evah wanted was for people to take

142

me serious as an actuh.'

'Let's start at the beginning of the scene. Read your first line.'

'No maw, Chawles. You've humiliated me lawng enuf.'

'Repeat after me: ah, fah, pah.'

'Auw, fauw, pauw.'

I modeled in the mirror in exaggerated rounds. 'Relax the back of your throat. Relax everything. Ahhhhh, fahhhhh, pahhhh. Drop your voice deeper, near your waist.'

'Ahrrr, fahrrrrr, parrrr.'

'Better. Now keep it relaxed. Don't pull in the drawstring. You have a stomachache. Keep those sweatpants loose. Ahhhh, fahhhh, pahhh.

'Ah fah pah.'

'By George, she's got it.'

'Ahfahpah,' she chanted deliriously. 'Ahfah-pah Ahfahpah. Oh, Maggie. What would oy do without you?'

'Concentrate. Say Chahills.'

'Chahh-illls.

'Now shorter, Chahills.'

'Charills.'

'Drop the R. It's Chah hills. Cha cha on the hills.'

'Chahills.'

'Good. Now shorter, and deeper: Chahls.'

'Chahills.'

'Almost. Again. Sharply. One syllable. He's been screwing around and making you look like a fool. Bite it off. Chahls.'

'Chahls.'

'Perfect.'

'No mah, Chahls! Oy did it right, Maggie. Oy can do this.'

'Yes, you can.'

Mommy Queerest

'Lots of babies are unplanned,' Rabbi Jennifer offered in my mother's lame defense.

'True. But I was also *unwanted*. Pearl has been very clear about that. Many times.'

'You call her Pearl?'

'Actually, I call her Mom, but only because I know how much it annoys her. She always does her very best to undermine and irritate me, so I figure it's only right to return the favor when I can.'

She frowned, troubled by this. Poor kid was much too sweet and innocent to appreciate the myriad joys of normal family sadism.

'Do you honestly think your mother means to hurt you?'

'Of course not. It has nothing to do with me. If my mother runs you over then too bad. In her way of thinking, it's your fault for standing where she chose to drive.'

'You truly believe she doesn't love you?'

'Truly? I don't know whether she's capable of loving anyone. She's not a bad person. I mean not compared to – say – Charles Manson. She's just completely, chronically, incurably self-absorbed.'

The rabbi's frown deepened, laying the template for a future worry line between her brows. 'That must be hard for you, Maggie.'

I shrugged. Rabbi Jennifer had me doing this a lot. And thinking, which probably wasn't such a hot idea. 'Actually, it's a good thing. If not for my mother's constant criticism, I bet I'd be much, much taller. At least six-four, I figure. Imagine what a problem I'd have buying clothes.'

'Humor helps. But it doesn't make the hurt go away.'

'OK. You're right. The truth is I wish she loved me in that wonderful, unconditional, blind, adoring way that June Cleaver loved Wally and the Beaver. But this is the real world. And Pearl is exactly like her namesake: a cold stone coughed up by a cranky oyster.'

'Who's June Cleaver?'

'Sorry. She was the mother on a popular sitcom, back in the olden days before they coined terms like abuse or dysfunctional and sugarcoated bullshit reigned supreme.'

Her baby face went tight.

'Sorry again. I probably shouldn't be saying things like bullshit to a Rabbi.'

'Bullshit,' she said. 'Don't you believe a parent can love a child in that way?'

'Sure I do. I know it. I love my kids that way. And my father adored me, which I'm sure kept my ego from shrinking to a dried shriveled pea.'

145

'What about your husband? How was Harold for your ego? Before all this, I mean.'

That gave me pause, which I used to pop a couple of therapeutic jelly beans.

'Pretty toxic, when I consider it now. He disapproved of me in pretty much every way imaginable. I was never serious enough and way too absorbed with my friends. I spent too much, earned too little and I wasn't even close to being interested enough in business, politics, or sports. And then there was my biggest sin of all: Harold always accused me of being anti-intellectual.'

'Are you?'

'Not really, but I do have a problem with pompous jerks. Whenever we'd get together with Harold's professor friends, they'd all bend over backwards to flaunt how know-ledgeable they were and what big vocabularies they had and how they'd all spent the weekend reading Aristotle in the original Greek. So when they'd ask me where I went to school, which they always did sooner or later even though they already knew, I'd tell them that I was in the home economics school at Cornell, where I majored in corn muffins. That made Harold so furious, his ears would turn purple.'

She laughed. 'I don't blame you. They sound awful.'

'They were, and so insecure. They actually wore their Phi Beta Kappa keys, which struck me as really sad.'

'So, what did you study in school?'

146

'Russian literature and Psychology. But I did minor in corn muffins.'

'I take it Harold doesn't have much of a sense of humor.'

'Wow. You used *Harold* and *sense of humor* in the same sentence. I wouldn't have thought that was possible.' I thought of Wop, which I did every three or four seconds. He got two big thumbs-up in the humor department, and the ego-building department and the fun department. But then, there was the giant thumbs-down he rated in the having-a-wife department.

Rabbi Jennifer was staring at me.

'Sorry?'

'I asked if you're being serious about Harold not having a sense of humor.'

'I am. To him, everything was dead serious, and strictly black and white. I was his spouse, and that meant I was supposed to act like a good, little, pompous ass, intellectual snob to impress his pompous ass, intellectual snob colleagues. What mattered above all to Harold was appearance.'

'Sounds as if you married your mother, Maggie.'

'Why would I do a boneheaded thing like that?'

'I don't know. What do you think?'

'I think you're going to help me figure it out.'

Out of Paprika

A lavish bouquet awaited me at home. Nerim, the evening doorman, handed it over with his typical gratuitous curiosity. 'Are these from Mr Megabucks with the Rolls Royce?'

'I have no idea.'

He whistled low. 'That car he came in has to go for six figures, easy. Plus the driver don't come cheap. So a bunch of flowers he can certainly afford.'

'Why thanks, Nerim. I can't tell you how comforting it is to have your expert assessment of my friend's financial well-being.'

He nodded. 'Florist they came from costs an arm and a leg. Bunch that big musta ran the guy two bills, two fifty even.'

'Is that so?'

'Minimum.'

'Fascinating.'

I waited until I was on the elevator to open the card.

Thanks for last night, Maggie, especially my first Brando lesson. I hope you don't look upon me as the biggest meatball you ever saw. Endeavoring to be appropriately yours, Anthony (Wop Carlucci) Sinclair.

This made me smile, which must have been his evil intent. I was still sporting the foolish grin when I ran into Mrs Feder, padding around the hall in her flowered chintz robe and bruise-blue scuffs.

'So what's with the fancy shmancy flowers?'

'Nothing. They're from a friend.'

'Oh yeah? And what's with you? You look like the cat that swallowed the canary.'

'I'm just in a good mood.'

'Let me guess. This friend of yours, he's a him?'

'It's someone I knew from junior high school, Mrs Feder. Just a friend, like I said.'

She trailed me down the hall, firing questions. 'What kind of a friend sends fancy flowers like that?'

'The thoughtful kind.'

'This friend? He's single?'

'I told you. He's just a friend.'

Her scowl deepened. 'So he's married and sending you flowers. If you don't mind my saying, Maggie, that doesn't sound exactly Glatt kosher to me.'

'Have a lovely evening, Mrs Feder.'

She stopped the door before I could shut it, and trailed me inside. 'You have any paprika, darling? I'm right in the middle of making goulash, and I ran out. Isn't that always the way?'

'I guess.'

'Wonderful. So, listen to me, Maggie. I'm not one to butt in, but a married man does

149

not send another woman flowers unless he wants another woman. *Ferstheh?*'

'Yes, I understand, but I don't agree.' Playing attempted footsie with another woman was probably a clearer sign, but I remained committed to complete, unequivocal and, if need be, strident denial. Seeing Anthony had been fun and what was wrong with having fun? In fact, there was nothing in the least inconsistent about having fun and being married, unless you happened to be married to Harold.

I set the flowers on the coffee table. Then, anxious to be done with Mrs Feder's carping, I went to the kitchen and started rummaging through the spice cabinet. I had dozens and dozens of herbs and spices, arranged in no particular order. I was one of those hopeless impulse condiment buyers. I saw recipes in the paper or on cooking shows, ran right out and bought the exotic specialty ingredients as if I might ever attempt to reproduce such concoctions, and then promptly forgot what they were for. My cupboard was crammed with odd-looking little tubes, cans and bottles labeled in languages I couldn't even identify, much less read. Many would qualify as genuine antiques by now, but for some reason, I was incapable of throwing any of them away. After all, who knew when I might need those little barf green pellets or that fuzzy gore-colored stuff or the gray paste that smelled like mint-flavored cow dung? Somewhere, in the midst of all that was the paprika, my

ticket to freedom from Mrs Feder's rabid –
and all too accurate – opinions. And so I rum-
maged with a vengeance: marjoram, allspice,
coriander seeds, geng wa ho.

'The wife. You know her? You're not best
friends I hope.'

'No. She lives in London.'

'Aha! You see? Just like that dirty so-and-so
in Madame Butterfly. He has a wife in London, and now he wants a comfort woman in
New York.'

Bay leaf, fenugreek, panko, saffron, dill
seeds, basil, bing mai lite.

'That's simply not true, Mrs Feder. You
don't even know the man.'

'No? Well don't come running to me when
his wife gives her little baby away and
commits hotsy totsy.'

Fennel seeds, oregano, whole black pepper,
Malabar pepper, cayenne.

'Don't you mean *hara-kiri*?'

'I most certainly do not. After the stunt they
pulled at Pearl Harbor, no way you'll catch
me speaking Japanese.'

Finally, I found the paprika. I handed it
over and herded her toward the door. On the
threshold, she wagged a knob-knuckled
finger at me. 'I can see you have a thing for
this two-timing flower sender, Maggie. It's
written all over you.'

'I don't have a thing for him.'

'Yes you do. I can tell.'

'That's good to know, Mrs Feder. Next time
I'm not sure what I'm feeling, I'll be sure to

151

check with you.'

'You could do worse.' Her eyes narrowed into ominous slits. 'They have a baby, this no-good flower sender and the wife in London?'

'No. Their youngest is twenty-four.'

She blew a breath. 'Well, at least we can be thankful for that.'

Try Hard With a Vengeance

7:55 a.m.

My appointment for my second free session with Dallas the personal trainer was at eight a.m. I waited at the health club fitness desk beside a pony-tailed redhead with a prom queen face and a body that could best be described as skimmed. I estimated she must be about Bethany's age. Though I'd never seen the slut brainiac Harold left me for up close, she was barely more than a child. I'd bet she had no cellulite. No stretch marks. Nothing prolapsed, occluded, abscessed, descended, varicosed or atrophied. Virtually nothing to recommend her at all.

I answered Red's affable grin with a sneer. Since I didn't have Bethany to kick around, she'd have to do. Soon Dallas loped over with another trainer, a scrawny guy with a buzz cut and sallow, acne-pitted skin. My trainer was hotter than her trainer – so there!

'Ready, Maggie?'

'Depends on your definition of ready.'

'Don't worry. I'll get you going. Why don't you hop on that treadmill and give me a couple of miles?'

'Sure, no problem.' I went full out, up to an astonishing three and a quarter miles per hour on the electronic gauge. I ran my little heart out for almost a full ninety seconds, at which point I feared I was too winded to make the necessary call to nine-one-one.

Dallas took pity and moved on to the floor exercises. He had me do lever lifts, knee lifts, crunches, crouches, squats – two ... three ... four...

'OK, now cross your left ankle over your right knee and lift from your shoulders. Relax your neck. That's it. Ten ... nine ... eight...

'Good. Now I want you to take your left foot, wrap it around your neck twice, and insert your big toe in your right ear.'

'What if something breaks off?'

'Relax,' he said behind the evil grin. 'That almost never happens.'

Dallas tried to distract me by asking questions like a typical annoying four-year-old. He wanted to know what I did, how I came to do it, what I liked, who I was.

'Separated,' I told him. 'Two grown kids.'

'You don't look old enough to have grown kids.'

'Thanks.'

'Twenty ... nineteen ... Now put your right leg back this time. Lower, deeper: One ... two ... three...'

'Oh my. I don't think I can do another...'

'Yes, you can. Push it: four ... five. That's it. Perfect. Six ... seven. That's good, Maggie. Keep it up. Gives you high, tight buns: Twenty ... nineteen...'

'More?' My rear end was not happy with me, and neither were my stomach, legs, arms, neck, or back. Even my earlobes ached. Nonetheless, I didn't want this to end. I imagined Wop admiring my imaginary high, tight buns. I imagined him imagining us together. I felt the phantom press of his stocking foot against my calf. Somehow, this registered much higher on my anatomy. That was the thing about prolonged starvation. A person could get positively obsessed with the idea of food.

'Are you feeling OK, Maggie? You're all red in the face.'

'I'm fine. Just a little warm.'

'That's how you're supposed to be. You're doing great. Just one more set and time's up. One ... two... '

By the time we finished, I could hardly move. The sweat blotches sprawled from the neckband of my T-shirt nearly to my waist. 'Believe it or not, I enjoyed that.'

'Great. See you again next week?'

Divorce meant splitting assets, so half of not much was what I'd get. My thoughts turned to legal fees, household expenses and Rabbi Jennifer, who now qualified as a bona fide and frequent necessity. 'I think I'll try exercising on my own for a while, Dallas. Do what you showed me and see how it goes.'

'Sure. I'll write down a few reminders. Just keep up the way you're doing and you'll get where you want to be.'

As Rude As It Gets

Janine accosted me as I stepped off the elevator.

'So how did it go? I was called out of town on a cocktail dress emergency, but I couldn't wait to get back and hear. Tell me everything. I want all the juicy details, including sound effects.'

'And I want an apology.'

'What for?'

'You had some nerve calling Anthony's office and pretending to be me.'

'That's outrageous. I did no such thing.'

'It had to be you, Janine. No one else even knows about Anthony.'

'OK, so I called him. You don't have to thank me.'

'I'm not thanking you, I'm telling you to butt out.'

'Sure. I hear you. I won't call him again unless it's absolutely necessary.'

'You will not call him again, period!'

'OK, whatever. Now give. How was the date? Tell me everything.'

Circling her warily, I pulled out my office keys. 'There's nothing to tell. It was exactly as advertised: dinner with an old friend. No big deal.'

She darted around and blocked my way. 'Don't give me that. I want the blow-by-blow. Not to mention the stroke-by-stroke and the ahh by ahh.'

'All right, Janine. Here goes. Anthony picked me up at seven. We went out to eat. We ate, and then he took me home. The food was good, and he was good company. I had a nice time. End of story.'

Her head was bobbing madly. 'Anthony Sinclair took you *home*, did he? And, pray tell, what did you two kids *do* once you got home?'

I glared at her. 'Get out of the way, Janine. I am not going to stand in the hall while you give me the first degree.'

She threw up her hands. 'Fine. No arguments. You can have your first degree inside.'

My office door was unlocked. Glaring harder, I held out my hand. 'Give me the key, Janine.'

'Don't be silly. How would I get your key?'

'I don't know and I don't care. Just give.'

'You're being paranoid, Maggie. I don't have your key. You must have left the office unlocked, or maybe the cleaning service did.'

'Give me my key or this conversation is over.'

She planted her hands on her leather-clad hips. 'Look, even if I had your key, which I don't, there would be no point in my giving it back. You'd just be putting me through all the bother of having to get it copied again.'

'There is no reason in the universe for you to have my key.'

'There is so. And it happens to be for your own good.'

'This I've got to hear.'

'What if you were locked in your office and suddenly you choked on – say – a candy bar and you couldn't speak. How would I get in to rescue you?'

'If I couldn't speak, how would you know I was choking in the first place?'

Her wink was chilling. 'Now you're asking me to spill trade secrets, sweetie. Just suffice it to say, I'd know.'

Feeling a little queasy, I went inside.

Janine followed close behind. 'So he took you home and then...'

'And then he dropped me off and went home and so did I.'

'You didn't.'

'I did.'

'And that was it? The end of the evening?'

'Of course not. I flossed; I brushed my teeth. I took off my make-up. I read a little. Pretty good book, in fact.'

'Jiminy Christ, Maggie. At least, tell me you did him in the car. Or better yet, in the restaurant! There's nothing quite as sexy as a little down and dirty under a nice, long, white tablecloth.'

'I did nothing of the kind. My God, Janine. What kind of person do you think I am?'

'Are you saying there was no down and dirty?'

'That's precisely what I'm saying.'

'No.'

'Yes.'

'Jiminy Christ!' She gesticulated, muttering under her breath. But then with jarring suddenness she went still and fixed me with a warm, generous smile. 'You know? I understand, sweetie. I honestly do.'

'You understand?'

'Absolutely. You've been through a lot. Of course, you're a little anxious and confused.'

I twisted a knuckle in my ear. 'Wow, I must be hearing things. For a minute there, I thought I heard you say you understood.'

'I do. This business about Harold leaving has been tough on you. I realize that. And all I want to do, as your friend, is try to make things easier.'

I looked her over. She didn't appear to be armed. 'I'd appreciate that, Janine. More than I can say. If you could just back off and give me a little time and space to figure things out, it would mean a lot.'

She rolled her eyes. 'I don't mean easier that way, goofy girl. I mean I'm going to lay everything out for you, clear and simple. I'm going to see to it you don't have a chance to screw things up with Anthony Sinclair ever again.'

'Stop, Janine. Please. You're right. I am anxious and confused. Nothing's clear or simple right now.'

158

'Yes it is, Maggie. You just refuse to look at it in clear, simple terms. Here's the deal. You woman; he man. He itches, you scratch. One and one equals ooh!'

'There's a lot more to it than that, Janine. There are consequences to what we do. People can get hurt.'

'No one's telling you to use the whips and chains, sweetie; unless, of course, he gets down on all fours and begs.'

'I'm talking about his wife and kids, me and my kids, not to mention Anthony and me.'

'Sheesh, Maggie. We're talking about a little fun here. You don't have to bring the whole League of Nations into it.'

'I can't simply pretend we're living in a vacuum, Janine. That's not how it is.'

'Enough. You need to get over yourself and lighten up!' She strode to the blackboard and wrote a new rule for the day: *When in doubt, put out!*

Runaway Brain

'Is everything all right, Maggie? You seem a little distracted.'

'What? Sorry. I'm afraid I'm a little distracted.'

'By?'

'Nothing in particular. Just a lot on my mind.'

Rabbi Jennifer moved a blue cookie tin from the bookcase behind her to the desk and popped the lid. Inside was nothing but gleaming emptiness. 'I offer this to people as a place to leave things they'd like to get off their minds. Feel free.'

The tin was perhaps eight inches wide. Wop was in good shape, but no way he'd fit in there. And why was I thinking about him anyway? Why had I been thinking about him pretty much non-stop? He was a married man. And even if he wasn't, a couple of oversized meatballs and a bouquet of flowers did not a future make.

'It's nothing really.'

'What kind of nothing?'

'Regular nothing. You know.'

She wove her fingers in a tidy ball. 'Such as?'

I shrugged. 'Brian's baby. Sore muscles. Whether to order take out sushi tonight or Chinese. Whether it would be more fun to murder Harold with an axe or a machete. The usual stuff.'

'Let's run through those then. What about Brian's baby?'

'Delia's a major cutie,' I had to admit. 'And she simply loves life. It's a pleasure to watch the way she embraces the newness and adventure.'

'Interesting.'

'What?'

160

'Your face changed when you talked about her. You got this faraway contented look.'

'Must have been gas.'

'Do you always do that, Maggie?'

'What?'

'Hide behind humor when something feels hard to face?'

'Always?'

'Do you?'

'I learned long ago never to say yes to a question involving always or never. I think it was one of those tips on how to ace the SATs. Which, of course, I didn't. My English was pretty good, but the math!'

She nodded. 'So sometimes you use humor and sometimes it's diversionary tactics.'

'Shouldn't we move on to talk about sore muscles now? Or spring rolls. Or assassinating Harold?'

'I'd rather you tell me what you're trying so hard to avoid.'

'Isn't that like asking me to eat something I'm allergic to?'

'It's a basic principle of psychotherapy that the very thing you least want to talk about is probably the most important thing for you to discuss, Maggie.'

'Is that true?'

'Yes.'

'Fascinating. What are the other basic principles?'

'That you should never get diverted from the subject at hand.'

'I agree. We were talking about the basic

161

principles of psychotherapy. Let's stick to that.'

'I mean the thing that's on your mind. Whatever it is, I'd really like to hear.'

'You know? What I'd really like to hear is how you decided to become a rabbi.'

She replaced the lid on the tin. 'When you're ready then, Maggie. Maybe next time.'

I wanted to tell her about Wop, but the words stuck in my throat. And it occurred to me that a basic principle of principles was that the very thing you were most reluctant to talk about was the very thing about which you had the most doubt.

Desperately Seeking New Man

Wop had not responded to the message I'd left nearly thirty-five hours, twenty-seven minutes and twelve seconds ago, thanking him for the flowers. OK, three messages, one to thank him, one to make sure he got my thank you and one to thank him yet again in case the two previous thanks somehow failed to get through. I was coming to the unpleasant conclusion that the bouquet he sent was not a hopeful come-on at all, as both Mrs Feder and I had suspected. I suppose it was the signature FTD kiss-off arrangement. *Roses are red; violets are pink. I found you lacking. Who wouldn't? You stink!*

All right, so I'd made five calls, but twice I hung up before they rang through, so according to the strict guidelines for insane, obsessive-compulsive behavior, those didn't count.

This was for the best, I told myself. Wop was a married man; after all. 'Pre-divorced', as Janine would put it, but off-limits nonetheless. And I'd had serious reservations about having anything to do with him, no matter how allegedly innocent. I resolved to march him out of my thoughts and be done with the ridiculous fantasy for good.

But why didn't he call? What did I say? What had I done wrong?

For starters, I shouldn't have wolfed down all that spaghetti and those monstrous meatballs at Rao's. You did not let a man see you grappling with messy pasta or your ravenous appetite. In fact, as I dimly recalled from my prehistoric single days, sensible women never ate on dates at all.

Plus, I'd had too much to drink, and I'd smiled too much, which laid wrinkle tracks in the under-eye concealer and gave Wop countless occasions to get an eyeful of the fetching gob of green matter I discovered much later at home that had no doubt been wedged between my front teeth since the antipasto.

Desperate to do anything but think of how I screwed things up with Wop, I popped the extra anti-anxiety pill I decided I was allowed under such circumstances. While I waited for the coma to kick in, I started trolling online

163

for old boyfriends. This turned out to be an excellent way to amuse yourself, if you were really, really easily amused.

First, I looked up Danny Chaskin, my steady squeeze at Camp Wisquamacutt when I was ten. I remembered him as a stubby, freckled boy with a cracked front tooth and horrendous food allergies. Diabolical bunkmates used to slip him forbidden pineapple juice and peanuts for the sheer sadistic joy of watching him gasp for breath and erupt in Vesuvius-quality hives. A website I found through Google reported that he was now a podiatrist, living in Indianapolis, where he ran the 'world renowned!' Chaskin Foot Care Centers. The homepage featured a smiling cartoon foot and the legend: 'Stroll on in, and we'll make those tootsies grin.'

I crossed him off my list so hard I tore the paper.

Maybe Anthony was turned off by my incessant calling. So maybe I should call and apologize for leaving all those messages. Better idea: why don't I just take a nice, well-sharpened No. 2 pencil and stick it in my eye!

Briefly, I considered Lawrence Kasden, the bumbling breast fondler from tenth grade, but the thought of him still made me cower behind crossed arms.

Geoff Steuben, whom I dated off and on during high school, didn't Google at all. For a moment, I considered that he might be dead, but then I rejected the thought as too depressing. No doubt good old Geoff was fine. Just serving an extended prison term or hospitalized for the past decade or so in a coma.

Then again, what if Wop didn't get my messages? They could get deleted by accident, after all. How many times had that happened to me?

Never, in fact. But, I was sure such a thing must be possible. So maybe I *should* try him just one more time to be sure.

I picked up the phone and dialed his number, which my fingers could now dance by heart. But I hung up before the call connected. The hell with him. I didn't need Anthony Sinclair. I'd bet the world was positively teeming with other, equally, if not more wildly inappropriate men for me to stalk.

Warren Kuperman, my senior prom date at Southside High in Rockville Centre, Long Island, turned out to be either a Toronto-based nuclear physicist, a chiropractor from Baltimore or the semi-retired president of the Golden Pines Condo Association in Tampa Beach, which was embroiled in a major lawsuit against the state to block an airport expansion project. Then again he could be W.M. Kuperman, who collected root beer paraphernalia and had opened what was purported to be the largest museum devoted to that venerable beverage in the entire Southwest! Or he might be W. B. Kuperman, who had been cast as Nathan Detroit in the forthcoming production of *Guys and Dolls* by the 'internationally famous' Pettibone Players in Des Moines.

No one would accuse me of having a rich romantic past. Harold and I had started dating in college when I was a freshman and he a senior, and during most of our frequent break ups, I'd hovered near the phone, breathing only when absolutely necessary, waiting for him to call. It struck me now that I could count my other love interests on one hand and still have plenty of fingers left over to hold a gun to my temple and pull the trigger.

Maybe that's why I was so fixated on Wop. Aside from Harold, he'd been one of the precious few abiding crushes in my life. Maybe unrequited love got lodged deep in some emotional crevice from which it could escape at any time and flare into a blazing bonfire of neurotic compulsion. Maybe an early crush acted like the virus that caused chicken pox. Decades later, that awful bug could kick up and cause a painful case of shingles. And who in her right mind would yearn for that?

So the hell with him, I told myself for about the millionth time. Anthony Sinclair, by any of his myriad names, was forgotten. He was history. Wop who?

With a resolute nod, I typed in the name Sam Weller, with whom I'd had a brief, tepid romance when Harold took up with a team-mate on the debating squad who'd had an especially large, firm, and well-rounded vocabulary. As it turned out, Sam was a successful realtor right here in the Big Hassle. The picture on his website showed a trim, attractive man, still recognizable, with no visible evidence of dangerous psychosis or contagious, unsightly disease.

My memory served up a tall, likeable guy with a wry sense of humor. Sam was also a very good kisser, as I dimly recalled. Eyes closed, I mustered the full sensation: sensuous lips, soft probing tongue. This caused a stirring, or so the author might have said if this was a steamy bodice ripper, and not my pathetic excuse for a life.

Unfortunately, Anthony Sinclair soon displaced Sam Weller as my co-star in this nerdo-erotic fantasy. I explored Wop's warm, fulsome mouth and pressed against his tantalizing nooks and crannies. The crannies, especially.

Stop!

Leaning closer to the monitor, I studied the site for clues to Sam's family situation. The picture had him seated at a broad mahogany desk. I saw no framed snapshots of a wife or kids, no ring on his left third finger, which I brilliantly concluded meant nothing.

But I was in desperate need of a substitute obsession, and for the time being, Sam would have to do. Tossing all sense and caution to the winds, I clicked on the *contact us* page and dashed off a breezy note. I thought about how proud Janine would be, and that terrified me.

Hi Sam.
Seems we're neighbors. Love to catch up.
Maggie (Evantoff, Cornell, 1978)

I read over the message, agonizing over every word. Was the tone too familiar? Too informal? Too uptight? Did *love to catch up* sound as lonely and desperate as I felt? Shouldn't there be a better sign-off? And if so, what? I couldn't say *sincerely* or *yours truly*, as if I was applying for a job. *Love* was way too strong, *warm regards* too weak, and *best* struck me as much too country club New Canaan. Plus, how did I signal that I was separated and seeking companionship, without being about as subtle as a Sherman tank?

I concluded that the whole thing was a terrible idea. But in my standard inept way with the keyboard, when I went for the Delete button, I hit Enter by mistake.

Your mail has been sent, my server taunted.

Sometimes, I really wished I lived in a simpler, more elegant era like the Renaissance, when 'instant communication' and its evil twin, 'instant regret' had not yet been invented. But then, they didn't have flush toilets or running water back then either, so it probably wasn't all that elegant, after all.

The Killing Meals

As I passed through the revolving door at Macy's, I spotted my mother waiting in the ladies' purse department. The look on her face eloquently expressed how she longed to see me, so she could rip me to shreds. I considered escaping while I had the chance, but given how depressed I was by Wop's continued silence, I reasoned that things couldn't get all that much worse.

'Hi, Mom. How's it going?'

'Lousy, thanks to you. You think I enjoy standing around on one foot waiting while you take your sweet time doing God knows what?'

I checked my own watch, which confirmed that it was not yet ten to noon. 'You're a hundred per cent right, Mom. I'm sorry.'

'Don't be flip.'

'I'm not. I'm expressing genuine remorse for my unconscionable behavior. It's after noon somewhere in the world. In fact, it's already late tomorrow in Australia. So depending on how you look at it, I've kept you waiting for hours and hours, which is unforgivable. So don't even try to forgive me. Please.'

'Don't talk nonsense. You need hose?

Socks? They're having a sale.'

'I don't actually.'

'Linens? They have thirty per cent off on those fuzzy towels you like. The ones that shed.'

'Nope. I've got all the dysfunctional towels I can use at the moment.'

'Small appliances, then? Who couldn't use a new toaster?'

'I couldn't.'

She huffed well, though not as well as Harold. 'You want to be in one of your moods, Miss Contrary-itis, go right ahead. No skin off my nose.'

'That's comforting.'

'Ready for lunch? I was thinking the coffee shop.'

'What an original idea!'

'Don't be smart.'

My mother's gait was not what anyone would term delicate. Walking down the street beside her, I could feel the sidewalk quake with each concussive strike. I imagined this must be what it was like to take a stroll with Godzilla, except the ape was so much more agreeable. For some reason, this, and most everything else, made me think of Wop. I wondered if he was OK. It occurred to me that he could be trapped unconscious under a construction crane, which before the advent of cell phones would have been a pretty decent excuse for not calling back.

'So I saw Frieda at canasta,' my mother said. 'And guess what?'

'She won.'

'Don't be ridiculous.'

'She's having a face lift.'

'She is? What is she, crazy?'

'That was a guess, Mom.'

'Don't try to be clever, Maggie. It doesn't become you.'

'OK. No more riddles. If you want me to know what's up with Aunt Frieda, tell me. I don't feel like guessing.'

'So I saw Frieda, who looks terrible by the way, and it turns out she knows a nice criminal lawyer.'

'Really? Is he going to represent her in the face lift?'

'Not for her, Maggie, for you. Frieda says he's a lovely man, a real gentleman.'

'Tell her thanks anyway.'

'Why not? You don't even know him. The least you could do is give it some thought.'

'Here's the code, Mom. *Nice* means ugly and *gentleman* means boring and/or loboto-mized.'

'Don't be a smart Alec. Frieda says he's very successful. She told me he dresses beautifully and he's a terrific dancer.'

'Divorced or widowed?'

'He's a bachelor.'

'Over thirty-five?'

'Of course. He's late fifties, I think. Sixty tops,' she said.

'So he's ugly, boring, knows a lot of charming murderers and drug dealers and he's gay. Sounds perfect. Sign me up.'

We entered the shabby coffee shop, where my mother did a perilous end-run around a frail old couple, so she could beat them out of the only available booth. The wizened little cotton-haired woman tottered like a bowling pin, but thankfully didn't topple. Her husband gasped in horror and turned pomegranate red. 'Please forgive her,' I said. 'I know she looks pretty normal, but in fact she was raised by wolves.'

My mother called the waiter over. 'Gimme two tunas on dry rye toast, two black coffees and a couple of good sized sides of slaw. Don't try to pass off those teeny little portions in the paper cups and charge us regular. I wasn't born yesterday.'

I braced myself. 'You know? I was thinking of having the chicken salad for a change.'

My mother looked as if I'd just requested a plate of sautéed human lung on a bed of chopped eyeballs. 'She'll have the tuna,' she told the waiter. 'And make sure the coffee's good and hot.'

'Thanks for the rescue, Mom. Chicken salad. What could I be thinking?'

'So when do you want to meet Frieda's friend? You could have a cocktail, maybe dinner and get to know each other.'

I thought it over. 'Never's good for me. Do you think never would work for him?'

'I don't see why you're being so picky. It's not like they're falling over themselves.'

'How do you know that? Maybe I have a secret lover who's crazy about me. Maybe he's incredibly successful and movie-star handsome. Maybe he takes me out to fabulous dinners in exclusive places and sends flowers to thank me the following day.'

And then maybe he drops me like a hot rock!

'Get real, Maggie. You think I'm about to believe that? Who do you think you are, J. Crew?'

'You mean J. Lo.'

'Jay shmay. Let's face it, darling. You're not exactly Marilyn Monroe.'

'For which I'm grateful, considering she's dead.'

'Look. If you don't want to meet Frieda's lawyer friend, who, by the way, happens to be a champion poker player.'

'I see. So he's ugly, boring, gay *and* gambling-addicted. Why didn't you say so in the first place?'

'Fine. You don't want to meet him, then how about Estelle's second cousin's brother's son's ex father-in-law from Pittsburgh? He's in gardening supply.'

'You mean he sells manure?'

'Don't be smart. He sells flowers and shrubbery. Things that make the world beautiful. What's wrong with that?'

'For one thing, Pittsburgh is a little far away.'

'You'll go there, he'll come here. You'll meet in the middle. You'll see. These things work out.'

'What's the catch?'

'No catch.' I studied her look of mock

innocence and the food swirling in her maw. 'Estelle says he's very good looking, and an absolute prince.'

'Divorced? Widowed?'

'Yes,' she said.

'Which?'

'Well, both. But just a couple of times,' she mumbled.

'How many wives has he had, Mom?'

'Oh, I don't know. Five, six maybe.'

'Will any of them give him a reference? The live ones?'

'Don't be fresh.'

I shrugged. 'I guess six wives could be viewed as a good thing. Practice makes perfect after all.'

'Now you're talking. So should I have Estelle give him your number?'

'No, Mom. You tell Estelle that if I'm ever in the market for manure, I'll be sure to look him up.'

An Affair to Dismember

Katie always found it comforting to discuss crucial matters in her place of worship: the tableware department at Tiffany's, and so she'd asked me to meet her there to talk about the party she and Roger were planning to celebrate Brian and Valerie's marriage. At five p.m. the store was packed. I made my way to the elevators, weaving to avoid bodily harm by the frantic shoppers struggling to unload those cumbersome wads of drug money or take advantage of the irresistible bargains one could snag now that the American dollar was pegged to the value of house dust.

Upstairs, I spotted Katie drifting in a covetous trance among the displays. My friend simply adored all things polished, pristine, cool, smooth, and costly. I imagined that fine china, silver and crystal reminded Katie, in an emotional sense, of herself.

'Marvelous news about the party, Mags! Bertie's available to cater. Can't tell you how relieved I was when she said yes.'

'Marvelous.'

'She is in such incredible demand.'

'Well I'm glad it worked out.' For the three decades that I'd known her, Katie had always hired Bertie, owner of Golden Spoon Catering, to provide the so-called food for her soirees. This amounted to starvation rations of passably attractive, inedible things on fancy trays, or as my mother might put it, you shouldn't know from it (and such small portions!).

Katie ran her finger seductively over the gold rim of a charger plate. 'So, I wanted to go over the menu with you.'

'Sure.'

'I thought I'd have Bertie do that fabulous crudité platter with the carrot sticks in the red cabbage bowl, and the cheese tray, and of course, she'll pass the rumaki and those little shrimp rolls and do a dip. Creamy onion or artichoke, do you think?'

'Either one's fine.' In fact, either one would work beautifully as library paste.

'Artichoke then. And what if I have her serve some of her little finger sandwiches: the ham, the cream cheese and olive, and the dried beef with brie and watercress?'

'Sounds perfect,' I said, delighting at the thought of my mother's apoplexy when she was confronted with all that technically forbidden fare. Not that Pearl was close to kosher, mind you. In truth, the only dietary law my mother had ever observed with any consistency was eating her young.

Katie paused to flirt with a soup tureen. Things got so heated for a moment there, I had to look away. 'Truly, Mags? You know how Rog and I adore Brian. We want everything to be just so.'

'I'm sure it'll be wonderful. It's really sweet of you to do this for the kids.'

'Our pleasure.' She cast one last longing at glance the tureen and then moved on, though I suspected she was not going to forget that sultry serving piece any time soon. 'You think it'll be OK if I have Bertie do her carrot cake for dessert?'

'I can't see why not.' True, Bertie's carrot cake tasted a lot like her dried beef with brie, but you didn't go to Katie's parties for the food.

'I'm worried that Valerie might be insulted if I don't order dessert from her company.'

'I doubt it, Katie. Valerie's not the easily insulted type. Anyway, she and Brian are thrilled that you're making a party for them. I should have thought of doing it myself.'

She cocked her head. 'Come now. Don't be hard on yourself. You've had a few little things on your mind.'

I watched in amazement as Katie honed in on a sterling gravy boat across the aisle. She approached with unabashed lust, as if the soup tureen had meant nothing to her at all.

'You think they have a color preference for the table cloths and napkins at the party, Mags? Because if not, I'd be inclined toward a classic pastel-and-ecru wedding look, if you agree.'

'Of course. Who could object to ecru?'

'Oh, and I've been meaning to ask. Where have Bri and Valerie registered?'

'For gifts, you mean? I don't think they have.'

'Well. They'd best get to it, Mags, and soon. Everyone's been asking about their patterns.'

'I'm not sure about Valerie, but Brian's pattern has always been pretty erratic.' I swerved to avoid a young woman choosing items for her registry. She was armed with a dangerous-looking diamond solitaire and a scanning gun.

'I'm serious. You do not marry without choosing patterns. It's not done.'

'I hear you. I'll explain that it's crucial they

177

choose tableware right away.'

'I'd think so. Which brings us to the guest list.'

'There aren't that many. Valerie's family is tiny and far away, and all I was thinking of asking were the closest people: my mother, Aunt Frieda, Darlys and her husband, and maybe Janine if I feel the need for extra stress. Bri and Valerie would probably like to invite some friends as well, but I'm sure it won't be many.'

'Perfect. So it'll be us, your list, the Vanderlips, the Claasens and some of the other old Connecticut friends, anyone Bri and Valerie want to ask, and the two of you.'

'I know I've put on a weight, Katie. But there's only one of me.'

Her blue eyes skittered away. 'Harold I mean. You can't expect us to have a wedding celebration for Bri and his bride and leave Harold out.'

'Why can't I?'

'Because whatever's happened between you, he's still the father of the groom.'

'Oh yeah? Prove it.'

Now she met my petulant gaze head-on. 'I know it's hard, but we all have to try to be grown-up about this thing.'

I bit my quivering lip. 'I'm trying to, believe me. But there's no way I can be at a party with Harold and Bethany right now. I understand it's bound to happen sooner or later, but I'm not ready to face that just yet.'

She put a finger under my chin. 'Come

now, Mags. You didn't think we were going to have Bethany there, did you?'

'I did, actually.'

'Well we're not. I've spoken to Harold about it. I told him we're not making any judgments, but the kids need to get to know Bethany under more casual circumstances first. He understands that this would not be a comfortable time for her to show up.'

'You're not making any judgments?'

'I told you. Rog and I are not going to take sides. We love you both, and we'll accept whoever you want to be with the same way we will with Harold.'

'Why do the kids have to get to know Bethany at all?'

She turned her back on the gravy boat. The woman had no loyalty. 'Because she's with their father, that's why. Be honest, Mags. In your heart you know that adults get to make their own life choices. We don't have to agree with them, but if we love someone, we do our best to accept the way they choose to live.'

'So if I showed up with – say – a married man it would be fine with you?'

'Things are never that black and white, Mags. I'm sure if you did, there would be much more to the story and it would all be perfectly reasonable.'

'What about if I decided to marry – say – a cannibal.'

'You're a sensible person, sweetie. If you chose to marry someone with odd food preferences, I'm sure he'd have lots of other redeeming qualities.'

'So basically, you'd approve of anyone I wound up with as long as we picked out silver and china patterns.'

Her look was sheer exasperation. 'And crystal, of course. A bride cannot fail to select her tableware, Mags. What would people say?'

The Prying Game

My last client of the day was barely out the door when Janine burst in. She was shrink-wrapped in a traffic-cone orange cat suit and wore rhinestone-studded spike heeled shoes and a sparkly silver top hat. Daphne trailed self-consciously behind cradling musical accompaniment in the form of a giant boom box. Her heels and top hat were identical to Janine's, but her cat suit was the red of an infected boil.

'Hit it, Daph!' Janine ordered.

Daphne dutifully set the boom box down, pressed the Play button, and posed beside Janine as the music began to play. The tune was 'Hokey Pokey'. The lyrics were classic Janine.

'You let your best parts show. You let your whole self go. You play him nice and slow, and you turn it all around. You do the hanky panky, and make sure the guy gets laid. That's how the game is played!'

This was accompanied by shimmies, hip thrusts and other suggestive gyrations which Janine and Daphne did more or less in synch.

'OK, Janine. Enough. This is a place of business for heaven's sake.'

The tune changed, as did Daphne and Janine. They busted out of their cat suits exposing the shimmering ice blue bathing suits beneath. 'She's got the whole world, in his gland; she's got the whole wide world, in his gland.'

'Stop!'

Now they stripped the Velcro side seams and the one-piece suits fell away, revealing tiny string bikinis in a tarnished-copper blue. As the music shifted yet again, Janine posed with an arm aloft like the statue of far too many liberties and crooned: 'Oh beautiful for soft, pale thighs for mysteries between. For sultry mounds of well-toned pounds above a belly lean—'

In a fury I switched off the boom box. 'I said stop, Janine. I don't play people and I am not interested in trying to manipulate Anthony Sinclair.'

'I know that, sweetie. So it's a good thing I'm here to straighten you out.'

'I don't need straightening out, Janine. I need you to leave me alone.'

While Janine puffed her exasperation, Daphne scurried about, collecting the costumes they'd shed. 'Sorry, Maggie,' she muttered as she passed.

I smiled at her, marveling at her courage.

The knock at my door heralded the arrival of my next client, Billy Griggs. At nine years old, Billy's acting career was rocketing. Recently, he had been signed to play a Russian chess prodigy in a major new Disney film. Our work on the accent he would need was scheduled to start today.

I herded Janine and Daphne toward the door and ushered in Billy and the young man escorting him. The child's eyes bugged at the sight of the women in their barely-there bikinis. 'Wow,' he said. 'What are they playing?'

'Unfair,' I told him. 'Unfair, out of bounds, and unconscionable.'

'Sounds cool,' he said. 'Think they have any parts for a kid?'

Why Noon?

Rabbi Jennifer looked like a kid faced with a perplexing math problem. If a train from New York and one from San Francisco departed at the same time and were traveling toward each other at a constant rate of speed and my mother was on one of them, wouldn't anyone in her right mind flee to Australia?

'So let me make sure I have this straight, Maggie. You go out to lunch with your mother regularly.'

Even though the subject was far from dear to me, anything was preferable to talking about my stubborn, continuing, maddening, and utterly fruitless fixation on the still AWOL Wop. 'Yes I do. At least once a week.'

'And it's always a miserable experience?'

'No. Usually it's miserable, but every so often it's much worse than that.'

'You're saying she gets mad at you for being late even though you're not late at all.'

'That's right.'

'You always go to the same awful place where the food and service are terrible. She always insists you order what she wants, and then all she does is undermine and insult you.'

'No. To be fair, she undermines and insults the waiters, too. And the short order cook and the cashier and sometimes the random customer. Pearl's an equal-opportunity destroyer.'

She eyed me strangely. 'I'm wondering why you keep it up.'

'Force of habit, I guess. Plus, call me crazy, but I've never had the least interest in being disemboweled.'

'What's happened in the past when you asserted yourself with your mother?'

'Nothing.'

'There you are.'

'Nothing happened because I never tried.'

'Then maybe it's time you did, Maggie. I bet her bark is much worse than her bite.'

'Her bite's pretty bad, believe me. I can show you the scars.'

'It can seem easier to cave in when somebody tries to bully you, but you pay for that by giving up part of yourself.'

'Maybe so, but it's still easier to cave in. I mean, what's the big deal? It's only an hour or so out of my life here and there. Plus, as Harold was always fond of saying, what doesn't kill us makes us stronger.'

'Doesn't sound as if Harold was exactly the self-sacrificing type.'

'No. Not exactly.'

'How did he get along with your mother?'

'You don't get along with Harold or my mother. The best you can do with either of them is get by.'

She folded her hands on the desk. 'I'd like to go back and talk a little more about something you said a while ago. How you always thought you and Harold would be together until you died.'

'That's true. I did.'

'Is that because you couldn't imagine life without marriage?'

'Of course not. I was a child for years, and I wasn't married then. Unless you count the mock ceremony Danny Chaskin and I had at the Camp Wisquamicutt carnival when I was ten, but I wanted six kids and he wanted a go-kart and two gerbils, so that relationship was pretty much doomed from the start.'

Rabbi Jennifer just sat there, patiently waiting for me to get real.

'OK, maybe you're right. Maybe I couldn't imagine not being married. I was raised on bride dolls and baby dolls. In my house, anything was more acceptable than an old maid. Even a child molester was preferable, as long as it was a married child molester. All my parents ever wanted me to be was a wife. They thought married was the only reasonable way for a woman to be.'

'And you still buy that?'

'Of course not. I may live by it, but I don't buy it at all. I think it's ridiculous and patently untrue. Plenty of women lead fabulous, happy, productive lives without ever getting married. And plenty do incredibly well after they're widowed or divorced, especially after a marriage that wasn't very good.'

'But?'

I threw up my hands. 'I get what you're trying to say, but here's the thing, Rabbi Jennifer. I'm not a shining star, and I have no interest whatsoever in being a beacon in the darkness. I'd make a lousy beacon. Trust me. I'm much better off as part of a nice, run-of-the-mill pair of socks.'

'You've been asked to accommodate a big, sudden change, and that's frightening, Maggie. It's only normal to do everything you can think of it to try to make it go away.'

'I haven't done everything I can think of, not by a long shot. I could annihilate Bethany, for example. I could have Harold lobotomized or castrated, though in his case that's

185

probably the same operation.'

She was wearing her indulgent smile again. 'I'm curious. If Harold came to you and said he'd made a terrible mistake and wanted to reconcile, what would you do?'

My stomach roiled. 'Harold's not going to do that.'

'What if he did?'

It's said that actions speak louder than words, and so I acted. I crammed my mouth full of jelly beans and chewed until our time ran out.

Chopped Liver Runs Through It

I had done my level best to repress cousin Jared's bar mitzvah, but sadly this failed to make the occasion go away. If it was anybody else, I would have begged off, but Jared is my cousin Ilona's son, and such a slight might well send her into a serious, prolonged tail-spin. It could take drastic therapy, like a round-the-world cruise or a major six-figure shopping spree in Milan, to lift Ilona from her frequent bouts of crushing despair.

The reception was at Tappan Hill, a sprawling former residence of Mark Twain's, perched on a bluff overlooking the Hudson River in Westchester County. The catering establishment had been done up to reflect the very essence of cousin Ilona, with a striking excess of absolutely everything, except taste.

My cousin had chosen a martial arts theme, which sadly magnified young Jared's obvious shortcomings. The boy was a scrawny runt, not to mention poorly coordinated, with glasses dense as snow globes and an unfortunate crop of spiky beige hair. To appease his impossible mother, he mugged for the photographers amid lifelike Styrofoam replicas of hugely muscled Ninjas. People viewing the photo album in millennia to come would be bound to wonder what this fierce band of hulking warriors was doing with a bespectacled whisk broom.

Bar mitzvahs were intended to mark a Jewish boy's religious coming-of-age, but this celebration was strictly about showing off. Ilona appeared to have cornered the market on tacky Mylar balloons, flashing neon, and annoying entertainments. Someone planted a hat on my head, fashioned from a paper plate to resemble the Empire State Building. Someone else plastered fake biker tattoos on my arms. I was draped with a cheesy necklace of flashing lights and forced to don a huge pair of gilt-framed dark glasses. When the caricaturist approached, brandishing a sketchpad and a nub of charcoal, I saw no choice but to hiss like a puff adder and scare her off.

During the cocktail hour, I kept my mouth full of nibbles and champagne, desperate to avoid having to answer the inevitable nosy

187

questions from my relatives. True, I was supposed to be on a diet, but slimming down wouldn't mean much if I allowed my nearest and queerest to make me suicidal. Some families had a genetic tendency toward heart disease or diabetes. For the Evantoff clan, the Darwinian scourge was tactlessness coupled with unmitigated gall, the dread family *chutzpah* gene.

At the sight of me, Aunt Esther's hand flew to her large, nasty mouth. 'Maggie. My God! You look awful!'

'Why thanks, Aunt Esther. That's always nice to hear.'

'I heard about Harold running off with some gorgeous young genius. So humiliating. No wonder.'

'Excuse me. I think I see a waiter with pigs in blankets.'

'Where? Hurry, darling! Go! I'm right behind you.'

I hadn't counted on that. 'Nope. False alarm. It's stuffed mushrooms.'

'Ah well. Keep an eye out. When it comes to pigs in blankets, you can't be too careful.'

'I couldn't agree more.'

'So tell me, Maggie. You think Harold's going to marry this girl?'

Hadn't counted on that either. The notion sent geysers of champagne shooting up my nasal passages. 'I don't know,' I croaked when I could speak again. 'You'd have to ask him.'

Uncle Eli cast a pleading glance at the ceiling. 'Esther, please.'

'OK, I suppose you're right,' she said. 'Why would he buy the milk if he's *shtupping* the cow for free?'

Eli set a comforting hand on my shoulder. 'Don't mind her, sweetheart. I've been searching for years, but I'm afraid that mouth of hers didn't come with an off button.'

I smiled at him. Poor shnook had to live with this woman every day, a fate that made the Ninth Circle of Hell look like two weeks on Maui. 'The Evantoff model rarely does.'

'Unless he knocked her up,' Esther prattled on. 'You think that's it?'

'I don't think, Aunt Esther, except in the event of an emergency.'

'Having a baby at his age. Ridiculous. Who does he think he is, Cary Grant?'

'You'd have to ask him.'

My mother was zeroing in, making her determined way past the soaring, swan-shaped chopped liver sculpture and then trying to part the dangerous crush of people at the smoked fish and caviar station. 'Excuse me, Aunt Esther. I need to go jump in the river now.'

'Of course, darling. Enjoy!'

I fantasized about being here with Wop, which would drive all my female relatives insane with jealousy (not that it was all that far a drive). But then, even if he hadn't already concluded that I was completely hopeless, meeting my family would do the trick.

At that moment, a Tony Bennett look-alike

with a road-kill toupee announced that dinner was about to be served. Several skittish-looking waiters in karate garb herded us toward the ballroom. I could well understand their concern. If a tray of pigs in blankets happened to appear right then, it might have triggered a perilous stampede.

We passed in single file through a passageway draped with acres of gold lamé. Choking vapor from a fog machine swirled around us, masking cousin Hannah's double-wide derrière and giving my great uncle Willie the look of a disembodied, liver-spotted head. At the end of the tunnel, the mist suddenly cleared to reveal – ta da! – Jared, the klutzy, myopic little warrior on a bejeweled, gold-painted throne. An oversized crown perched on his head, bending his ears so he resembled a Jack Russell terrier. His three piece mini-banker's suit and tiny Hermès tie peeked out from under an ornate Japanese robe. He looked, in other words, exactly the way you'd expect a lad to look at his bar mitzvah if his mother was a histrionic, over-privileged loon.

The ballroom was festooned with enormous cardboard swords and too many black and silver balloons to contemplate. Towering black and white floral arrangements lent the occasion an atmosphere that could only be described as morbidly depressing. As the guests swarmed in, the band played 'Celebrate', the classic migraine-inducing refrain.

According to my reception card, which in Ilona's typical understated way was inset in an engraved sterling silver frame, I was at table 28. This took a while to find, wedged as it was between the men's room and the emergency exit. Soon, I was joined by six other wary-looking souls. We circled the table in strained silence, searching for our assigned chairs.

The seating arrangement was not easy to dope out. My dinner date was either Sofi, Ilona's blowsy Guatemalan housekeeper, who was on my left, or Ilona's husband's gay cousin Neil on my right, whose life partner, Karl, was in Vegas for a menswear show. The stooped old man beside Neil introduced himself as Morris Plotnick, the family's long-time accountant. He was aptly paired with a surly girl of sixteen or so with more piercings than a dartboard and a bare midriff that showcased her Betty-Boop-astride-a-motor-cycle tattoo. She sneered by way of greeting, flaring her ring-studded nostrils, and then tossed back a Cosmopolitan, which was obviously far from her first of the day. Beside her sat a daisy-blonde woman, who courage-ously confessed to having prepared Jared for his part in the ceremony. Last, though it would have been difficult to determine the least, was an unsavory-looking fellow, wildly underdressed in soiled jeans and a grubby T-shirt, who bopped to the frenzied beat of a musical hallucination and, to my great relief, declined to introduce himself at all.

I swallowed hard. So it had come to this. Throughout my life, I had followed the orderly progression from the children's table to the young singles' to the young marrieds' and finally, the established couples' section at family events. I'd expected to continue on in due course to the elders' table, the one all the younger people clucked at smugly and said, 'Look at her, a hundred and three and still sharp as a tack,' or simply, 'God Bless, Uncle Fred!' which was another way to say: *if I ever get that feeble, shoot me!* But now that was not to be. I'd been relegated to the odds-and-ends table, the pointy-headed misfits left over after the host had assigned everyone else to his or her logical spot. We were only seven, in a room packed with tables of ten or twelve. A shortage of odds, I reasoned. Or perhaps, it was a tragic paucity of ends.

A deep ache of loneliness lodged in my chest. I longed for someone to gaze at me admiringly and pass secret signals while we ate. I yearned for the press of someone's leg against mine and strong arms to hold me as we made our way around the dance floor. Rabbi Jennifer was right, no matter how ridiculous it might look from the outside, you never stopped yearning for love and romance. I didn't care if my glass slipper would need the orthopedic insert. So what if my prince had jowls?

'*Demasiado, no?*' Sofi asked, with a sweep of her chunky arm. 'Ees too much.'

I blotted my eyes. 'Too much doesn't begin to cover it.'

The housekeeper leaned close as if anyone

else in earshot was in any danger of understanding her, and I caught a whiff of misguided cologne: something in the tutti-frutti and fried onion family. '*Senora Ilona es poca loca.*'

'*Más que poca,*' I said, with a healing surge of spite.

She jabbed my upper arm and laughed in great, snorting bursts. '*Boca loca.* That woomin, she talk so much sheet.'

I smiled stiffly and turned to cousin Neil on my left. It wasn't so much that I felt disloyal trashing my cousin Ilona with her hired help as I was terrified that she'd somehow find out and stab me in my sleep.

Neil told me he worked as a molecular pathologist, doing microscopic battle with cancer cells. I asked him to explain, imagining it would be fascinating. And no doubt it would have been, if I'd had the vaguest capacity to understand a word of it. Soon, he was going on and on about monoclonal antibodies and high-throughput gene array analysis, and I was sinking into a deep – and probably irreversible – coma with my eyes open.

Luckily, Brian and Valerie came over and spirited me off to join the enormous throng on the dance floor doing the *hora*. At the center of the clomping, kicking, bobbing crowd, six men hoisted cousin Ilona on a chair. They bounced her up and down, so her absurdly enhanced breasts threatened to pop out of her low-cut, sequined silver gown. Her husband Fred went next, looking so alarmed, I feared he'd have a coronary before the one he was bound to have when he saw the bill for this shindig. Jared's homely little sister Alyssa, a scrawny, hair-challenged version of her brother in drag, was next up, and then, the bar mitzvah boy himself. Aloft in the chair, Jared went chalk-pale and rigid with fear. This was going to be one indelible memory for that kid. No question. I predicted he'd be talking about it decades from now, on a couch.

When the dancers dispersed to eat their appetizers of sautéed tiger prawns with melon and *prosciutto*, I caught a distant glimpse of someone who bore an uncanny resemblance to Harold. Beside him stood a young, attractive, slender, self-possessed brunette in a lovely blue gown, who bore an uncanny resemblance to my worst nightmare.

Furious, I caught Ilona's eye. She had the nerve to smile at me in all her phony, eye-lifted innocence, as if she hadn't invited Harold and his Phi Beta Bimbo out of sheer meanness.

My blood heated to a boil. Leave it to that crazy bitch Ilona. Leave it to that inconsiderate bastard Harold to skip the service and show up for the party. Leave it to that home-wrecker Bethany to have the nerve to look so fabulous.

'*Mira. La loca* she have shreemp and *jamón* at a bar meet-zah,' Sofi said with an arrogant sniff at her plate.

'Shrimp and ham are nothing,' I said. 'There's also a pig on the hoof.'

Look Who's Stalking Now

I was in a ratty blue robe and matching mood, mainlining coffee, when a key clacked in my front door lock. Before I had the chance to wet myself, Harold strutted into the living room as if he owned the place, which he technically did, but still.

'Who let you in?' I demanded.

'I let myself in.'

'Well, you can let yourself out. Right now!'

'I'll leave after we have that talk, Margaret.'

'This is my place, and you have no right to barge in uninvited. Now leave.'

He ambled into the kitchen, poured himself a cup of coffee and opened the refrigerator door. 'There's no milk.'

'That's because everyone who lives here takes her coffee black. Now, for the last time, Harold, I'm asking you to give me that key and get the hell out of my home *immediately.*'

He chuckled. '*Your* home, indeed. It so happens that this residence is jointly held and shall remain so until the separation agreement is signed. If you wish to avoid such impromptu encounters in the future, all you need to do is execute the papers our lawyers have prepared at considerable expense. In fact, I've brought a copy with me for your convenience.'

'All I'm willing to execute for my convenience is you.'

'I see you are still your mature, charming self.'

'I'll count to three. If you're not out of here, my mature, charming self is going to call the police and charge you with trespassing, harassment and impersonating an ass.'

He twirled the phantom tip of his former mustache. 'You wouldn't dare.'

'And stalking. Don't worry. I'll think of others by the time they get here. One ... two...'

'Don't be ridiculous. The authorities would hardly be interested in an innocent discussion between two people attempting to reach a rational agreement in a simple divorce.'

'Two and a half.' I lifted the receiver and tapped nine-one-one.

'All right. If you must be so childish and unreasonable, I'll go. But you will be sorry, Margaret. I can promise you that. If you refuse to do this the easy way, I see no choice but to respond accordingly.'

I held out my hand. 'The key.'

Grudgingly, he handed it over.

'And don't even think about trying to bribe one of the doormen to get you in here again, Harold. I know how to bribe them way better. I know how to tip them twice as much as you could ever stand to do without a general anesthetic.'

'How many times have I told you? Such

overblown largesse does nothing whatsoever to win you respect. Quite the contrary.'

'I don't want respect. Paid loyalty suits me fine.'

'My Lord, Margaret. Will you never learn?'

I felt a smile coming on. 'It was dicey there for a while. But right now, I believe I will.'

Million Dollar Maybe

When the house phone shrilled, I charged dripping wet from the tub.

Tabrik (the night doorman, who was filling in for Lucius the day doorman during one of his regularly scheduled benders): Someone here to see you, Mrs Strickland.

Me: Who?

Tabrik: Mr Something Something. Didn't quite catch the name.

Me: Then why don't you ask again?

Tabrik (checking to see if such a demand was covered by the contract between the New York Board of Professional Tenant Gougers and the American Federation of Overpaid, Attitude-Disabled Doormen): So you want me to send him up?

Me: No, Tabrik. I want you to ask his name and then tell me what it is, in that order.

Tabrik (contemplating the tragic inadequacy of my Christmas tip): It's Mr Sinclair,

Mrs Strickland. He's on the way.

Me: No, Tabrik! Stop him! He can't come up here now!

Tabrik: (doing an uncanny imitation of a dial tone).

Me: Tabrik? Are you there? Tabrik?

The good news was that our elevator was painfully slow. I charged into the bedroom and tugged on my ancient gray sweats. Next, I raced to the bathroom, brushed my lank, sodden hair and waved the mascara wand in the general neighborhood of my eyes. Blush followed that and a swipe of lip gloss, at which point, the doorbell rang.

Wop looked heart-thumpingly handsome, though a tad exhausted and morose. 'Sorry to barge in on you, Maggie. Have a minute?'

'Sure. Come in. Are you all right?'

He pulled a breath. 'Not exactly.'

'What's wrong, Anthony? Are you sick?'

'No. Nothing like that. Things have just been a little crazy the past few days. That's why I haven't called.'

'You haven't?' I took his coat. 'Can I make you something? Tea? Coffee?' *Mine?*

'No thanks. I wasn't even planning to come here. I was out walking, trying to clear my head, and somehow I wound up at your door. I should have called first.'

'That's OK. What's going on?'

He perched on the couch. 'Stephanie – my wife – showed up unexpectedly. She says if I don't quit my job and move back to London, she wants a divorce.'

198

I offered the wisest comment that came to mind. 'Hmmm.'

'I've tried to reason with her, but it's no use. Either I promise to pack it in, or she's out.'

'Hmmm.'

'It's crazy. I know. But I honestly can't decide whether to chase her to the ends of the earth or toss in the towel.'

Though I refrained from saying so, the obvious answer was B. After all, global pursuit was so expensive and time-consuming. Much simpler to buy a new towel.

He shook his head. 'When she mentioned divorce, I panicked. We've been together since high school. Stephanie was my first and only serious girlfriend, if you can believe it. As bad as things have been between us, it's hard to imagine life without her.'

'I'm sure.'

'But she wants me to spend all my time playing golf and puttering around the house, and I can't imagine that either. I'd go nuts.'

'Sometimes people grow apart.'

'You can say that again. Stephanie used to be a regular firebrand, full of life and energy. Now all she does is hang around, buy things she doesn't need from catalogues, do crossword puzzles and sleep.'

'Maybe she's depressed.'

'Oh, she's that all right, and depressing. I can't tell you how many times I've begged her to see a psychiatrist, maybe try medication. But she says there's nothing wrong with her, it's all my fault. She blames everything on my spending too much time at work, not paying enough attention to her. If I would just give up my career and live the way she wants me to, things would be perfect.'

'You think?'

'Of course not.' His lips pressed in an angry seam. 'You know what her problem is? She's not happy unless she's not happy. When I was offered the job in London, she was dead set against it. How could I possibly ask her to leave New York? She loved it here and never wanted to live anywhere else. We talked and talked, and she finally agreed to try it for a year. But she never gave it a chance. She was so miserable I finally convinced the Board to move the executive offices here. Took months and all the good will I could muster. I thought Stephanie would be thrilled, but no. When I told her, she went ballistic. How could I possibly ask her to move again? She claimed she'd always hated New York and loved London.'

He stood and started pacing. 'For thirty years, I've been trying to please that woman. Well, I'm sick of giving in. Sick to death of it. What a ridiculous waste!'

'So what are you going to do?'

That stopped him cold. His face fell, and he slumped again on the couch. 'I'm so confused.'

'This is hard, complicated stuff, Anthony. You need time to think it through.'

'You're right. Steph doesn't get to write the rules. I'll figure out what's right for me in my own good time.'

'I'm sure you will.'

He blew a breath. 'You know what you are, Maggie? You're a smart, sane, sensible grown-up, and I can't tell you how much that means to me right now.'

'Thanks. I can't tell you how much it means to me right now to be wildly overestimated.'

Wop responded with his feet, which he got to, and his arms, which he wrapped me with, and his mouth. His kiss was probing, and melting, and wonderful beyond words.

My body was waving a big white flag of unconditional surrender, but somehow, I managed to pull away. 'This is not what you need right now, Anthony.'

'I don't?'

'No.'

'Are you sure?'

'Go, Anthony. Think. Maybe talk to a counselor. Take your time.'

'Can't I think later?'

'Go.'

'Are you sure?'

'Go.'

Lotions Eleven

On the phone my mother sounded breathless, and mildly insane. This rendered me sufficiently curious to cease second, third, and fourth-guessing what I had – or more accurately – what I hadn't done with Wop. I couldn't remember what the righteous were supposed to inherit, but I'd bet the taxes on whatever it happened to be were hell.

'Thank God I caught you, Maggie!' my mother said. 'Get your coat. You have to go to Bloomingdales right away!'

'What for?'

'Don't ask questions. Just go! Run! Call me back from your cell phone, and I'll explain.'

'Calm down and tell me now.'

'I'm almost afraid to talk about it. It's amazing! A miracle! Promise you won't tell a soul!' I hadn't heard my mother this excited since her sister's husband went bankrupt, unless you counted how thrilled she was last winter when Aunt Frieda fell on an icy sidewalk and broke her hip.

'OK, I promise.'

'How do I know I can trust you?'

'You don't. And you probably shouldn't take the chance.'

202

'Don't be a stupid idiot. This is the opportunity of a lifetime!'

'Now you sound like you're trying to sell me an Amway franchise.'

'Don't be fresh. Write this down. Capital L-a—Wait! Is anybody there?'

'Not unless you count me, which, of course, you don't.'

'How can you be sure no one's listening in?'

'Please, Mom. If this is such a big secret, do me a favor and keep it to yourself. I'm not in the mood for intrigue.' I couldn't shake the image of Wop slogging out the door in utter dejection. Leave it to me. I had the perfect chance to act reprehensibly, and I blew it.

'Don't give me your moods,' my mother snapped. 'Capital L-a, capital R-e-c-h-a-r-g-e. You got that?'

'Sounds like something naughty you do with French batteries.'

She puffed her exasperation. 'It just happens to be the most incredible line of skin care products ever. Costs a fortune, but it's worth every cent. I read about it at the dentist's office, when I was getting my gold on-lay. Seventeen hundred dollars and it hurt like hell.'

'You're suggesting that I spend $1700 for a skin cream that hurts? Forgive me for asking, but are you on some new medication?'

'Don't be snide. I was talking the on-lay. Dr Constantine had to drill practically to China to put the damn thing in. The skin cream is a regular bargain considering how it works.

Only $125 an ounce for the renewing moisturizer.'

'You're making that up.'

'OK, so it's actually 7/10 of an ounce for $130 plus tax, but I'd pay more. Of course, you have to get the whole line to do it right. There are eleven products: toner, cleanser, night cream, day cream, neck scrub, exfoliating mask, soothing mask, and so on. But it's better than a facelift. One month on the stuff and my wrinkles are practically gone. Especially the ones around my mouth. Remember those?'

'I'm going to plead the Fifth on that.'

'Don't be cute. I wanted to show you at Ilona's bar mitzvah, but you kept running away.'

'You mean Jared's bar mitzvah?'

'Don't contradict.'

'Fine. I'm sure you look wonderful. But I'm not spending that kind of money on skin cream.'

I swear I could hear her eyes rolling. 'For this, I had an episiotomy. And piles. Listen to me, Maggie. Don't be a horse's ass. Losing a few of those wrinkles of yours wouldn't hurt. If you want to compete with that *shiksa* chickie of Harold's you will run, not walk, to Bloomingdale's and get the whole line.'

'I don't want to compete with her. If first prize is Harold, I think I want Bethany to win.'

'Don't be stubborn. When the word gets out, you won't be able to buy this stuff for love or money.'

'I hear you, Mom. I'll think about it.'

'There's no time. I'm telling you – go. Run!'

'Sure, Mom. I'm going. I'm running. Speak to you soon.'

Hanging up, this struck me as weird. Normally, my mother was more sensible, at least when it comes to absurd anti-aging hype. Sure, I was as vain as the next person, and I certainly wouldn't mind a magic youth pill, especially now. But come on.

Then again, it wouldn't hurt me to get out and take a walk. And if I happened to pass by Bloomingdales' La Recharge counter, I suppose there was no harm in checking the fool stuff out. With the way things were going, Lord knew I needed all the help I could get.

Three Ten and a Baby

3:10:32 p.m. and counting.

'Gammy pay dubeye tong?'

'Sure, sweetie. Whatever you say.' Valerie and Brian were due home in 49 minutes and 28 seconds. I was watching the baby and the clock.

'Dubeye tong?'

'Sorry. I don't understand.'

'Gammy pay it?'

'I have an idea. How about a cookie?'

So far, either the cookie or the cloying purple-juice-in-a-sippy-cup gambit had succeeded in distracting her from whatever it was she wanted that I could not comprehend. This was evident in Delia's tummy, which had expanded under the juice-stained Hello Kitty T-shirt so she was beginning to resemble a Strasbourg goose.

And now, it seemed she had reached capacity. When I approached, wielding one of her Mommy's 'world-famous' peanut butter wafers, she clamped her lips and shook her ringlet-studded head.

'How about an oatmeal raisin, then? How about a yummy chocolate chip?'

'Dee-duh wan dubeye tong NOW!'

Her lower lip curled, striking raw terror in my heart. There was ample evidence that I once knew how to manage such a creature, but I also once knew how to body surf, wear micro-mini skirts and do the funky chicken. One did not try such stunts at my age.

'I have an idea. Why don't you show me?'

This was a brilliant solution, which of course, failed brilliantly. The baby stomped around in frightening disarray like a poorly loaded washing machine. 'GAMMY PAY DUBEYE TONG NOW!'

'How about I tell you a story?'

That quieted her down. 'Gammy tory?'

She sat on my lap, and I cast a desperate net for inspiration. All I could think of was Anthony trudging out the door after I rejected his advances; that and how he met a

25-year-old supermodel half a block from my apartment and fell madly in love.

'OK. Once upon a time there was a chubby old crow whose husband flew off with a really smart young starling. For a while, the old crow was very sad, but then she met the most amazing eagle that she used to know way back when they were both baby birds.'

Delia nodded in preliminary approval. 'Maw koh tory.'

'Right. So one day, the eagle flew to the old crow's nest and said he wanted to sleep over. The old crow really wanted to let him, but she didn't, which turned out to be really dumb. And so the eagle left to find a much better crow. The end.'

'Maw koh tory.'

'No more, sweetie. That story's over.'

'Dee-duh wan dubeye tong NOW.'

'Soon, sweetie. Mommy will be back and she'll do whatever it is for you.'

'Wan Mommy!'

'No more than I do, *believe* me.' This was not how I should be spending my time. I was supposed to be out there in the big world of possibilities, waiting for fate to suffer a twinge of conscience and toss me a bone.

'Mommy home!' she commanded.

'Soon, sweetie. Mommy and Daddy are meeting with someone really important at Zabar's, remember? I think it's the actual chief mucky-muck in charge of desserts you eat without a fork. Isn't that exciting?'

Delia went still, eyeing me in that tentative

way toddlers had, trying to decide whether I was tolerably amusing or criminally insane.

She edged closer and worked my face, patting and molding, trying to stick her fingers in my eye sockets, under my lips and up my nose, testing to see whether the pasty, odd-looking appliance mounted on my neck had any decent play value.

I set my voice at a low, hypnotic lilt. 'So Mommy and Daddy are at their meeting. And they'll be home veeery, veeery soon. Just 38 minutes and 26 seconds, if there is a God.'

She bobbled my lips as I said this, so I sounded like a demented kazoo.

'Mommy home soo-nuh,' she intoned.

'Veeeerrreeeee veerree soon,' I agreed, silently begging the hands on the wall clock to hurry along.

'Mommy meeting,' she confirmed.

'Very important meeting. The future of Valerie's sweet treats, and quite possibly the fate of independent cookie entrepreneurs everywhere, might well hang on the verdict of Zabar's chief executive of finger desserts. That's right.'

'Daddy meeting?'

'Yes he is. Your Daddy has undergone a miracle conversion from devout non-conformist to born-again, buttoned down entrepreneur. I believe he's put together a major PowerPoint presentation on the lemon squares alone.'

'Daddy home soo-nuh?'

'That's right. Daddy and Mommy are at a

meeting, and Nanny Grace is out sick, I suspect with a sudden, acute attack of irresistible President's Day sales at the department stores, so Granny is staying with you for just a little while longer.'

'No GATE!'

'Definitely not. Nanny Grace called in sick, and unreliable.'

'Wan Mommy NOW!'

'As do I, sweetie. Right this minute! In fact, if I wasn't required by law to imitate an adult, I'd cry for her myself.'

'DEEDUH WAN MOMMY!' She held her breath for a long time, and then did an uncanny imitation of an ambulance siren.

'Ssh. Easy. I've got it. Why don't we watch TV? Mommy and Daddy don't allow that, so it'll be really, *really* fun.'

'Wan dubeye tong,' she wept. 'Dubeye tong peeze.'

'Hush, sweetheart. I understand. I mean I don't understand, but I can empathize. I know what it feels like when someone doesn't get what you say. Try spending thirty years with your Grandpa Harold. Try thirty minutes, for that matter.' I knelt down and held out my arms. 'Want Granny to pick you up and rock you?'

She shrieked harder, like Harold always did when he saw the MasterCard bill. 'Gammy pay dubeye tong NOW!'

'Maybe you're sleepy. Why don't I take you in for a nice, long nap?'

I carried her to the bedroom, wedged her

209

into the tiny vacancy between the staggering profusion of toys in the crib, and sang the song that had been Brian's hands-down favorite lullaby:

A hundred bottles of beer on the wall. A hundred bottles of beer. If one of those bottles should happen to fall...

For a blessed moment, she stayed still. Head down, rump up. Yes!

I was halfway to the door when she scrambled to her feet and started howling.

'Ssh. What, sweetie? I know. Maybe you're wet.'

I laid her on the changing table where she squirmed like a beached fish. Somehow, I managed to wrestle her out of the tiny denim cargo pants and undid the diaper. Naturally, Valerie used cloth.

Naturally, she was not just wet. Her flailing spread the mess, which rapidly crossed the line from merely gross to revolting.

I was grabbing wipes, swiping madly. 'Oh, yuck! Phooey. Gack! Icky poo!'

This inspired hysterical laughter. 'Poopee diepuh.'

'You think it's funny?'

'Gammy poopee.'

'Indeed I am. And I'm pretty sure this calls for an emergency bath.'

'Bubboo duck!' she chortled in delight.

'Whatever.'

I ferried her to the bathroom like a ticking

bomb. She pranced about happily as I filled the tub with lukewarm water, baby bubble bath, waterproof picture books, pouring toys, animal-shaped sponges, and a staggering assortment of smug-faced rubber ducks.

With glee, she assaulted the soapy water, splashing wildly, soaking me to the skin. 'Bubboo duck,' she shrilled. 'Gammy bubboo duck?'

'Thanks, anyway. I think I'll wait and take my bubble duck alone.'

At that moment, Brian and Valerie returned.

'Good meeting?' I asked.

Brian flashed a big thumbs-up. 'Excellent. They want us back next week to meet the head of the entire pastry division.'

'How wonderful.'

He leaned in and kissed Delia's sodden head. 'Hey, Boobly Woobly. Who's the best widdoo dirl in the whole wide world?'

'Dee-duh is,' she declared with admirable self-assurance.

'Did you and Granny have fun?' Valerie asked.

'Gammy no pay dubeye tong.'

Rotten whistleblower.

'That's OK, sweetie. I'll put on the goodbye song soon as you finish your bubble duck. That's her favorite,' my daughter-in-law explained. 'I must play that silly thing a dozen times a day.'

'Too bad I didn't know,' I said, resisting the urge to lunge for her soft, pink throat.

'It doesn't matter, Mom. Believe me. Having a granny who loves her is all Delia needs.'

The Princess Tried

Amelia Burkart was doing remarkably well. In character, she now sounded exactly like Princess Diana, albeit on a bad day with a head cold, and before the novocaine for her dental work had fully worn off. But this was incredible progress, nonetheless.

'You know, Maggie. Maybe yaw gonna think oy'm crazy, but when oy put awn that accent, oy really feel like a princess.'

'Not crazy at all. You look the part and you're starting to sound it. I'm proud of you, Amelia.'

'Come awn. It's awl because of you, Maggie. Every woid.'

'Not true. You're working very hard.'

She wrapped me in a hug. 'I could nevah do it without you. No way, no how. Yaw my inspuhrayshin.'

'I'm flattered, Amelia, but all I'm doing is helping you to bring out what you're already capable of doing. You should be proud of yourself.'

She paused and frowned at her dressing room mirror. 'Oy'm not proud at all. Oy'm ashamed of moyself. Heah oy am, awl about me. Let's tawk about you faw a change, Maggie. Tell me about yawself.'

'Nothing much to tell.'

'You married?'

'Getting divorced.'

'Sorry.'

'It's OK. Probably for the best.'

'Yaw so philosophical.'

'Tranquilized, mostly. Anyway, I've got two grown kids,' I told her. 'And a baby grand-daughter.'

'Yaw kidding. You look like a baby yawself.'

'That's sweet, but I'm a whole lot older than I act.'

Her face fell. 'People like you should be the rich, famous stahs, Maggie, not no-talent actuhs like me. It's not right that you don't get the recunishin you dissoive.'

'Watching you do so well is all the recognition I could ever ask for, Amelia.'

'It's not enough,' she said. 'Oy'm not gonna settle for that, Maggie. Oy can't.'

'You're sweet, Amelia, but you shouldn't be worrying about me. Let's focus on making you the best Lady Diana you can be.'

She giggled. 'Can oy make a confeshin?'

'Sure.'

'Oy'm so wrapped up in the role, oy actually had a romantic dream about Prince Charles. Can you believe?'

'Not entirely.'

'There has to be more to him than meets the oy, don't you think?'

'I suppose.'

'Oy wish oy could always sound like a princess, Maggie. Not just faw the film.'

'You can if you want to, Amelia. You can use the accent any time you like.'

'Oy can? Oy mean, I can?'

'It's a simple matter of practicing until it becomes your regular way to talk.'

'That's possible? You really think I could pull it awf, I mean off?'

'I do. Just keep working at it.'

'That's awl? I mean all?'

'It is.'

'Really?'

'Really.'

'Wow!'

Track to the Future

'What about your friends, Maggie?' Rabbi Jennifer wanted to know.

'What about them?'

'Do you have a good support system? People who get you?'

'Interesting question.'

'And?'

Until then, I'd resisted the siren song of the jelly beans. But what the hell? I reached for the pale yellow gem that had been calling out to me, which I was willing to bet was my favorite flavor: buttered popcorn.

And it was!

I chewed slowly, savoring the gluey sweetness. Avoiding my baby rabbi's laser gaze, I stared at the Hebrew scroll behind her desk. Though I had no idea what it said, but I imagined it must be one of those unassailable spiritual truths like: *If you think life sucks now, tune in tomorrow.*

'And?' Rabbi Jennifer said again.

'Well, Katie has that stiff-upper-lip WASP thing going, so she's not comfortable dealing with my sloppy emotions. Then there's Ellie, who was so put off by my divorce, even though she's been divorced for years herself, that she won't have anything to do with me.'

'Some people don't make a lot of sense.'

'And some people make no sense, which brings me to Janine, who works down the hall. She considers herself a good friend, but with Janine, it's all about what she thinks and what she wants. I'm pretty sure her ears are ornamental.'

'So why are you friendly with her?'

'Strange as it sounds, I enjoy Janine, in reasonable doses. She's everything I'm not: completely self-assured and uninhibited with no capacity for guilt and a really enviable screw-you attitude toward the world. Plus, you never know. I may need her to organize a special outfit or a contract murder for me some day.'

Rabbi Jennifer dug into the jelly beans, taking care to leave the buttered popcorns behind for me. What a total sweetheart! I couldn't imagine a better, more reasonable, or more improbable shrink. If she only had one lousy little Y chromosome, I'd find someone else to whine to and ask her out.

'Anyone else?'

I thought of Wop, but somehow, I couldn't bring myself to discuss my irrational, hopeless, and maddeningly unflagging affection for a married man, especially with someone so G-rated. Plus, I was sure I'd never hear from him again. Anthony and his wife would work things out and ride off into their sunset years together. Failing that, I had no doubt he'd live ecstatically ever after with the imaginary teenage supermodel he'd met five minutes after I kicked him out. So why should I book a costly one-way ticket to Hell that might well be non-refundable?

I thought awhile. 'There's Darlys, my college roommate. She's a great listener, but we rarely get together.'

'Because?'

'Because she's busy being a brilliant, internationally renowned fertility expert; and I'm busy feeling sorry for myself. You know how it goes. Also, she and Harold never got along.'

'But Harold's not an issue anymore.'

'Good point.' I passed up two popcorn-flavored jelly beans and settled for a mango instead. Fair was fair. 'The truth is Harold wasn't comfortable with most of the people I liked, so I lost touch with a lot of them.'

She nodded. 'So why don't you get back in touch now?'

'I could do that, couldn't I?'

'You could. And I recommend it. You can't have too many good friends.'

'True. And you *can* have too many bad ones.'

She smiled, which I swear made her glow. 'I bet you're an excellent friend, Maggie.'

'Oh yeah? Try me.'

'I certainly will.'

Bar Dreck

'Margarita, *buona sera.*'

'Giuseppe?'

'Si. Tu mi hai telefonato?'

'Yes, I called you. Speak English, OK? I'm suffering from rusty tongue syndrome. Plus divorce dementia, and don't ask.'

'English it is. It was so nice to get your message.'

'I'm glad. I can't tell you how nice it is to hear your voice.'

'Been way too long. What are you up to?' he asked.

'Wallowing in regret, mostly. With a little time off now and then to get furious or have a panic attack.'

'You can do those things any time. I'm leaving work now. Meet me at Zarela. We'll have margaritas in your honor.'

217

'I'm in a crappy mood, plus looking lousy and feeling lazy. So tell me you won't take no for an answer, OK?'

'I won't take no for an answer.'

'I'm also cranky and testy. So you have every right to back out while you have the chance.'

'Merry Sunshine Strickland: crappy, lousy, lazy, cranky and testy? Three more and you'll beat the dwarves.'

'How's lumpy, dumpy and depressed?'

'Excellent! Wouldn't miss it for the world. See you in a bit.'

Giuseppe, whose real name was Joe Salvato, became a pal when we were classmates years ago at *Parliamo Italiano*, a small Italian language school on 65th Street and Lexington Avenue. He was a bright, sweet, funny soul, a decade younger than me, who'd gotten divorced from a world-class horror that had left him more than a little doubtful about love. Every so often, he put a toe back in the game and, generally, got it stepped on. I saw my future in him, and my past.

Zarela was a boisterous Mexican place on Second Avenue near 51st Street. On a Thursday night, it was filled to bursting with raucous, booze-soaked revelers. The instant I stepped inside, several male faces swerved in eerie unison. Bleary eyes ran over me, slowing when they reached select body parts as if my modest indents and paltry protrusions qualified as serious speed bumps. You could almost see their libidinous brains flashing

218

neon: Live possibility! Fresh meat! Pounce!

I searched for Giuseppe, but he had not yet arrived. I tried to ignore the inebriated smiles and rabid leering, but I felt as if I'd landed in a lion's cage and the slavering beasts hadn't eaten for days.

I raced outside, heart hammering. Several hard-pulled breaths brought my blood pressure all the way down to stroke level. I'd been married for three decades. I had no idea how to deal with strange men who weren't fixing my plumbing, directing traffic, calculating my taxes, or trying to sell me shoes.

I couldn't remember the last time I was on my own in a situation like this. Harold always hung on me like body armor, making sure that I never so much as looked at another man. Not that I was interested – except in Paul McCartney way back when – but Paul and I were so discreet, Harold never had the teensiest clue.

Still, though I gave him no cause to be, Harold was jealous, suspicious and overbearing. He insisted on accompanying me everywhere and snooping into everything I did. His paranoia extended to anyone who was even remotely of the opposite sex. He grilled me endlessly about clients, including 80-year-old Mr Winston with the laryngotomy and six-year-old Rory Starkwell, who was playing Oliver in *Oliver, the Twisted Musical* off Broadway and needed to master a Cockney accent and trash his lazy, lolling Tom Brokaw L.

No male was exempt. If Brian happened to

plop down next to me on the couch, Harold made him move so he could claim the seat himself. Before the separation, Giuseppe and I would get together once a month or so at lunchtime to practice our halting Italian. I did this on the sly in fear of Harold's huffing indignation, always feeling a little sordid as I skulked in and out of the cheapo Indian places where these forbidden *rendezvous* (or *reunioni*, as they say in *Italia*) took place.

Harold's jealous lunacy had always struck me as incomprehensible. Now, I realized he must have imagined that I was a two-faced cheating slime like him. In psychological terms, this was called projection. To live it felt like cohabiting with a pathologically clingy, enormous, bearded, two-year-old.

A grin broke through my shock at the display of galloping testosterone in the bar. For the first time in decades, I realized I was free to go where I pleased, do what I pleased, say what I pleased and wear what I pleased. I no longer had to suffer insinuating Harold huffs, as I did if I ever had the audacity to wear black underwear. No more outraged harrumphing, as I used to get if something was deemed too tight, short, low cut, see-through, clingy, sexy, sultry, provocative or young. No sniffing snit if I appeared to flirt or, heaven forbid, enjoy myself.

Giuseppe turned the corner and wrapped me in a hug. 'Ready for that margarita, Margarita?'

'I am, but before we go in there, I have to

warn you the natives are mighty restless. I actually felt safer out here among the muggers and garden-variety psychotics.'

He shook his head. 'Sometimes I'm not proud of my species.'

'I can't believe they'd take any interest in me, for heaven's sake. I'm old enough to be their mother.'

'Oh? You thought Oedipus was fiction?'

'Promise to protect me?'

'Yea, and forsooth, fair lady. That I will.'

We found a pair of free stools among the Sabine warriors and ordered nachos and drinks. Except for the jelly beans, this was the first serious breach in my diet in nearly two whole days.

'So?' he said. 'How are things in Splitsville?'

'Strange and packed with surprises. Like a monster roller coaster, only scarier and a lot more expensive.'

'Tell me about it. My favorite definition of divorce is the screwing you get for the screwing you got, which with Wendy was infrequent and forgettable.'

'Tell me about it.'

'You know what they say is the best way to get back at the woman who stole your husband?'

'No, what?'

'Let her keep him.'

'This feels so weird, Giuseppe.'

'What? Being out after dark without Harold?'

'No. I mean this. Laughing. Letting my hair

down. Having fun.'

'You and Harold didn't have fun?'

I slurped the frothy remains of my margarita and twirled my finger to summon another round.

'Sometimes I did. But he made it clear he didn't approve.'

'It's pretty amazing to consider what you were willing to put up with when you look back, isn't it?' he said.

'What amazes me is how content I thought I was, even lucky. I used to speculate about other people's marriages and imagine they were dealing with much worse. After all, Harold didn't beat me or anything, at least not with any blunt instrument other than his tongue. He wasn't a drunk or a compulsive gambler or a serial killer like some women's husbands. He didn't disappear for weeks at a time or chain me in the cellar or put me through a wood chipper.'

He winced. 'Wendy did that to me once, and boy, did it smart.'

'I'm serious. The truth is I got used to things the way they were, and I convinced myself that was the way they had to be. But they can be like this. Light and peaceful. Catching up with an old friend. Which feels incredibly good.'

'I'm delighted.'

Right then, of all times, I got teary-eyed. 'I'm happy, Giuseppe. I am.'

'That's fine, *cara*. Nothing wrong with a little liquid happiness.'

222

I mopped my face with a cocktail napkin. 'Did I tell you I've become a grandmother?'

'Allison had a baby? Congratulations.'

'Not Allison, Brian. He married someone who had a love child with a turkey baster.'

'Seriously?'

'Little girl named Delia. Brian's adopting her.'

'Love, babies. All good things.'

'That's true. What's up with you, Giuseppe? Any new love interest?'

'Not to speak of. Actually, I've given up looking for Ms Right. I've decided I'm willing to settle for Ms Right Now.'

'Sounds sensible.'

'We'll see. You?'

'Believe it or not, I ran into someone I haven't seen since eighth grade. Nice Italian boy, in fact.'

'*Fantastico!*'

'He took me to dinner at Rao's.'

'*Perfetto!* How was it? And more importantly, how was he?'

'*Perfetto*, like you said, except for being ever-so-slightly married.'

He munched on a nacho. 'How slightly?'

'He's miserable, from what he describes. Says he has been for years.'

He nodded. 'Miserable is good. Something to work with.'

'Plus, he's here and she lives in London.'

'Separated by a major body of water is promising.'

'Plus she's done the ultimatum thing. Said

it's either her or his job.'

'Kiss of death. The ultimatum thing is practically always followed by the consultation-with-a-divorce-lawyer thing. I'd say the prognosis is excellent.'

'I don't know. Even if the marriage thing goes away, there's the ambivalence thing and the emotional recovery thing and the rebound thing, for starters. And then there's the he-could-have-anyone-he-wants-so-why-would-he-choose-me thing.'

'Oh, I could think of a few reasons.'

'In any event, I'm pretty sure I blew whatever chance I might have had with him. He came on to me, and I put him off.'

'Hard to get is extremely effective, Maggie. Take it from someone who's been put off a lot.'

I shrugged. 'We'll see.'

'True enough. Nothing wrong with living in the present. Making the best of what there is.'

'There isn't, is there?' I felt a big, old grin coming on.

The bartender set down our drinks, and we raised them. 'To *la mia bella amica*, Margarita,' Giuseppe said. 'And to lots and lots of feeling incredibly good.'

Shove Story

True to his threat, Harold was determined to make things as difficult as he could. Federal Express delivered a chunky box to my office. Inside I found a giant stack of detailed questions and a cover letter demanding that I answer them all and return the lot to Harold's lawyer within five business days.

I leafed through the pages with mounting horror. Harold had always handled the finances, and I had no clue about most of these things. Stock bases? Long or short term capital gains? Discounted present values? True, I could respond to the basics. I knew my maiden name, where and when we got married, the names and ages of our children. Things like that. But I thought it was fair to assume that Harold could somehow come by that information on his own.

Outraged, I called my lawyer. 'I just got a huge pile of something called interrogatories. Please tell me I can toss them down the incinerator.'

'Sorry. I'm afraid you have to fill them out.'

'Why?'

'Because the law says Harold's entitled to have you answer pertinent questions.'

'That's ridiculous. He has all this stuff.

Anyway, finances make my nose run.'

'I understand, Maggie. But it's part of the deal. If it's any consolation, he'll have to do it, too.'

'It's no consolation. This stuff is easy for Harold. He's an anal-retentive, obsessive-compulsive, criminally organized record keeper. Harold alphabetizes his ties. He still has his report cards from pre-school.'

'If you don't have the records, just indicate in the appropriate places that Harold has them.'

'But that's ridiculous. It's like a punishment assignment. It's like having to write one hundred times that I won't ever put chewing gum in Stevie Duberstein's hair ever again.'

'And I'm sure you won't,' Lena said. 'My recommendation is to just dig in and get it over with.'

'What if I don't like your recommendation?'

'Wish I could give you a different answer, Maggie, but it is what it is.'

My next appointment had canceled with the flu. I decided to use the time to follow Lena's advice and put this annoyance behind me. I printed my name and vital statistics. I answered Harold's absurd demands to know where we had been married, the names and ages of our children and when and where they were born. I detailed our last three addresses, including how long we were at each, whether we rented or owned and the approximate carrying costs. Under major assets, I listed the modest cottage in the Berkshires we'd bought ten years ago and our car, a fourteen-year-old Volvo wagon with a chronic cough and unsightly skin condition that lived at the house in Massachusetts. It occurred to me that we hadn't built much in the way of assets in thirty years. Of course, we'd made Ali and Brian, but they didn't count as part of our 'marital estate'.

It took me most of an hour to get through all the niggling, annoying, and often incomprehensible questions, even though I answered the majority as Lena had suggested, noting that the records were in Harold Strickland's possession. I refused to refer to him as *Plaintiff*, though he still was. The word simply stuck in my craw.

When I finished, restless anger pushed me to the corner deli for ice cream. Back in the office, I ate with grim determination. I was furious with myself and others, not necessarily in that order. Every last spoonful of Cherry Garcia was Harold's fault. If there was any justice, he'd gain the weight, not me.

On the Daughter Front

My anxiety mounted with every riser as I trudged up the monumental stone steps to the Metropolitan Museum. I couldn't remember the last time I'd seen my daughter on a weekday during business hours, except for her occasional appearance on CNBC's *Power Lunch*. Under normal circumstances, to do so otherwise, I would have to be a client, for which I would need to have an investment portfolio containing more zeroes than all the men I'd ever dated, combined.

While the security guard at the entrance searched among the crumpled Kleenex, loose change and lint-encrusted Tic Tacs in my purse for weapons of mass destruction, I spotted Ali waiting near the information desk at the center of the giant rotunda. The sight of her in casual khaki pants, tan driving moccasins and a pink ribbed turtleneck deepened my dread certainty that something was terribly wrong.

Ali glanced my way. She waved. She managed a brave, little smile.

My heart lurched against my ribs. 'Hi, honey. Hope I didn't keep you waiting. I got here as soon as I could.'

'Just got here myself. Glad you were able to make it on such short notice.'

I kissed her forehead. It felt cool, but low temperature could be every bit as ominous as high. 'Of course. Any time. What's going on?'

She shrugged. 'Same old—'

'Honestly? You're not sick? You didn't find a lump?'

'Of course not. I'm fine.'

'Look. If work isn't going well, try not to take it too hard. Every career has ups and downs.'

'Work is going well. In fact, I just landed a major new account. And I mean major with a B.'

So maybe the poor kid couldn't deal with such success. Imagine someone handing you a billion of their dollars to invest. 'That's great, honey. Don't you think?'

'You bet I do.' She perused a museum leaflet. 'Want to see the new surrealist exhibit first? I absolutely adore Dali and Magritte. So imaginative and playful.'

'You like imaginative and playful?'

'Definitely. Interested?'

'Sure, sweetie. Whatever you like.' She looked a little pale, but then she normally looked *very* pale, so in itself, this was probably not a harbinger of doom.

She flashed her major-donor membership card. After the woman at the desk did the requisite scraping and fawning, she handed us little barbell-shaped metal tags to clip to our collars. The entry color for today – and

229

my daughter's hands-down favorite – was a bright, freshly-minted-currency green.

I trailed her upstairs. She wasn't limping. She hadn't lost a significant amount of weight. 'How's Jon?'

'Fine. He sends his love.'

'Everything going well with his job, too?'

'Terrific. Busy, crazy as usual.'

'And the two of you? Things OK there?'

'Everything's fine, Mom. Why the inquisition?'

'It's not exactly like you to take off in the middle of the day.'

She shrugged. 'Once in awhile I do something out of character.'

'Nothing's wrong? You're sure?'

'OK, Mom. I give up. You caught me.'

'What?'

'I wanted to spend some time with you. A little quality Ali-and-Mom time like we used to do when I was a kid. There it is.'

Now I was really scared. I caged her fine-boned hand. Mine had gone clammy and cold. 'That's what I'm here for, sweetheart. Talk to me. Whatever it is, you'll feel better if you get it out.'

She wrested her hand free and scowled. 'Cut it out, Mom! There's nothing wrong. It's just been forever since we spent some together, the two of us. That's all.'

'Really?'

'Cross my heart and hope to under-perform the Standard and Poor's.'

'You're serious.'

'Yes, I am. I love you, Mom. I even like you a little.'

'Oh, sweetheart. That means more to me than you can imagine.'

'Come on. What's the big deal?'

'It's just nice to know that you want to spend time with me. That's all.'

She caught me trying to nab a runaway tear.

'What's wrong, Mom?'

'Nothing.'

'Are you sure? Are you sick or something? Did you find a lump?'

'No. I'm fine.'

She draped her slender arm across my shoulder. 'Job problems then? Because every career has its ups and downs.'

'Don't be fresh.'

She patted my back as we passed the Rodin bronzes on our way to the exhibit entitled 'Soul of the Surreal'. 'You'd better watch it, Mom. You're starting to sound like Grandma.'

'Oh yeah? Well, my darling daughter, you'd better watch it, too. You're starting to sound like me.'

Cradle Attraction

Rabbi Jennifer smiled at the picture of Delia I'd brought to show her. 'What a doll.'

'Yes, and lucky thing.'

She laughed, though in a sad way. 'I guess that's right. Imagine what might happen if babies weren't so irresistible.'

'You learn to resist them after awhile. It becomes easier and easier as they get bigger and more willful and keep mastering new and ever improved ways to drive you up the wall.'

'I'm sure that's true. But it's hard to imagine when you look at a precious little one like this.'

'You'd be surprised. Even by Delia's age, babies instinctively understand how to drive their parent's insane. Must be some sort of twisted survival mechanism.'

Her smile went wistful. 'I'm sure.'

'You'll see when you're ready to have kids. If you want them, that is.'

'Oh, I do, and I'm more than ready. Have been for years. But no luck so far.' Her mouth smiled while her dark chocolate eyes welled up in the human equivalent of a sun shower.

'I'm so sorry. Here I am complaining about becoming an instant grandmother and you're

232

wishing for a child of your own.'

She squared her shoulders. 'One thing has nothing to do with the other.'

'You must think I'm a selfish, insensitive fool.'

'Nothing of the kind. I think you're thoughtful, caring, generous and kind. You're one of those rare souls who work hard to make sense of what's going on and do the right thing. You can't imagine how many people I talk to who believe that they're completely OK and therefore, whatever goes wrong in their life must be somebody else's fault.'

'Oh, I can imagine. So happens I was born to such a person and married one. And I work down the hall from Janine, queen of the buck-passers.' Desperate to atone for my insensitivity, I pushed the bowl of jelly beans her way. 'I'm sorry you're going through that. It must be tough.'

'Lots of ups and downs. There's hope, then disappointment, then more hope and bigger disappointment. Then, just when you hit a new low, there's hope again, and on and on. Gets a little wearing after a while.'

'It's no excuse, but I really thought you were too young to be worrying about having kids.'

'Michael and I both always wanted a big family. When we decided to get married four years ago, we also agreed we might as well get started on that big brood right away. But the powers that be seem to have other plans.'

'I don't know what to say.'

'That's exactly the right thing to say, Maggie. What I usually get is a story about someone who tried to get pregnant for years and years and then had a baby the minute she adopted and "relaxed" or suddenly started cranking them out like nobody's business and then couldn't turn off the spout. Then there are the people who assure me I'm much better off, that kids have made their lives hell, and if I'm crazy enough to want to have them anyway, I'm welcome to theirs.'

'Doesn't sound like a tempting offer.'

'To say the least.' She nudged the jelly bean bowl back to the precise center of the desk. 'So tell me what's happening with Delia.'

'Brian's completely besotted. This is nothing like he was with the parakeets. And my daughter Allison seems to be pretty besotted, too, which is amazing given that babies are not-for-profit.'

'And you?'

My eye lit on the snapshot of Delia. Brian had captured her on a baby swing at the peak of a forward arc. Delia's arms were outstretched, her expression drunk with joy. I found myself musing about how she would be when she got a bit older. Would she like to play dress-up? To dance? Would she be good at sports? What would be her favorite song? Subject? Jelly bean? And it occurred to me that with a little luck, I'd eventually find out.

The Sum of All Beers

'Sorry to bother you, Mom. Hope it's not a bad time.' Valerie's voice was pinched. In the background, Delia was shrieking like Harold did when the Yanks struck out with the bases loaded.

'It's fine. What's going on? Delia sounds pretty upset.'

'Poor baby's having a terrible time teething. And Bri's out at a business dinner, so that makes it even worse. She so looks forward to seeing her Daddy before beddy-bye.'

'Have you tried rubbing Scotch on her gums?'

'Oh, gosh. I couldn't do that. Giving a baby alcohol is illegal.'

'Self-defense isn't legal any more?'

Delia's screams were growing more insistent.

'How about a piece of frozen bagel, then? Or a frozen washcloth? Both worked pretty well with Ali, though Brian definitely preferred the Scotch.'

'Thanks. I'll try those. But that's not why I called. Delia keeps asking for you. Every time I try to put her down to sleep, she cries for her Granny.'

'Are you sure she's not crying *about* me? She may still be miffed about my not playing her favorite CD.'

It was hard to hear over the baby's Banshee howls. 'Hush, sweetie,' Valerie pleaded. 'Guess what? Granny's on the phone. Want to talk to her?'

The crying stopped. 'Gammy phone?'

'That's right. Here. Talk to Granny.'

I heard heavy breathing. 'Hi, Delia. How are you? I hear you're having a little trouble with your teeth.'

'Boo boo buddy?'

'Yes, sweetie. I'm sure Mommy will be glad to give you your boo boo buddy. That's the little blue teddy bear head with the plastic ice cube inside that Mommy keeps in the freezer for when something hurts – right?'

'Mommy feezuh.'

'Exactly. Clever bit of modern technology designed to replace the magic kiss and make bundles of money for the manufacturer. See? Granny's learning, slowly but she's learning.'

'Gammy?'

'Yes, honey. Mommy says you've been asking for me.'

'Gammy!' she exulted in a voice that reminded me of marshmallow fluff.

'None other. Mommy is delusional enough to believe you'd be comforted by a visit from me. Absurd, right?'

'Wan Gammy.'

'Are you absolutely sure, sweetie? Granny hasn't been able to sleep for months and months, so she was planning to spend the evening in a nice, cozy catatonic stupor.'

'Gammy hep you?'

'How about I help you tomorrow, baby?'

'Deeduh wan Gammy – peeze!'

'Are you sure this is necessary?'

An exploratory snuffle was followed by one far more ominous.

'OK. Don't cry. I'm on my way.'

Valerie took up the phone. 'So I hate to ask, but is there any way you could come over and see her, Mom? Just for a little while?'

'I'll be there in ten minutes. And since Delia's not allowed hard liquor, I'll have hers.'

The baby was ecstatic to see me, as if I was the American Idol of aging relatives. She shrilled in delight and did a happy dance, jangling her short, pudgy limbs. She soon wore herself out and crumpled to the floor, rubbing her eyes.

'I think some little girl is ready for nighty-night,' Valerie said with the dewy-eyed, deluded optimism of youth.

Delia offered up her dimpled arms. 'Gammy nie-nie.'

This was a Janine-quality order, not a request.

'OK,' I said, with considerable trepidation. The modern nighty-night protocol, like all things to do with small children today, could well be fraught with far more peril than I imagined. 'What do I do?'

Valerie smiled. 'I tell her a little story and

sing a lullaby. Normally, she drifts off in no time.'

'Story – song – drift off. Roger that, ground control.' I hoisted the baby on to my hip and headed for her room. 'You'll be right here in case I need you?'

'Sure.'

'Promise?'

'Of course. But don't worry, Mom. There's nothing to it.'

I sat in the rocker and cradled Delia in my arms. She gazed up at me expectantly. 'Maw koh tory?'

'Sure. Why not? So after the chubby old crow made a big mess of things with the eagle, she—' A sudden power outage spread through my brain.

'Gammy tinkin?'

'I'm trying to.'

'Koh tory – peeze?'

'OK. I have it. So since the old crow had no idea what was going to happen next, she decided to just forget the whole thing, get into her coziest crow pajamas and go nighty-night. And she drifted right off to sleep and had lots of wonderful dreams. The end. Time for a song.'

Delia's lids were lolling at half mast. She grew slack and heavy as I rocked her. 'Lullaby, and good night—'

Her eyes snapped open again. 'Bee-na-wa tong, Gammy?'

'What, baby?'

'Bee-na-wa tong?'

This time I got it, which felt indescribably good. 'Sure, kiddo. Here goes. "A hundred bottles of beer on the wall, a hundred bottles of beer. If one of those bottles should happen to fall. Ninety nine—" '

'Bah-toos a beeee-na-wah.' A soft grin settled on her face as she drifted off in my arms.

In The Line of Ire

Janine was pacing in my office when I showed up for work. 'I am seriously pissed off at you, Maggie!'

'*You're* pissed off at *me*?'

'Seriously!'

'What for?'

'You don't turn Anthony Sinclair down. It's just not done.'

'Who says I turned him down?'

'He does, that's who. What could you be thinking? Answer me that.'

'When did you talk to him?' Now I was getting worried. I scanned the office anxiously. It was not beyond Janine to be holding Wop prisoner in a file drawer.

'Who says I talked to him?'

'How would you know what he said if you didn't talk to him?'

'Three guesses.'

239

'I am not in the mood for games, Janine.'

'Bad guess. That leaves two.'

'Hmm, OK. Let me think. I guess that if I throw you out the window, you're going to break a lot more than your nail.'

'I swear, Maggie, you are no fun at all.'

'Tell me, Janine. Now!'

'All right. Don't get your bowels in an uproar. Anthony left a message on your machine.'

'So you just broke into my office and listened to my messages like any normal person would do?'

'Right!'

'No. That's *not* right. You are to stay out of my office, out of my business and out of my life. I've had it with your meddling, Janine. I'm done!'

She attempted to strut around the office, but her skirt was so tight it was all she could do to make little lurching moves like an antique wind-up toy. 'I don't think you understand, Maggie. I truly don't think you comprehend what an amazing and rare opportunity Anthony Sinclair is. Now, you're going to stop all this nonsensical carrying on. You're going to call him right now, apologize from the heart for not jumping his bones, and then offer to meet him at the location of his choice for a nooner. I recommend the Museum of Modern Art or Rockefeller Center. Sex in a public place is a big turn-on, and we're looking at a desperate situation here.'

'I mean it, Janine! No more!'

'Fine. Now call. Tell him you're not wearing any panties. You want a love slave? That gets them every time.'

'Goddamnit! Didn't you hear a word I said?'

'Of course I did. What did you say?'

'I said you're to butt out. You have no idea what's going on, and no place in it.'

She perched on the desk and tried to look demure. 'In what, sweetie? If you want me to understand, tell me. I'm all ears.'

'I've told you, I'm not ready for a new relationship. And neither is Anthony. He has to work things out in his own life first. It's complicated.'

'That's not what he said in his message,' Janine said.

'What did he say?'

She pressed a finger to her lips. 'Hmmm. I forget.'

'Fine. I'll listen for myself.' My heart hammered as I strode toward the answering machine and hit the Playback button. Zero flashed on the digital counter, and a robot voice declared that I had no new messages.

Janine's hand flew to her cheek. 'Oops. I must have erased it.'

'You didn't.'

'Yes, I believe I did.'

'Why would you do a thing like that?'

'Why would anyone rely on a silly answering machine? That's the question you should be asking, Maggie. Who do you trust more, your own ears or some cheap, unreliable, foreign-made electronic device?'

My reply was a slow, silent burn.

'It's simple, sweetie.' Janine lifted the receiver and offered it up. 'You want to know what Anthony has to say, call and ask.'

Bummer of Sam

The Cornell Club was on 44th Street half a block from Grand Central Station. A giggling gaggle of geriatric sorority snobs trailed me into the elevator. Every smug look and snotty gesture screamed that they were all lifelong members of Alpha Ralpha Hotsie Totsie Poo Poo – or something close – and I was pitiably, despicably not.

This propelled me back to freshman year, when I'd decided not to go Greek and found myself consigned by women such as these to the permanent out basket.

I addressed my elevator mates in sign language, which I'd learned years ago when I worked with a deaf and adorably churlish teenager. I'd taught her how to make herself understood with the hearing jackasses (as she affectionately called those of us who were so afflicted). In exchange, she'd taught me a number of signs that were not in the dictionary. *You are a sorry bunch of shallow, self-*

242

important assholes, I gestured to the Alphas with a smile.

One dowdy witch bit her lip to keep from laughing. The lizard-skinned crone in the middle showed her palms. 'Deaf,' explained a desiccated blonde bean pole to the others, pointing at her outsized ear.

When the elevator stopped on five, I hurried out. Thankfully, the Alphas continued their ascent.

The first club room I passed was deserted. The second was crammed with people who sported stick-on nametags and unconvincing grins. At the door a sign read 'Reunion kick-off, class of '78'. I ventured in and searched for Sam Weller who had answered my e-mail with a phone call, suggesting we meet here tonight. I spotted him near the window and waved, trying without success to capture his attention.

'Can I help you?' An officious young woman insisted on checking my name against an invitation list and fitting me with a 'Hello my name is...' tag.

I wove through the crowd, trying not to spill the cheap merlot. Glancing down at my shapeless black slacks and lackluster white blouse, I suffered a pang of regret. Maybe I should have allowed Janine to dress me in something fabulous despite the fact that I was finished and furious with her.

Halfway across the room, I was accosted by a woman with a vintage '50s flip hairdo bound by a thick velvet band. I could barely breathe through the cloying lavender cloud of her perfume. 'Maggie Evantoff? How great to see you!'

I checked her nametag. 'Estelle Hinkle. How have you been?'

'Great. Just fabulous. Tons going on, as usual. Eric is a junior in the engineering school. Betsy got in of course, but she simply insisted on going to Yale. Kids. Anyhow, Herb's semi-retired, so we've been wintering in Florida, summering in the Hamptons and playing tons and tons of golf. Of course, we still have the Dix Hills place, which we keep expanding and expanding – you know how it is. We're also traveling tons. In fact we're just back from Costa Rica and we're off to Australia and New Zealand in a week. You?'

'Great. Tons and tons. If you'll excuse me.'

I moved two paces closer to Sam before I was assailed again. This time I recognized the supercilious face of Vince Fenold, a wormy little creep who'd latched on to me like a cold I couldn't shake for most of sophomore year. He had aged into a paunchy, balding wormy little creep. What a surprise!

His eyes swam like bloated fish behind the trifocals. 'Maggie Evantoff. How the hell are you?'

'Actually, I'm meeting someone. Better run.'

He eyed his diamond-encrusted Rolex. 'Me too. Meeting with the major givers. You know, people who donate upwards of a hundred thousand dollars a year to the school. Perhaps

244

you'd like to join us.'

'Why? Are you looking for a token poor person?'

He snickered. 'You always were such a card, Maggie.'

And you were always such a discard. 'Bye, bye, Vince. Have fun.'

I pressed on, avoiding eye contact. But soon, a hand clamped my arm. The attractive brunette behind the grip looked familiar, but she was not wearing a hello tag and I couldn't dredge up her name.

'Maggie? It's Suzanne Haskel. We were in Psych 101 together, and I lived down the hall from you freshman year.'

'Suzanne, of course. Good to see you. Sorry I didn't get it right away, but it's been about two billion years.'

'Bless you for being honest. Most of these characters come up to you, squint at your name tag because they're too vain to put on their glasses, and then say: "Suzanne! You haven't changed a bit. I mean – what a crock." '

'Exactly. Are they suggesting we look nineteen now? Or that we looked forty-nine in college?'

'Exactly. Which is why I finally rebelled and lost the damned name tag.'

I peeled mine off as well. 'Excellent idea.'

At that moment, Sam Weller spotted me. He approached with a tiny snub-nosed blonde in tow. This one looked even younger than Bethany, if that was possible for someone still up at this hour.

'Who's that?' Suzanne rasped.

'Sam Weller. I thought he was my date for the evening, but it would seem I thought wrong. Be a pal and stick around?'

'Sure.'

'And shoot me when you get the chance, OK?'

'I'd much rather shoot *him*,' she rasped through a broad, steady smile.

Sam and Tinkerbell soon reached us. 'There you are, Maggie. So glad you could come. You too, Suzie. This is my daughter, Emily. She's starting Cornell in the fall.'

'Your *daughter*! How wonderful that she's your *daughter*!' Sam looked great. He was taller than I remembered, and the years had etched appealing little details on his face. A trace of silver ran through his thick, dark, senatorial hair. 'It has been forever.'

'Certainly wouldn't know it to look at you. I swear you haven't changed a bit.'

I winked at Suzanne. 'Are you trying to tell me I looked forty-nine in college?'

His smile was a bright toothy blaze. 'Let's go downstairs and catch up, shall we?'

Suzanne sent us off with a nod of approval.

We took the elevator down to the grill room and settled at a table in the rear. 'So tell me about yourself, Maggie. What's been going on?'

I shrugged. 'Standard stuff. Kids, work, silver anniversary, divorce court.'

'You married Harold Strickland, right?'

'Wrong, as it turned out.'

'If you don't mind my saying so, I never did like that guy.'

'Now you tell me.'

His eyes scrunched like an eager kid when he smiled. 'You didn't ask.'

'Fair enough. How about you?'

His grin fell away. 'The business, the one daughter you met, and that's about it. Sally, my wife, died four years ago of ovarian cancer.'

'I'm so sorry.'

He showed his palms. 'Hasn't been easy, but I found that it helped to be busy, so I threw myself into my work, and other things.'

'Like what?'

'Skiing and sailing when I get the chance. Going to theater. Volunteering. I've gotten pretty active in alumni affairs.'

'Sounds busy.'

'Busy is good. What about you? Aside from work, what do you do?'

My answer was an enigmatic little smile. Weeping and sucking down ice cream didn't have quite the panache of *alumni affairs*.

He looked me hard in the eye. 'Would you be offended if I come right out and tell you exactly what's on my mind?'

'That would depend what it is.'

'I've always admired you, Maggie. I'm sure you know that.'

'No, but I'm not offended in the least.'

'You've always struck me as such a smart, independent woman. Charming and likeable

247

and fun.'

'I'm flattered, Sam. Thanks.'

'It's true. And it's amazing that you wrote me that note when you did. I don't know why I didn't think of it before, but you're just the woman I've been looking for—'

'That's sweet, Sam, but—'

'—to run the independent affinity group for reunion,' he said.

'The what?'

'The independent affinity group. I've agreed to chair the reunion. My idea is to appoint a bunch of committee heads to seek out classmates who shared a particular affiliation, or in your case, people who were alike in not belonging to any of the sororities, fraternities or major clubs. I'm determined to get the biggest possible turnout for our thirtieth, and I'm convinced the affinity group approach will get us there. What do you say?'

'You want me to be in charge of the affinity group for people who have no affinities?'

This time his grin showed too many teeth. 'See? You always have the perfect sharp comeback. All you need to do is take the list of people who were unaffiliated and get on the horn. You'll convince them to come, Maggie. I know you will. Who could say no to you?'

The Mouth That Scored

The sun rose in the east; taxes were due April 15th, and Janine lied. Those were the fundamentals. So Anthony might have called as she'd claimed and left a message that she had erased, or she could have invented the entire story to hasten my descent into incurable twitching schizophrenia, for the fun of it.

Having agonized over this for days, I concluded that the only reasonable course of action would be to leave an offhanded message on Wop's voicemail: 'Anthony, hi. It's Maggie. If you left a message for me, I didn't get it, so if you did call and wanted to talk to me, you're welcome to try again if you like, or not if you don't, and if you didn't call in the first place, please disregard this and don't feel the slightest need to let me know that you didn't or why or anything – OK? Hope all's well.'

Cringing at how ridiculous that had sounded, I called back. 'Anthony, hi. Maggie again. What I meant to say was that your message got erased, unless you didn't leave one, of course, in which case, it obviously didn't get erased because it wasn't there in the first place (insert desperate giggle here).

249

In any event, I didn't want you to think I was being rude by not returning your call, so that's what I'm doing, returning your call, that is, not being rude, unless you didn't call at all, in which case, there's no call to return, now is there? (Desperate giggle reprise). Over and out.'

And people wondered why I had no affiliations.

'Anthony, hi. Look, I feel like a total idiot, so let me try to explain. What happened was someone broke into my office and told me you'd called and that she'd erased your message, but she's a pathological liar, so she probably made the whole thing up, except it would be just like her to be telling the truth the one time I was convinced she was lying her head off. And if that was the case, you would have wondered why I didn't return your call. So please feel free to ignore the whole thing and forget you ever heard from me. In fact, you didn't hear from me. This is just a hallucination that sounds like me, only dumber.'

'Maggie? Is that you?'

'You're there?'

'Just walked in.'

'I was trying to figure out whether you left me a message or not. You don't have to get involved, though. Your machine and I have gotten to know each other very well, and I'm sure we can sort it out between us.'

'Not necessary. I did leave a message. More than one. I've been trying to reach you for days.'

'You have?'

'Yes. I wanted to tell you I've been doing a lot of thinking and talking things over, as you wisely suggested, and I've figured out what I want to do.'

'Oh? What's that?'

'I'd like to tell you in person, Maggie. Would that be all right?'

'Fine. Of course. You can't give me a hint?'

'I think it'd be better face to face. I can be there in ten minutes if you're free.'

'I'm not. I have a bunch of clients back to back and then two appointments out of the office. I'll be tied up until six thirty.'

'How's seven then?'

'That would work.'

'Great. Would it be OK if I come to your place? It would be good to be somewhere we have privacy to talk.'

'Sure. You're welcome to come here.'

'Thanks. I'll arrange to have dinner brought in.'

'That's not necessary. I can make something, Anthony. Or we can call up and have something delivered when you get here.'

'I'll take care of everything. Don't give it another thought.'

That Touch of Stink

This time it was Rabbi Jennifer who seemed distracted. You know your life has turned into a hopeless snooze when you can't even hold your shrink's attention. This spurred me to open up about Wop, as did my complete preoccupation with the fact that he would be showing up at my apartment in a couple of hours.

'Remember when we discussed my having dinner with Liam Neeson, Rabbi Jennifer?'

'The friend from junior high school? Did you have dinner with him?'

'I did. And then he pretty much disappeared for a while, and then he showed up again. Turns out he's having big problems with his wife. He's been trying to figure out if they have a future. Doesn't look good.' I bit back an unseemly smile.

'You sound like an interested party.'

'He's wonderful. I can't deny that. And if his marriage is over, I can't say I'd be altogether disinterested.'

She went grim. 'He's not exactly in a stable situation, Maggie. Don't you think the figuring out and being certain should come way before the jumping in?'

'I'm not talking about jumping into anything. It would be dipping a toe to begin with, that's all.'

Her frown deepened. 'If you dip your toe in a nice warm pool with plenty of chlorine, that's one thing. Dipping it in a tank filled with piranhas or a vat of boiling oil is quite another.'

'Anthony is neither of those, I can assure you. He's a brilliant, charming, successful grown-up.'

Her brow edged higher. 'Anthony?'

'Yes. It isn't actually Liam Neeson at all. His name is Anthony Sinclair, and he's an extraordinary person.'

Her expression reminded me, in a chilling way, of my mother. I had a fleeting hallucination of Rabbi Jennifer remarking that Anthony certainly wasn't a Jewish name with her mouth full of tuna on rye. *Don't be an idiot*, I imagined her saying. *If he's so wonderful, what would he possibly want with you?*

'I don't doubt that he's a wonderful person,' Rabbi Jennifer said. 'The problem is that he's in an unstable, transitional situation, and so are you. That's a set up for uncertainty, confusion and hurt.'

'I knew Harold for more than thirty years and that turned out to be a set up for major uncertainty, confusion and hurt. So by that standard, the right answer would be to wait and not even consider getting into a new relationship until many decades after I'm dead.'

'I understand there aren't any guarantees,

Maggie, but you can avoid getting into something where the odds are against you from the start. If this man is right for you, how could it hurt to wait a bit until things settle down?'

'I waited to get tickets to *The Producers*, and I got shut out, that's how. With a man like Anthony, the right approach is definitely *carpe he-um*. Anyway, I've known him since eighth grade. He's far from a stranger.'

'I thought you said he just came back into your life?'

'He did. But he and I survived Miss Crawshaw's homeroom together. That's an entire lifetime of foxhole camaraderie right there.'

'I understand that you don't want to miss what looks like an important opportunity. But if it's meant to be, taking your time won't destroy it.'

'How do you know that? *The Producers* sold out in a heartbeat, and then Nathan Lane and Matthew Broderick left. You either jumped at the chance when you first heard about it or you missed the boat.'

'I'm on your side, Maggie.'

'So am I.'

'I hope that's true. I'm concerned that you might be selling yourself a bill of goods because you're anxious to be with someone.'

'That's not it at all, Rabbi Jennifer. Anthony's a great guy. He's thoughtful and funny and fun to be with, and if it so happens that I have the chance to be with him, why not? I can tell you I seriously regret not seeing

The Producers with Nathan Lane.'

She frowned. 'Does that mean that if someone had offered you stolen tickets to see the show you would have taken them?'

'Of course not. I'm not a thief.'

'No, you're not.'

Now, I scowled at her. 'What you're saying is: *Don't be.* You're suggesting that I'd be stealing Anthony, as if it would be wrong to have anything to do with him, whether his marriage is over or not.'

'Is that what you think I'm saying?'

'You said what if someone offered me stolen tickets. Wasn't that meant to suggest that this would be a theft as well?'

'What do you think, Maggie? That's what counts.'

'I think you're being judgmental and disapproving. This feels like talking to my mother. If I'd had fifth row center tickets to *The Producers* with Nathan Lane that I bought before the show opened, and I invited you to join me, I think you'd still find something to criticize. Don't shlump, Maggie. And that's what you wear to the theater?'

'Don't be stupid!' Rabbi Jennifer said. Or at least, that's what it felt like to me. True, I didn't see her lips move, so this might have been in my head, which was jammed to the bursting point with a lifetime supply of nasty pearls.

Legally Conned

Lena paced her office, glaring at the forensic accountant's report. 'Jim Brockton didn't find anything. He checked out Harold's finances, and everything seems to be clean.'

'I'm not surprised, Lena. Harold may be lots of things, but he's not a crook.'

She puffed her lips. 'I can't say I'm convinced of that, but it doesn't make sense to pursue it further. If there was a smoking gun, Brockton would have found it. He's very thorough, very clever, very good.'

'All I want to do at this point is to get things settled and over with.'

'I'm going to cover Brockton's bill, Maggie. It was my idea.'

'That's OK. I agreed to it. You didn't give me any guarantee.'

She tossed the report on her desk. 'Nevertheless. It's on me. Now there's another bit of unpleasantness we need to discuss.' She removed a letter from my file. 'It showed up this morning.'

The message was from Harold's lawyer, Randy Schlam. I gazed at the Slam Dunk firm logo, two stylized interlocking fists, and then read with growing disbelief.

'Squandering assets? What is he on about?'

'It's nothing but mumbo-jumbo. Keep reading.'

'Mounting indebtedness? All I spent in the last week was $49 at the grocery store, $15 worth of take-out Chinese, and the cost of a daily frappuccino with an espresso shot at Starbucks. But that's a medical necessity.'

'Doesn't matter. That letter is nothing but an attempt to put a positive spin on what Harold has done. He's closed all your joint charge and checking accounts. Froze the savings.'

'That's ridiculous. He can't do that.'

'He can, Maggie. He did. The accounts were in joint names, which means either of you could close them any time.'

'But that was my money. I earned it. I deposited a bunch of client checks last week. What am I supposed to live on? How am I supposed to pay my bills?'

'I'll petition the court for an emergency distribution as quickly as I can.'

'How long will that take?'

'Shouldn't be more than a couple of days, a week at the outside. Try not to worry.'

'I have to worry. I can't afford to do anything else.'

'Try to look on the bright side, Maggie. The court does not take kindly to a divorcing spouse causing deliberate financial hardship or absconding with joint funds. Randy Schlam must be ready to kill Harold.'

'He can kill him after I do. I definitely get to kill the bastard first.'

Pillow Squawk

Anthony showed up with a tuxedo-clad waiter in tow. Between them, they wheeled a room service cart covered with tableware that would have given Katie palpitations. Dinner, which crouched under bright silver domes, was from Daniel, one of the city's top restaurants. I'd never been there, but both the cuisine and the prices were reputed to be breathtaking. At the center of the cart was a glorious floral arrangement flanked by flickering votive candles in cut crystal holders. Soft music was provided courtesy of yet another man in a tuxedo, wielding a violin.

'You didn't have to go to all this trouble, Anthony. Pizza or Chinese would have been fine.'

'No trouble at all. My pleasure. I wanted to make it special. To thank you for being such a pal.'

He poured Dom Perignon and I somehow managed to drink, despite the lump in my throat, to my being his *pal*. 'I thought you wanted privacy to talk.'

'I do, and we'll have that, as soon as we finish dinner.'

That was not entirely true. After we finished dinner, the waiter and the violinist moved my furniture to the periphery of the room. The violinist switched from his classical repertoire to Cole Porter and played 'All of Me'.

Anthony stood and took me in his arms. He was a wonderful dancer, especially compared to Harold who moved on the dance floor as if he was stepping on hot coals while trying to deflect a swarm of mosquitoes. I loved how Wop pressed my back firmly and moved with such graceful assurance that all I had to do was let myself go along. I loved how he sang the lyrics, pouring breathy shivers in my ear. His voice was deep, rich and incredibly seductive, like the rest of him.

After a few turns, he stopped singing and spoke in a conspiratorial hush. 'Stephanie and I are finished, Maggie. Sad as it is, I recognize that the marriage has been over for years.'

'Are you sure?'

'Completely. We met with a counselor several times, and there's just no way we can work things out. It's obvious to both of us, and we agree the only sensible thing to do is call it quits.'

'Sounds civilized.'

I felt him shrug. 'Why shouldn't it be? We'll figure out how to divide things and that will be that. There's no reason for a battle.'

'Sure there is. It's called bile. People get angry in a divorce. I don't know why it has to be that way, but it almost always is. I don't want to be discouraging, but I wouldn't be much of a *pal* if I didn't tell you the truth.'

'You are a pal, Maggie. I think if you as a very *close* pal and getting closer all the time.' He held me tighter and started singing again. This time it was 'When We Begin the Beguine'. His hand rubbed the small of my back and slipped lower. His lips grazed my cheek and then brushed the corner of my mouth. At some point, he passed a silent signal to the violinist, who switched on a Cole Porter CD and drifted with the waiter out the door.

'Being friends is a great basis for a relation-ship, don't you think?' He exempted me from answering with a deep, probing kiss. Then we continued dancing.

I closed my eyes and let the dizzy rush from his kiss wash over me. I don't know how much time passed, punctuated by more and more urgent kisses, but eventually, we danced into the bedroom.

Anthony set me down on the bed. He spent a long, languid time touching and exploring and transforming me from a sensible woman of a certain age into a large, quivering sigh.

'Is that good for you? Do you like that?' he asked, again and again.

'Mmmm.'

'You're a beautiful woman, Maggie.'

Items of clothing were unfastened, shed and tossed aside. I kept my eyes shut so he couldn't see my copious figure flaws, or so I tried my damnedest to believe.

Mercifully, we soon slid beneath the covers. I had a brief battle with myself about whether this was a good idea, and it ended in a draw. That left Anthony to cast the tie-breaking vote. With my eyes still closed, I yielded to the flood of sensations: the touch, the warmth, the incredible rush of feeling desirable and desired. I reveled in the soft, urgent sounds of his mounting excitement: low moans, shallow breathing, a harsh gravelly squawk.

'Anthony? Are you OK?'

'God damn it,' he said. 'I'm so sorry.'

'Don't be embarrassed. It's nothing.'

The squawk sounded again, and he fumbled beneath the pillow. 'It's my damned cell phone.'

'You don't have to answer it,' I said, as he did.

His expression registered shock, then fear and desperation. 'Steph, wait. No. That's not true.' He scrambled out of bed and struggled into his clothes while he continued to stammer excuses. 'I'm just finishing up a meeting. I'll be right there.' He slipped on his shoes and grabbed his coat. 'I'm on my way. Just wait.'

He shot me the shamed, desperate look of someone caught dead to rights with his hand in the nooky jar. That was the self-same look I'd seen on Harold's face when he realized he'd been busted with Bethany. True, it had been replaced mere moments later with that chilling look that said he was glad to have everything out in the open, that he didn't give a damn, that what he felt, above all, was relief. Now, he could stop wasting time on annoying pretense and have what he wanted full time. But Anthony did care, that was obvious, only not about me.

'I'm sorry, Maggie. That was Stephanie. She's upset.'

My voice was quaking. 'Get out.'

'It's an emotional time, Maggie. Confusing. Please try to understand.'

'Leave, Anthony. Now!'

'These things take time to sink in. Steph's having a hard time.'

'Now!'

He held up his hands. 'OK. Fine. I'm going.'

'Go faster.'

'I'll call you.'

'Do me a big favor – don't!'

Bridge On the River Why?

What happened next was almost too strange and unsettling to recount. For a long time after Wop left, I lay unmoving on the bed, curled on my side like an overcooked shrimp, staring at the wall. I braced for the violent feeling storm that was bound to erupt once the worst of the shock wore off. I was sure I'd suffer hot waves of humiliation, brutal surges of rage and disgust, ruinous assaults on my shriveled prune of an ego that would reduce me to an ugly ooze of self-loathing, with flabby thighs.

Hard as I tried, I couldn't come up with any way to ease the coming pain. Under other circumstances, I might have attempted to ride out the emotional tempest in a bottle of merlot, but at that moment, wine held absolutely no appeal. I saw no comfort in tearing a pile of Harold pictures to bits. I couldn't muster any interest in whipping myself to a pained frenzy at the gym or trying to assuage the hurt with Rocky Road. For once, even ice cream held no allure. Maybe I was simply too fed up. I wasn't even amused by my all-time favorite fantasy, the one in which I'm looking down my automatic rifle sights at Harold and my mother as they cower in front of an enormous bull's-eye, pleading for their lives. OK, I was a tiny bit amused, but not much. I considered popping one of my anti-anxiety pills, or two or three, but a firm little voice inside my head kept telling me I could get through this without chemical help. I was strong, the voice insisted, resilient and fully capable of handling this.

Atta-girl!

And so I did the unthinkable. I got myself in position, emptied my mind, and fell asleep.

It was a deep, still, dreamless, seamless sleep, the kind I hadn't experienced since Harold admitted he'd put a sizeable deposit down on a shiny new model and had decided to trade me in. When I awoke nearly ten hours later, my mind was ice clear and I was fairly fizzing with energy. The face I glimpsed in the mirror while brushing the fuzz off my teeth looked fresh and vibrant, nothing like the droopy, under-filled balloon I'd come to expect.

For breakfast, I had cereal and fruit with skimmed milk and a cup of decaf green tea. Feeling as I did, a double frappucino with an espresso shot would have been redundant.

With remarkable efficiency, I read the paper, made the bed, straightened the apartment, showered and dressed. My first appointment wasn't until eleven, so I still had a couple of hours to pass as I pleased. The day was bright and promising, an irresistible tease of spring. And at that moment, two startling things struck me.

One: I had not given Anthony Sinclair a single thought. And now that I thought about not thinking of him, I found that incredibly, I was not outraged, devastated, mournful, depressed or hurt. What I felt was simple, delightful contempt. Wop was a lying, phony, overrated jerk, pure and simple. I was glad he'd moved to Tenafly, New Jersey in junior high. I wished he'd stayed there where he belonged; flipping burgers at a Wendy's or selling used Chevrolets at his dull wife's overbearing father's dealership. But fate in its endless perversity had willed him to be wildly successful and then sent a giant carrot to arrange for us to meet again. On the upside, he was Stephanie's problem, not mine. Harold was Bethany's, Wop was Stephanie's la de dah de day.

The second thing that struck me was that I knew exactly what I wanted to do with my remaining free time. I grabbed my purse, walked the few blocks and rang upstairs.

'Valerie? Hi. Hope it's not too early.'

'Of course not. You're welcome any time, Mom. Come on up.'

'Actually, if you don't mind, I thought I'd take Delia for a walk. Give you some time to yourself.'

'That would be wonderful. Guess what, Delia. Granny came to take you for a walk!'

'Gammy wok!' Delia exulted. 'Gammy wok NOW!'

'Yes, sweetie. Delia's thrilled, Mom. I'll have her ready in a jiff.'

'Take your time.'

Moments later they emerged from the elevator. Valerie pushed Delia in a stroller crammed with drinks, snacks, a diaper bag, blankets, toys, books and all manner of other emergency supplies, as if we were going off to tackle Everest's north face instead of the upper Eastside. Still, her face tensed with concern. 'I think you have everything, Mom, but you can always reach me on the cell phone if there's something I forgot.'

There was barely room for the baby. 'I'm sure you didn't forget anything. Ready to go, sweetie?'

She bobbled gently in her buggy. 'Deduh weddy go.'

'Say bye-bye, Mommy. See you soon.'

'Bye bye doon.'

A nocturnal rain had washed the city clean. The air smelled fresh and encouraging and the sky shone like Tiffany silver.

Delia was bouncing hard now. 'Deduh wok, Gammy.'

'Yes sweetie. We're going for a walk.'

Agitation rocked her back and forth. 'Wok!'

'On your own, you mean? Sure. You can walk if you want.' I lifted her out. 'Isn't it pretty out?'

'Peeyeow,' she agreed. 'Wook, Gammy. Tuck.'

'Yes. That's a great big Fedex truck.'

'Why tuck?

'Trucks deliver things to people.'

She dipped her chin, satisfied with the explanation. 'Tuck peepoo. Why toor, Gammy?'

'Stores sell things, baby. That's how Mommy and Daddy get food and clothes and toys for you. They go to stores.'

We had come to a playground tucked beside the East River. Delia rushed headlong toward the toddler-sized equipment. She loved it all: the labored ascents and dizzying dips on the slide, the heady arcs of the swing, the uncertain footing on the rubbery surface near the fountain. Not yet two years old, and she already knew what I was just beginning to understand. Life was an endless series of ups and downs, trials and triumphs, false starts and dizzying turns, and every one, good or ill, elevating or excruciating, could help you learn and grow.

'Maw fing, Gammy.'

'I'll be glad to swing you some more, sweetie, but we have to wait our turn.'

To pass the time, she exercised her curiosity. 'Why boy fing?'

'The little boy is on the swing because it was his turn.'

'Why wady?'

'The lady is here taking care of the little boy.'

Delia pointed at her chest. 'Gammy care you.'

'That's right. Granny's delighted to take care of you, sweetie. Granny thinks you're wonderful, and she loves you very much.'

'Gammy lub you.'

'Indeed I do.' I wanted to tell her more, to explain that love wasn't all of it. There was magic here. She was my baby's baby, after all. Someday, if everything went according to plan, she'd grow up and get on in years and have a baby's baby of her own.

Delia toddled closer to the tall fence that separated the playground from the river. The water churned with the determined pull of the tides. Sunlight glinted off her buttercup curls. Waxing serious, she leveled a tiny finger at the giant steel filigree of the 59th Street Bridge. 'Whazzat, Gammy?'

'That's a bridge, sweetheart.'

'Why bidge?'

'The bridge goes over the river.'

'Why bidge oba ribber?'

Something shifted inside me, chased by a

267

tiny chill. Ask, and the answers will be given. Seek, and ye shall find. 'To connect things, baby. The bridge is there so people who want to can cross to the other side.'

A Touch of Gas

In my mother's view, nature had placed her foot at the end of her leg so she could kick people most efficiently when they were down. I wasn't down at the moment, but she didn't know that, so she started in on me the minute I met her in the purse department at Macy's.

'You could be on time you know, Maggie. It wouldn't kill you.'

She said this at 11.42. 'Actually, it might.'

'Don't be fresh. So I was thinking of buying a wedding gift for Brian and his *shiksa*.'

'You mean Valerie.'

'That's what I said. So I was thinking to myself, what do those kids need? And the one thing that kept running through my head was dental work for the *shiksa*.'

'Don't be nasty, Mom. Valerie happens to be a wonderful, kind, lovely young woman.'

Her face stretched with mock innocence as she pointedly examined the tusk-like adornments on a large black tote. 'So don't you think her teeth should be lovely, too? They're so – how can I put this delicately?

They're so *goyish*.'

'Lay off, Mom. I don't appreciate your bigotry. Teeth have nothing to do with being Christian. And anyway, Valerie's teeth are her business.'

'Don't be ridiculous. Teeth are public. You open your mouth, and there they are for everyone to see. When that girl opens her mouth, it's like she's wearing a neon sign that says: *Shiksa from Wisconsin*.'

'If you want to get them a gift, they could use a Dutch oven.'

'Why? Is their Dutch oven stained and crooked too?'

I glared at her. 'Why don't you give them a check?'

She nodded. 'A check is a good idea. Miss Wisconsin could use it for a down payment on the dental work. I could recommend someone excellent on the card.' She framed the text with her fingers. 'How about: *Wishing you a wonderful life together and a much better bite*? Dr Smithline, I think his name is. He did Ilona's mouth. Remember how bad her teeth used to be before she had them capped?'

'The only thing that would help Ilona would be to cap her entire head.'

'So you want to go for lunch?'

'Not really. I'm not very hungry.'

'Don't be ridiculous. It's way past noon. Your problem is you need lunch.'

'Then why don't we go someplace where they serve food?'

'Don't be difficult.'

The midday sun shone fiercely, inspiring Pearl to do the same. 'So let me guess. You bought those La Recharge skin lotions.'

'A couple,' I admitted. 'But I'm not convinced they work.'

She sniffed. 'Leave it to you to fall for such *michigas*. Of course they don't work. A few cents worth of ingredients in a fancy package, and you believed they were going to make your skin look like a baby's *tuchas*?'

'You swore they worked on you, that they were a miracle.'

She flapped away the thought. 'Miracle, shmiracle. Turns out I'd put on a couple of pounds, probably retaining water.'

'Water. Sure.'

'So guess who I happened to run into?'

'Hmm. Were you in a car or on foot?'

'Don't be a smart mouth. I was at the post office getting stamps, and Alma Feder, your neighbor, was standing eight people behind me on line. So naturally, we got to talking.'

I could sense what was coming, but the sidewalk stubbornly refused to open up and swallow me whole. 'Naturally.'

'So she tells me you have a boyfriend with a little baby and a depressed Japanese wife.'

I stopped in my tracks and faced her. 'Let's get this straight, Mom. I do not have a boyfriend, and the rest isn't even remotely close to true. I want you to drop this line of discussion, right now.'

Her attempt to look innocent was a miserable failure. 'I'm just interested in you, darling. Alma told me some man sent you fancy flowers and you seemed to be very pleased with the whole business. Also, she heard in the building that he picked you up and took you out in a fancy limo and that another night he showed up with dinner from some fancy schmancy restaurant. Except for the crazy Japanese wife and the baby, it all sounds very good. I was just wondering why I have to hear it from a stranger rather than my own flesh and blood.'

'I told you, Mom, I don't want to talk about it. Anyway, there's nothing to talk about. I was catching up with someone I knew as a kid who grew up to be a major jackass. That's all.'

'Don't be hasty, Maggie. If a man has a few little faults, you can change him. That's what I did. When I met your father, he was a regular pushover, but I told him, look Marvin, you're not going to get anyplace if you don't open your mouth. Don't be a shrinking violet, I said. You have to tell your boss you want a raise; you want a promotion. You have to speak up and stand your ground and make demands, and that's exactly how he got to be such a big shot in housewares. If it wasn't for me, that man would have been dried on the vine in small electrics.'

'You certainly wanted him to be a pushover at home. You wouldn't even let him decide whether to have cold or hot cereal for breakfast.'

'Hot's better. Everyone knows that. Anyway, your father had more than enough responsibility at the store. You think its easy deciding whether to stock more drip or perk? Do you have any idea what goes into the two-slice versus four-slice equation, much less whether the Crock pot is a passing fad? But don't try to change the subject. Who is this man? Where did you meet him? Is he Jewish? And how come he married a Japanese *kvetch*?'

As soon as we entered the diner, my mother charged like a crazed rhino toward her favorite booth at the rear. It was occupied, but that was of no consequence to her. 'I see you're done, we'll take the table.'

'We'll be finished in just a few minutes,' said the nice young woman who was having lunch with her two tow-headed little girls.

'Mom, stop. They're still eating.'

'Nonsense. Look. Those girls can't wait to get out of here. You're finished, sweetheart. Aren't you? You don't want to eat too much and get sick.'

'I'm finished,' the smaller one said.

'Me, too,' said her sister. 'We're finished, Mom.'

Pearl showed her teeth. 'You see. I'll just put my things down while you get the check.' She proceeded to crowd them out with her coat, gloves, scarf, hat, purse and several overstuffed shopping bags.

'OK, girls,' the mother said pleasantly. 'Let's go somewhere else for dessert.'

They hastened to leave, a feeling I could well understand.

'Sit, Maggie. We'll order, and then you'll tell me everything.'

I stared in a fury at the menu. And I decided, right then and there, that I'd had enough. When the waiter approached, I took a deep breath and ordered a Greek salad.

'She'll have the tuna on rye,' my mother said.

'I'll have a Greek salad with extra feta cheese, no onions and the dressing on the side,' I said. 'And hot tea with lemon.'

'Don't be ridiculous.'

I smiled at the waiter. 'Let me make sure you got that. I'm not having tuna or lettuce and tomato or dry rye toast or coffee or coleslaw. None of those.'

'Greek salad, tea with lemon, extra feta, no onions, dressing on the side,' he confirmed.

'That's exactly right. Thanks.'

As he walked off, my mother fixed me with a killer look. 'So Alma Feder was right. You've gone off the deep end, Maggie. I can see you're not anywhere close to your regular self.'

'I'm not. That's true, Mom, and thanks for noticing. Maybe there's hope for me yet.'

The Big Spill

Roger and Katie's party was scheduled for Saturday night at 6 p.m. Brian and Valerie picked me up for the drive to Connecticut in a Valerie's Sweet Treats van. The cab was infused with the powerful essence of freshly baked cookies, and by the time we crossed the state border, both Delia and I were riding a cinnamon sugar chocolate vanilla high.

The baby spoke to the beat as we jolted over the bumper crop of late winter potholes. 'Gammy ting hippo happy nowit.'

'What's that, sweetie?'

'Gammy tingit.'

Valerie bailed me out. 'If you're happy and you know it, clap your hands.'

The verses went on and on. To demonstrate our contentment, we clapped her hands, stomped our feet, winked, attempted ear-wiggling, mussed our hair and honked our noses. We made silly faces, stuck out our tongues, brayed like donkeys and mooed like demented cows. Still, while Delia's happiness was the genuine item; mine rested on a house of tottering cards. The closer we got to Roger and Katie's colonial manse in northern New Canaan, the more anxious I became. The party was for and about Brian and Valerie, but Harold would be there, too. This was the same Harold who'd thought it understandable, rather than adorable and absurd, when Brian was little and thought that the words to the Lord's Prayer were, *Our Father who art in heaven, Harold be thy name.* For the entirety of our marriage, Harold had managed to make himself the central, sole, overpowering issue in most everything, including my pregnancies, Ali's dance recitals and Brian's little difficulties with the law. And so I had no doubt that he would do his intrusive best to make this party all about nothing but him.

I endeavored to set these negative thoughts aside as we entered Roger and Katie's foyer, where effusive greetings and copious air kisses were exchanged. The hall table was piled with elaborate gifts. Many of the guests were friends we'd made while we lived in Connecticut. And I hadn't seen most of them since Harold and I split.

'Maggie, darling. Don't you look simply divine!' said Taffy McNally, a neighbor of Katie's I liked a lot despite her fixation on cockroach-sized dogs and a tragic addiction to Lilly Pulitzer pastels.

Having refused Janine's offer to dress me for the event, I was decked out in my standard see-no-evil tunic top and shape-free black slacks. 'Thanks, Taff. You're a wonderful liar.'

'And you're such a breath of fresh air. So how's it going? Oh my. I can see.'

All I could see was the horror etched on her Palm Beach-burnished face. An inner voice warned that I should not, under any circumstances, turn around and find out what had put it there.

Then I heard Roger's booming hysterical voice, the one I'd last experienced when his son came out as a registered Democrat. 'There you are, Harold. And Bethany, hello.'

At that instant, I had a powerful craving for a drink, something tall, cool and bracing that I could pour over Harold's head. But this was about Brian and Valerie, I said to myself over and over again. I decided the best course was to keep as far away from them as possible and wait for a more appropriate occasion to slice off Harold's ears.

Katie descended in a fury. 'Son of a bitch. Don't you worry, Mags. I'm going to tell him to leave.'

'Don't. You've made a wonderful party. Let's not spoil it with an ugly scene.'

'But this is outrageous. Rog and I asked Harold to come on his own, and he agreed. He had no right to go back on his word.'

'It is what it is. Let's just deal with it.'

She looked suspicious. 'That's totally big of you, Mags. Incredibly big. Are you sure you're OK?'

'I'm sure.'

'Well I say you're acting incredibly big. How about I get you a nice, stiff martini?'

'That's not necessary, Katie. Really, I'm fine.'

'Sure it is, Mags. It's dandy. Anything you say.'

Harold squired Bethany to the bar where he bullied the bartender into opening one of Roger's best burgundies in lieu of the perfectly wonderful Bordeaux he'd elected to serve. He then bullied a waiter into retrieving two special burgundy glasses from a cabinet in the kitchen. Then, drinks in hand; Harold led Bethany to the couch where he bullied their way into the prime seats beside Brian and Valerie. This involved edging out my mother and her sister Frieda, an act akin to milking lethal venom from a pair of cranky snakes. Everyone gaped as all this transpired.

Brian was seething. Valerie, ever the sweetheart, tried to defuse the situation with the best she could think to do. 'Delia, honey, say hi to Grandpa Harold and Bethany.'

'Hi, gampuh wawoo. Hi, Befnee!'

Harold recoiled, pressing his back against the couch as if Delia was a hairy insect crawling on the floor. As Harold had charmingly observed on many occasions, babies were profoundly incontinent and incapable of rational discourse, so why would anyone venture close enough to risk soiling himself with their repulsive effusions and grubby little hands?

Bethany, to her undeserved credit, leaned toward the baby and smiled. 'Aren't you a beautiful little girl?'

'Deduh booful,' the baby preened, and she was resplendent indeed in a white party dress with a smocked pink bodice, a full skirt, a bow in the back and puffed sleeves.

'And so smart,' Bethany went on. 'Do you know what the cow says?'

Animal noises happened to be Delia's specialty. 'Moo!'

Everyone save Harold joined Bethany in hearty applause. 'That's right. What does the horse say?'

'Neigh!' Spurred by the enthusiastic audience, the baby put her all into the performance. 'Neigh, neigh!'

'And what does the mule say?' asked my mother, for whom mule was a native tongue.

Delia scrunched her nose. 'Ee aw!'

'And what does a—' Aunt Frieda said, but then her face went blank as she dropped the mental thread.

'Monkey eee eee aah aah,' Delia exulted. 'Bird cheep, cheep!'

Harold continued to regard Delia with distaste.

'Wook, Gampuh Wawoo. Wook!' she demanded. 'Woostuh – cock a doo doo!'

Harold reached for the comfort of his wine. 'Heh heh.'

Delia went through the rest of her repertoire, determined to win him over. She imitated a frog, a pig, a lion and a duck. Finished with her selection of animal sounds, she moved on. 'Bunny hop!' She crouched low and sprang forward. 'Hop hop hop!' On the fourth hop, she lost her balance and staggered toward Harold. Outrage bloomed on his lipless, chinless face as the outsized burgundy glass toppled, dousing his pimp-blue jacket, striped shirt and silver trousers.

Harold handled this with his customary good humor. He leapt to his feet, turned the color of an infected boil, and hollered, 'Shit!'

'Easy, Hal. It was an accident,' Bethany said.

Hal?

'Goddamn it to hell! That's going to stain.'

'Try some club soda,' Rog ventured.

'White wine takes out red wine,' Katie said. 'Scissors cuts paper. And paper covers rock.'

'This is not funny,' Harold harrumphed. 'Not in the least!' He glared at Brian and Valerie. 'The least you two could do is control that child!'

'Why don't you control yours, Hal?' I couldn't help but mutter. At least, I intended to mutter.

'Maggie's right for a change,' my mother said. 'Don't act like such a *putz*, Harold. The baby's a baby, for chrissakes.'

'She has no place at a civilized gathering if she can't behave.'

'Quit it, Dad,' Brian said. 'She's our baby, and she has more right to be here than you.'

Harold fiddled with his phantom moustache. 'You could teach her some manners, if you had any.'

The cords bulged in Roger's neck. 'That's quite enough, Harold. You're the one whose being uncivilized.'

'Well I never.'

'Yes you have, Harold. More times than I can count,' Katie said. 'What's that thing you called him, Pearl? A poots?'

'A *putz*,' my mother said. 'It means *shmekel*.'

'Pardon?' Katie said.

'A *shmekel*, a *shmuck*, a *shlong*. I don't know what your people call it.' She motioned for Katie to bend down and whispered in her ear.

'Oh,' Katie said. 'Yes. Harold, you're acting precisely like one of those insufferable smickle slongs.'

Delia chimed in. 'Wawoo mickalong.'

'Mickalong, my butt,' Janine sniffed. 'The man's a mother ducking dickhead.'

'Duck quack quack,' Delia said.

'Forget all that,' Pearl said, leaning close to Delia. '*Putz* is easier. Say it like this, sweetheart. Say Grampa Harold is a *putz*.'

Guess Who's Coming to Win Her

The flowers made me furious, and they made me sneeze. Stargazer iris poked forth from the opulent arrangement, and their overbearing fragrance shot up my nostrils to the area of my brain responsible for giant, exuberant, allergy-induced ah-choos. One sneeze led to another, and in short order, I was red-eyed and itching madly in places I was unable to scratch.

'Damn you, Wop!' I declared between the nasal explosions, though it came out: *Dab you, Wab!*

The square glass vase weighed a ton, stuffed to bursting as it was with pricey blooms. I hefted it off the living room table and wrestled it into the kitchen, slopping water on the carpet as I went. I shut the door, planning to trap the itch bugs on the other side, but safely back in the living room, my sneezing bout continued.

Dab you, you suduvabidge!

When I lifted the massive centerpiece again, my lower back screeched in protest. So, in addition to giving me red, swollen eyes and causing a fireworks display to shoot from my nose, Wop's idiotic attempt to make nice would probably leave me bent like a horse destined for the glue-factory. Still, I had to get rid of the thing. Barefoot, I walked out to haul the arrangement to the garbage room.

I could hardly see where I was going, much less the pan of piping hot brownies Mrs Feder had deposited on my welcome mat. My foot was scorched by the steaming pastry and the scalding hot pan.

'Oh shid!' I hollered. 'Shid fug!'

'Oh my. I hope you didn't hurt yourself, Maggie. Though if you don't mind my saying, that's what happens when a person doesn't look where she's going.'

'Shid!'

'It's OK, darling. Just a little boo boo. You'll eat a brownie, you'll feel much better.'

I would have felt much better making her eat the pan, but I held back.

281

'More flowers from Mr Hanky Panky, I see. You know, Maggie, some women wouldn't keep a gift under these circumstances.'

'Agshilly, I wuz just geddig rid ob it.'

'You're throwing out such beautiful flowers?'

'I done wan dem. You can hab dem iv you like.'

She planted her hands on her chintz-covered hips. 'Well, it would be a sin to waste them. I bet they cost a fortune.'

'OK fide. I'll bring dem to your place.' The flowers gained weight with every step as I trudged past my apartment and down to the very end of the hall where Mrs Feder lived. My back ached, my foot stung, and a fresh round of sneezes was poised to commence. I felt the teasing itch, the pressure building.

Try sneezing while holding something heavy that you detest. Try it while your spinal cord is imploding, your nose and ears are about to pop off, your foot is melting and your nosy neighbor is taking forever to find her house keys, even though she's wearing a house coat with one pocket.

'Blease, Bissis Fedur. Hurry ub!'

'You shouldn't be in such a rush all the time, Maggie. Stop and smell the roses.'

The sneeze broke loose, spraying the arrangement with the atomized contents of my sinuses, my spinal column and my lymphatic system, whatever that was. This was of no consequence to Mrs Feder, who led me around the apartment, demanding that I

282

move the vase five times before she decided where she wished it to remain.

Free at last, I hobbled back to my apartment, retrieved a bag of peas from the freezer to put on my foot, opened the window to air out the flower smell, and sat gingerly on the couch. I blew my nose again and again, trying to clear my head enough so I could concentrate on complaining about my back and foot. This was all going as well as could be expected, until about thirty seconds later when Mrs Feder knocked.

'Maggie darling, it's me.'

'Whadizit, Bissis Fedur?'

'I thought you'd want the card from the arrangement.'

'Do thangs. I hodestly dode.'

'Yes you do want it, sweetheart,' she crooned. 'It's not what we thought at all. In fact it's a wonderful surprise!'

'You keeb it. I dode wad a suhprise'

'Just open the door and I'll give it to you. You'll be glad you listened. Take my word.'

Mrs Feder could be almost as tenacious as Janine. I got more or less to my feet and hobbled to the door.

She caught me in a hug that unhinged the few vertebrae that hadn't yet been knocked loose. *Mazel tov!* I'm so happy for you, for both of you. Wait until your mother hears!'

'What?'

She stiffened. 'You'll have to see for yourself, Maggie. I'm not the type to read someone else's mail.' She handed me a small white

283

envelope and strode off.

I shuffled back to the couch and stared at the envelope, fearful of what it might contain. Any news that had delighted Mrs Feder and threatened to please my mother was likely not cause for me to celebrate. Dreadful things ran through my mind. Maybe the flowers were from Frieda's gay, gambling-addicted criminal attorney or the florist from Pittsburgh who'd been married twenty-seven times. Maybe they were from Sam Weller, congratulating me for being voted Most Pathetic in our Entire Graduating Class! Maybe Wop was pretending to have split up with Stephanie again. Or worse, maybe this was Harold's way of trying to murder me so he wouldn't have to split assets in the divorce. He knew how allergic I was to stargazer iris. The diabolical troll might well have calculated that a couple of hundred dollars worth of flowers was a hell of a lot cheaper than half the house in the Berkshires, half the IRAs and the Marriott points.

I pulled the card up just enough to view the top line of writing. And sure enough, there was *Dear Margaret* in Harold's swaggering scrawl.

'Hah, you jagass! Your burder plan didit work!' All right, to be perfectly fair, he'd almost managed to murder me, but as everyone knows, almost doesn't count.

Cringing, I tugged at the note until I could read the next line. *Please forgive me...*

Fat chance.

Next line: ... *for being such a fool.*

Now I was curious. Why on earth was Harold begging forgiveness for being himself?

I miss you, and long to resurrect what we had. Please allow me to make things up to you so that we can move on to a wonderful future together. With all my love, Harold

I sat back, trying to absorb the stunning turn of events. The life I'd lost was mine again for the taking. All I had to do was say the word and I could be Mrs Harold Strickland again, part of a nice, normal, no-raised-eyebrows pair. I could check off 'married' on forms and resume my place at the married couples' table at family events. If I cared to, I could slip my rings back on to cover the permanent dent in my left ring finger. I wouldn't have to suffer pitying or distrusting glances from smugly still-married women. Perhaps most importantly, if something catastrophic happened to me and I was left brain-dead, I'd have a husband on hand to pull the plug. Then again, if Harold was my husband, he'd probably pull the plug no matter what condition I was in as soon as he heard what the medical care would cost. With Harold as my guardian, a simple nap could prove to be a fatal mistake.

As I was pondering this, the house phone rang.

Tabrik: Got something for you, Mrs Strickland. I'll bring it up.

Me: Please dode Tabrig. I'll gedit laydur.'

Tabrik: OK then. Be right up.'

I hung up shaking my head. I told myself this was a simple miscommunication. When I said *no*, I meant I didn't care to be bothered right now and would get whatever it was later. What Tabrik heard was *Sure, come on up and I'll give you a big, fat tip.*

The doorbell rang, and I shuffled to answer. I thought to gently rebuke Tabrik, but instead of the doorman, there stood Harold, his face warped with an attempted grin.

'How wonderful to see you, Margaret. You look lovely.'

The sight of him somehow cleared my head. 'Hello, Harold.'

'May I come in?'

'What for?'

'I want to talk to you, to try to explain.'

'Explain why you've behaved like such an ass? Why you froze my charge cards, why you raided the accounts?'

'I've reversed all that, Margaret. It was a foolish, impulsive thing to do, and I'm terribly sorry if I inconvenienced you in any way.'

'You *inconvenienced* me? You've got a mighty strange idea of inconvenience, Harold. Running off with Bethany, hiring Jaws as your divorce lawyer, leaving me penniless. Calling that an *inconvenience* is like calling World War Two a *little misunderstanding.*'

'You're right. Please, sweetie. Don't make this any more difficult than it already is.'

'Sweetie? Who are you trying to kid, Harold? You never called anyone a pet name in your life. You didn't even call the pets pet names. It was Mr Fish, Ms Bird and small feline of uncertain lineage.'

Now he looked me in the eye. 'I love you, Margaret. I love you and I always have. I know I lost my way for a time, and I'm thoroughly ashamed of myself. I'm sorrier than you can imagine, and I want to make it up to you.'

I stared at this total stranger trying to pass himself off as my ex, but for the life of me, I couldn't detect the place where the mask and the real face met. Nevertheless, this could not be the Harold I had been with for all those years. This Harold was much too in touch with himself. He was far too honest, open, caring, decent and sweet.

'I've changed, Margaret. I've come to my senses and realized what's important in this life. You mean the world to me. You, us, and the family we used to be. Give me a chance to prove it, and I'll do anything. Anything you want. Say the word.'

Miss is Doubt Mired

Rabbi Jennifer was having trouble keeping still. Her wide dark eyes kept skittering about and she shifted again and again in her chair. 'You say you've never seen him like this before?'

'Contrite, humble and conciliatory? No way. I saw Harold laugh a time or two years ago, but this was even weirder.'

'And you think he was being sincere?'

'I don't know what to think. But I'll tell you one thing, if he's had a psychotic break, it's mighty attractive.'

She fidgeted some more. 'You found it attractive?'

'I didn't say that. I mean I said it, but that's not what I meant.'

'What did you mean?'

That called for a jelly bean, or actually six, which was not enough to get the subject changed.

'Are you thinking of trying to reconcile with him?'

My response was a quick, forceful, no-doubt-about-it shrug. 'In a way, yes, and in a way, definitely no.'

'Meaning?'

The breath escaped me in a rush. 'Meaning

I'm confused, Rabbi Jennifer. I want my old life back, only not the one I actually had. In many ways, I'm much happier now, but in a semi-miserable way, if you know what I mean.'

She squirmed in her seat again and my maternal side started fretting that her underwear must be too tight. Or perhaps, considering her age, she had diaper rash. 'I'm afraid I don't, Maggie. Why don't you explain?'

I lost the stare-down. 'OK, fine. You win. When it comes right down to it, I'd still rather be a sock than a beacon. Being a sock is what I know.'

'And the thought of becoming a beacon is scary.'

'For a sock, sure. I'd guess born beacons don't find it scary at all.'

She went still. 'What if you're not a sock at all, Maggie? What if you've always been a beacon, but you never had a chance to act like one?'

'Now I need you to explain.'

Her hands cupped air. 'Imagine a hatchling. All it has known is first being safe and warm in the egg and then contained in the nest and protected by its mother. But sooner or later, the day comes when it's time for that baby bird to try its wings.

'The sky is a vast unknown, and the nest so cozy and familiar. That little bird wants to stay where it is and cling to what it knows, and it refuses to fly. So the mother bird, or perhaps the father, decides to help it on its way.' She raised her hands slowly, and then in a rush, spread them apart, releasing the trapped air between. 'And you know what happens?'

'What?'

'The little bird flies, Maggie. It tests its wings and finds its way, and it soars. And before you know it, that bird can't imagine ever not knowing how to take to the skies. Being up there feels like second nature; not to mention exhilarating. In short order, that young bird can barely imagine any hatchling being afraid to leave the nest.'

'So you don't think I should consider taking Harold back.'

'I think you should do what's right for you.'

'I agree. The only problem is – I don't know what's right for me.'

'You'll figure it out. I know you will.'

Her cell phone sounded a chirpy *Hava nagila*.

'Would you excuse me, Maggie? I need to get that.' Her look went grave as she answered. Nodding ensued, interspersed by the occasional *mmhmm*. Rabbi Jennifer tucked her left hand in her right armpit, and the start of a smile tugged the corners of her mouth.

'Really?' she said.

She nodded again, followed by several more *mmhmm*s.

'No! You mean it? Are you sure?'

Her smile stretched with joyous astonishment. 'Oh thank you, thank you, thank you!'

She leapt from her chair and seized my

hands. Next thing I knew, we were dancing in
dizzy rounds, both of us laughing.

'Good news?' I brilliantly surmised.

'No, Maggie. Great news! I'm carrying
twins!'

'Twins?'

'Yes!'

'*Mazel tov*, or I should say *mazel tov* times
two? I'm so happy for you!'

Now she went still and her chocolate eyes
brimmed with tears. 'You see? That's the
thing of it, Maggie. Anything can happen.
That's why you shouldn't be afraid to spread
your wings and try.'

The Lying King

I agreed to have lunch with Harold on the
theory that even beacons have to eat. He
asked me to meet him on the corner of 63rd
Street and Park Avenue. Only after I arrived
there did it occur to me that this was the
precise place where I'd spotted the seven-foot
carrot, causing my life to collide head-on with
Wop's.

This time no giant vegetables appeared.
The oddest sight I encountered was Harold
walking down the street. His lush pewter
beard was back, as were his tweedy, elbow-
patched sports coat and baggy corduroy

pants. He wore his familiar tortoise-shell glasses as well, all of which made him look disturbingly like himself. The sole off-note was the wide, aw-shucks smile plastered between the moustache and the beard. Harold grinning boyishly was about as believable as an opera-singing pig.

'How wonderful to see you, Maggie. Ready for lunch?'

'Do me a favor, Harold. Call me Margaret like you always have, or bitch.'

'Sure, sweetie. Whatever you say.'

I cringed. 'Don't call me sweetie either. I can't imagine you saying that to anyone who wasn't terminally ill.'

'Of course. Whatever pleases you, my dear. Thanks for letting me know. I want you to tell me about anything I do that makes you uncomfortable.'

The fact that he was still breathing came to mind, but I doubted even the new Harold would be accommodating enough to cut that out.

'I made a reservation at the Park Avenue Café. Does that meet with your approval?'

'You want to take me someplace elegant and expensive for lunch? I'm wondering if you've suffered a blow to the head.'

'Quite the opposite. I'm seeing things clearer than I ever have. You deserve the very best, Margaret, and I'm going to do everything in my power to see that you get it.'

'That sounds as if you've hired the finest possible hit man.'

'Heh heh.'

Harold squired me to the restaurant and held the door. He accepted the first table we were offered without so much as a raised eyebrow. I would have been less surprised had he sprouted fins.

'Would you care for champagne, Margaret? Being here with you, I do feel like celebrating.'

'Go right ahead, Harold. I'll stick with water.'

We ordered, and incredibly, Harold failed to go on and on about how he wanted his dish prepared. Typically, he demanded his chosen dish with a different sauce and other accompaniments than the ones listed. Often, he requested ingredients that didn't even appear on the menu in a style that had nothing to do with what the restaurant served. Under ordinary circumstances, having Harold as a dinner patron was about as stressful as having your restaurant torched, but right then he was the model of good-natured cooperation. 'I'll have the same,' he said, after I requested the sole.

'You will?' I asked. 'Just like that?'

'However the chef suggests.' He said this almost exactly like a normal person, so I presumed he had been practicing for weeks.

While we waited for the food, he gazed at me with an expression that in anyone else, I would have judged to be mooning. But Harold Strickland did not moon, except at the Yankees. And so, the picture finally came clear.

'Let me guess, Harold, Bethany dumped you.'

He harrumphed. 'She did nothing of the kind!'

'What did happen then?'

'Nothing productive will come from dwelling on that, Margaret. I say, let's not.'

'I say let's. You told me you're willing to do anything I want, and what I want is to hear what broke you two lovebirds up.'

That inspired a host of quintessential Haroldian behaviors. He fiddled with the edge of his moustache, sniffed a time or two, and huffed.

'What, Harold? And don't even try to bull-shit me. I can assure you I'll smell anything but the whole, unsanitized truth.'

'All right then, as you wish. I discovered that she was absurdly unrealistic, not nearly as sound and intelligent as I'd presumed, at least in an emotional sense. After Delia behaved so appallingly at the party, I was naturally perturbed. But when we discussed it on the way home, Bethany's reaction to the entire incident was astonishing. She said I was overreacting. And then she started bab-bling on about how she adores children and can't wait to have three, or perhaps even more. She actually envisioned a future in which she and I might marry and have off-spring. Can you imagine such a thing? The girl must be insane.'

'Wanting marriage and children! What

could she be thinking?'

'Indeed. It was bad enough having to go through all that the first time. Imagine dealing with such idiocy at my age.'

'Idiocy? That's it you describe bringing up two terrific kids?'

'Let's stay on point, shall we? All I could think of was Bethany losing her figure, becoming a dowdy, sexless soul obsessed with potty training and all that mindless nonsense. Imagine a young woman with such brilliant potential reduced to conversing with a barely sentient, blithering, incontinent child!'

'Instead of conversing with a barely sentient, blithering fool like you? I can imagine that just fine. In fact, there's a terrific little child I'd much rather be with right this very minute. Goodbye, Harold. Have a nice life.'

Bringing Down the Louse

Back in the office, I found my message light blinking. A moment later, Janine barged in. She was costumed in a short plaid pleated skirt and a tight red jersey with a large silver J on the front, brandishing a red and white pom-pom. Before I could speak, she launched a cheerleading routine, complete with high kicks, jumps and whirling arms. 'Hit 'em again, hit 'em again, lower lower. Yay team!'

'What's going on, Janine? Or maybe I don't want to know.'

'This, you definitely want to know. Brace yourself for some fabulous news!'

I filled my lungs. 'OK, I suppose I'm ready.'

She began another cheer. 'Harold, Harold, he's a crook. But now he's busted. What a shnook! Yaaaaaay team!'

'Cut it out, Janine. If you have something to say, please do it in plain English.'

'I swear, Maggie. You are no fun at all. Anyway, I don't have to explain. You can hear for yourself.' She pressed the Play button on the message machine.

Maggie, hi. It's Lon Thrasher. Thought you'd like to see what just came over the wire, so I'm faxing it to your machine. Hope everything's going well with you.

At that, Janine retrieved a page from the fax machine. 'Here you go, Maggie. Read it and whoop.'

The story ran one paragraph, but that was more than enough.

Lakewood Press has just announced a two-book deal with Columbia ethics Prof Dr Harold Strickland for timely tomes on ethics in the workplace and in personal matters. Given the continuing spate of headlines about the seeming collapse of corporate and interpersonal scruples in the US, the publisher has high hopes that the so-called Strickland Principles will prove to be more than profitable enough to justify the mid-six

figure advance. The franchise should be fur-
thered by a deal in the works for Strickland
to do regular commentary on ethical ques-
tions for NPR.

I read the piece again, thinking that perhaps this time it would make at least a little bit of sense. A book deal didn't happen overnight. I knew this from my ex-friend Ellie Matthias who worked in publishing. An idea had to be divined, developed, sat upon and hatched. Next, someone, often several someones, had to get interested enough to give it the green light. Typically, it took writing a proposal and then getting an agent to represent the author to find a publisher willing to take the project on. And even then, the process was far from over. There were negotiations, endless points to bicker about, a contract written and dissected and rewritten, again and again. The publisher's announcement of the deal meant that all those things had transpired, which meant Harold had known about this for many, many months.

And while I stood there, limp-jawed, a giant herd of pissed-off imaginary cows stampeded through my mind. 'That lying shit.'

'Exactly. And I say we see to it he gets what he deserves. Picture this all over the news.' With a sweep of her pom-pom, she defined the banner headline. 'Greed-crazed un-scrupulous ethicist exposed as lying, asshole, mother-ducking scum. Or do you think that's too refined?'

'No. That sounds about right.'

She clapped her hands, and the pom-pom made a great ruffling din. 'Oh, Maggie. I can't wait to spread the word. This is going to be such fun!' She did another high jump. 'Harold, Harold. Here's our plan. You'll be rooting for food in a garbage can. Yaaaay team!'

Numbly, I watched her exult. She wrapped up her routine and headed for the door. 'I'm calling all my media contacts. I'm calling everyone. I'm getting on it right away.'

'Wait.'

'It can't wait, sweetie. We don't want to miss the evening news.'

'Hear me, Janine, I don't want you to do anything yet. I need to think this through.'

She puffed her exasperation. 'There's nothing to think about. We caught him with his pants down, trying to commit a fraud, and it's our civic duty to turn the bastard in. There's no other choice in a situation like this, except, of course, blackmail. If that's the way you want to go, all right. It's true that you might come out better financially by squeezing Harold, and I can't deny that. But I have to tell you, Maggie, when it comes to revenge; blackmail is not nearly as satisfying as public humiliation.'

'Give me time. I'll think it over and let you know.'

'OK. But think fast. The man is asking for it, Maggie. Begging. So I say we give it to him, but good.'

The Mensch Connection

'I hope you're feeling as wonderful as you look,' I said to Rabbi Jennifer. She was not far along, but her contours had already softened and rounded, a perfect compliment to her warm, contented glow.

'I am,' she said. 'How about you, Maggie? I hope you're not feeling as troubled as you look.'

'It's nothing. We probably shouldn't discuss it in front of the twins.'

She ran an affectionate hand over the tiny swell of her belly. 'Don't worry. They'll be fine.'

'Maybe we shouldn't discuss it anyway. It's too upsetting.'

'Maybe if we discuss it, we can find a way to make it less so.'

'You think?'

'We'll never know unless we try.'

I tried. I told her the whole sordid story about Harold's new book and radio deals, and his attempts to keep them secret so I wouldn't make a claim on his windfall. 'How could I be so stupid? I always thought he was a decent, honest man. Even after all that business with Bethany, I believed in my heart that Harold was a fundamentally good person. The truth is our marriage was a teardown way before the affair. I realize we both had a hand in the way things fell apart, not just Harold.'

She nodded. 'Accepting responsibility is what a grown-up person does, Maggie. And that's what you are, a grown-up *mensch*. But you weren't stupid to trust Harold. You can't make judgments about things you don't know.'

'I'll never trust that lying, cheating, scum-sucking creep again, I'll tell you that much. For once, Janine's right. Harold should be exposed for what he is; he should be brought down and publicly humiliated. He should lose his precious deals, not to mention his job. Imagine Harold Strickland teaching ethics, of all things. It's like taking anger management classes from Attila the Hun. I'm going to tell Janine to break the story. Let that jackass get the medicine he deserves.'

She tamped the air. 'You're angry, and understandably so, Maggie. But before you react, I'd urge you to consider the conse-quences.'

'I have; I am. If it gets out that Harold was trying to perpetrate a fraud, he'll get exactly what's coming to him. That's a fitting con-sequence for what he's done.'

She plucked two jelly beans from the jar, a licorice and a coconut, and set them at extreme opposite corners of the desk. 'Let me ask you a question, Maggie. How do you see things between you and Harold going forward?'

'Non-existent, that's how.'

Her brow peaked. 'You'll have children together, grandchildren. There will be birthdays, graduations, times when the family will gather for joyous and difficult occasions alike. How do you see things between you two then?'

I looked from the black jelly bean to the white one and it struck me as absurd for them to be so far apart. I nudged the white one closer, but just a bit. 'I'd hope we'll be civil.'

'You think that's for the best?'

I shrugged. 'There's nothing to be gained by battling.'

'I agree.' She picked up the black and white jelly beans and set them down much nearer the center. They weren't close, not touching jelly bean elbows or anything, but if they needed to trade a few civil words, they wouldn't have to shout.

I felt my bitter resolve softening. 'I guess going public with this would make it hard to deal with him later on.'

'The question is: what's best for all concerned?'

My face heated. I'd been focused on the sheer joy of juvenile spite, not thinking about what really mattered. 'It would be terrible for Ali and Brian to hear a thing like that about their father. The divorce has been plenty for them to deal with. More than plenty.'

'I'm sure.'

'And to be honest, I don't really want to get

301

caught up in a mess like that either. This is between me and Harold, and that's where it should stay.'

'Makes sense.'

I pushed the feuding jelly beans off to the side, where they belonged. 'Anyway, Harold gets a life sentence with himself. That's punishment enough for anyone.'

'Sounds pretty harsh from what you've told me.'

A smile replaced the seething frown I'd been wearing for days. 'Cruel and unusual,' I said happily. 'Better him than me.'

The Money Split

Randy Schlam fired a warning glance at Harold as he passed the amended agreements across the conference table to Lena and me.

'A couple of things were inadvertently omitted from the earlier draft,' Schlam said. 'You'll find the significant changes in paragraph 6a and 7c.'

Lena's brow shot up as she flipped the pages. 'Omitted inadvertently were they?'

'It's all there now,' Schlam said.

'We'll see.'

While she read, Harold studied his fingernails. I passed the time strafing my ex with loaded looks.

My lawyer drew Schlam's attention to page five. 'Mrs Strickland gets half of all proceeds from the books and radio contract, I see, but of course, since the *Strickland Principles* were conceived during the marriage, she is also entitled to half of the proceeds in everything emanating from the concept, in perpetuity.'

'That's absurd! I will not stand for it!' Harold jumped to his feet and punctuated the declaration with a concussive strike of his fist against the glass table.

'Harold,' Schlam said sharply, 'come with me! If you ladies will excuse us, I need a moment to confer with my client.'

They straggled out like a timorous kid and a furious parent en route to the woodshed. After the door shut behind them, Lena sat back, smiled, and laced her hands behind her neck.

'Is there anything else you want me to put on the table? If you have a wish list, Maggie, now's the time.'

'Like Harold's head on a plate, you mean?'

Her grin was diabolical. 'That, we already have.'

'What then? What would I wish for?'

Her shoulders hitched. 'Don't know, but say the word, and it's yours. I've never seen Randy Schlam so pissed off. If this matter ever got to court, the judge would rip Harold up, and Schlam knows it. Their backs are to the wall.'

'All I want is what's fair, Lena. The law says that's a fifty-fifty split.'

'All may be fair in love and war, Maggie. But divorce is a whole different story. You have an advantage and you're well within your rights to use it.'

I eyed her sheepishly. 'Call me nuts, but I just want what's fair. I want that, and to get this over with. That's my wish list.'

She nodded firmly. 'Then that's how it's going to be.'

Sweet Parity

Even the most tumultuous divorce ends with neither a bang nor a whimper. What it came down to was the simple anti-climactic act of signing on the appropriate line. Harold and I signed our separation agreement before the lawyers and a notary, and a few weeks later, a divorce decree arrived in the mail. I looked it over, amazed at how light and insubstantial it was, and then I filed it away at the bottom of a drawer.

And that was that. Harold and I were a thing of the past. We had no more legal ties or obligations; in fact we were legally bound to go our separate ways. Strangely, getting the decree felt like a non-event. I didn't feel like celebrating or mourning. I guess I'd already done more than plenty of both. Instead, I headed out to my appointment at the Sun-

shine Studios in Queens, where Amelia Burkhart was scheduled to film Lady Di's final
scene.

Amelia greeted me warmly. 'Hi, Maggie.
Ready to go over today's loins?' OK, so she
sounded as she wished to most of the time,
but every so often she still slipped.

'Lines, you mean? Sure.'

'Lines,' she said. 'Lines, lines, lines. Damn
it. Why can't I stop messing up?'

'You will, Amelia. You're amazing now and
getting better all the time. Before you know
it, it's going to feel like second nature.'

There was a meek rapping on the dressing
room door. Marty Colossi, the film's famed
director, entered. He cast his adoring sights
on Amelia. 'How's my gorgeous star? Almost
ready to roll?'

'We were just going over the final monologue, Marty. I'll be right out.'

He turned to me. 'Can I speak with you
after you wrap up with Amelia, Maggie?'

'I have to get back to the office, but I guess
so, if it's quick.'

'Fine. We'll make it quick.'

After we finished our rehearsal, I walked
Amelia to make-up. Colossi's office was
directly across the way.

'Come in, come in, Maggie. Sit.'

I did, discomfited by his rare pleasantness,
trying to anticipate what he might be planning to fry me for, and in what kind of oil.

He folded his thick, hairy hands. 'I know
you're in a hurry, so I'll make this short and

to the point. I've seen what you've done with Amelia, and I'm completely blown away.'

'Thank you.'

'No, thank *you*! You saved my bacon on this. Casting her was a mistake that you turned into a triumph. You should see the dailies, she looks and sounds fabulous. I'll bet this will be the turning point in Amelia Burkhart's career, sex kitten to serious actress, thanks to you.'

'Amelia did the work, Mr Colossi.'

'Call me Marty. And don't bother with the bullshit. She could have worked till the cows came home and still sounded like one of them. You were the magic here, and I want that magic.'

'Excuse me?'

'On the team, I mean. I want you to come work for me, coach my stars. It was Amelia's idea, and I have to admit, it's brilliant.'

'That's flattering, but I can't give up my practice.'

'Sure you can. I'll double what you make in a year.'

'Sorry. There are clients who depend on me.'

He flapped at the air. 'OK, OK. I'll triple it. Plus full benefits and all expenses. Listen to me, kiddo. I want you on board, so name it, and I'll give you what you want.'

I caught his cool, calculating gaze. 'What I want is my independence.'

His eyes rolled. 'Christ. You drive a hard bargain. OK, how about this? You sign on as a consultant. I pay you a fat retainer, and you're available when I need you for a shoot.'

'With reasonable notice, so I can adjust my schedule?'

'Reasonable, sure.'

'How fat a retainer were you thinking?'

He wrote a number that was one hundred times higher than I'd dared to imagine. Still, somehow I refrained from shrieking with delight.

I stood, and we shook hands. 'Sounds like a deal.'

'Glad to have you on board, Maggie. You're really something else. If you play your cards right I predict you're going to make it huge.'

'This is big enough.'

'Not for someone with your talent. In fact, I was talking about you to a couple of people the other day at lunch. One guy was head of a major publishing house, and he thought you sounded like the perfect person to write a book that can help people sound their best. *The Voice of Success*, or something like that. He thinks it could be big.'

'Interesting.'

'That's not all. This other guy at the table does programming for a major cable network. He jumped right on it, said he thinks there should be a companion show. He'd have you do voice makeovers for people with accents they want to ditch, speech problems, stuff like that. There could be videos, a line of speech improvement aids. Sky's the limit.'

'Whoa. This is all a bit much.'

Marty stuck a fat cigar in his mouth and bit off the end. 'You're right, kid. One thing at a time. I'll have my lawyer draw up the agreement, and we'll get you signed on.'

The Swing and Eye

It's said things happen when you least expect them, and on this day, that's how it went. Valerie had a crucial order to fill, Brian was busy with an out-of-town client and Nanny Grace had suffered a flare-up of her chronic lazy-itis, so Delia and I were keeping each other company in the playground.

The slide was her latest fixation, and for the past hour, she had trudged up again and again for the fleeting thrill of the short glide down. My job was to watch and applaud each death-defying three-foot descent, which I did with admirable enthusiasm given that many of my brain cells had long since succumbed to lethal boredom and nodded off.

'Wook, Gammy. Wook!'

I wooked. Stuporous or not, I kept a keen eye on her, understanding that no matter how adorable and innocent they might seem, toddlers were the human equivalent of a loaded gun. You couldn't be too careful with them, or careful enough.

'Wook, Gammy!'

I must have blinked, or something similarly irresponsible, because when I fixed on her again, she was teetering at the top of the slide, about to fall backwards on to her head and trade her brilliant future as an astrophysicist, concert pianist and Olympic figure skating champion for a job scooping up elephant dung at the zoo.

'Sit, Delia. Get down!'

'Dow!' she chortled, tickled pink by my terror. 'Deeduh dow!'

'I mean it, young lady. Sit!'

'Wady thit!' She was giggling madly now, teetering like a duck pin at the top.

I raced over, grabbed her and set her on safe ground. Heart thwacking, I knelt to face her eye-to-eye. 'No standing on the slide, Delia. Understand?'

Her eyes went wide. 'No danda.'

'You have to sit on the slide. Understand?'

'Thit thide,' she said gravely.

'That's right. Good girl. I want you to play safely.'

She made a beeline for the slide again, and I watched smiling, confident that she would behave. And she did behave, like a loaded gun. She scrambled up the ladder and once again, stood wobbling at the top.

And again, I snatched her from the brink of disaster. 'That's it. No more slide.'

'Maw thide.'

'No more. You can go on the swing.'

This would have been a fine solution, except all the swings were occupied. This meant Delia had to wait patiently, and loaded guns are not known for their serenity. In fact, what loaded guns do, best of all, is whine. 'Wan fing. Deeduh wan fing NOW!'

'You have to wait, sweetie. It'll be your turn soon.'

'Wan thoon NOW!'

'I know. Try to be patient.'

'Wan fing.'

'I know.'

About six days later, or so it seemed, a little boy was plucked from one of the baby swings by his nanny. Delia raced headlong for the vacant treasure while it was still jerking in a wild, unpredictable arc.

'Delia NO!' I shrieked, as the swing zigged and she zagged, colliding with the metal bracket that fixed the seat to the chain. 'Oh my God!'

The impact knocked Delia backward. She landed on her rump and started to howl. Tears streamed down her face and mixed with the blood that gushed from the cut that had bloomed a breath away from her eye.

I picked her up, held her tightly, and raced down the block. Thankfully, just last week, Valerie had pointed out that this was the site of Delia's pediatrician's office. His name was Dr Ben Berwick, a great guy from Valerie's description, that they treasured as a doctor and a friend. The doorman directed me to an office down the hall.

By then, Delia had screamed herself hoarse. 'Shhh, baby. It's OK.'

Of course, it was anything but OK. It was my fault that this beautiful little girl had been hurt and quite possibly disfigured for life. I imagined cruel kids taunting, calling her scar face and worse. I imagined Brian and Valerie having me locked up for attempting to impersonate a responsible adult.

We were installed in an examining room, where I sat holding Delia on my lap. Soon, a tall, kindly looking man strode in. 'Hi, Delia. I hear you have a boo-boo to show me.' He smiled at me and extended a hand. 'I'm Ben Berwick. And you're?'

'Sorrier than you can imagine. I'm Maggie Strickland, Delia's granny. I should've watched her better. I should have moved faster. This was entirely my fault.'

'Take it easy, Maggie. She'll be fine.'

He took Delia from me, checked her over and cleaned the wound. Then he sealed the cut with a slim trail of glue.

'You don't use stitches?'

'No need. The surgical glue works better on little ones. It should heal nicely, without a scar.'

He applied a tiny bandage and set Delia down on her feet. 'There now. Good as new.'

'Bye bye, Docka Ben,' Delia said.

'Bye, Delia. Bye, Maggie. Say hello to Brian and Valerie for me.'

'Will do.'

'I'll check in later.'

'Thanks.'

Delia did seem fine, in fact. I took her

home, gave her lunch and settled her down for a nap. While she slept, I indulged in an orgy of guilty fretting. I continued to do so until Valerie came home. The sound of her key in the lock made me ill.

'What's wrong, Mom? You look so pale.'

'Valerie, I'm so sorry. I took Delia to the playground and she got hit in the face by a swing. It's all my fault. I wish I could just disappear.'

'Oh my. How is she? Where is she?'

'Taking a nap. She's all right. I took her to your friend Dr Berwick and he sealed the cut with surgical glue. He said it won't scar. But I'll never get over it, that's for sure. Will you ever forgive me?'

Her answer was a reassuring hug. 'Don't be silly, Mom. There's nothing to forgive. Kids fall and run into things and bump themselves all the time. It happens. All that matters is that everyone's all right.'

'I feel so terrible.'

'Well don't. It was an accident. It's not your fault at all.'

'Of course it is. Everything's my fault. Ask my mother.'

'Poor thing, you're all shaken up. Sit down and I'll make you a nice, relaxing cup of chamomile tea.'

'You're not mad at me? You don't hate me? Are you sure?'

'Of course not. You're the best. Now put your feet up and take it easy. I'll fix that tea.'

The phone rang while she was in the

kitchen. Valerie emerged moments later sporting a coy, little grin. 'It's Ben Berwick, Mom. He wants to talk to you.'

'Me?'

She nodded broadly and put her hand over the phone. 'He's a widower,' she said in a whisper. 'Bright as they come, and a total sweetheart. And so cute!'

'Why does he want to talk to me?'

'Only one way to find out.'

I braced for a safety lecture, at best. Maybe he'd thought it over and decided to press negligence charges. What I did not expect, not in my wildest imagining, was what he said.

'I was wondering if you might be free for dinner Friday night, Maggie.'

'Dinner?'

'Yes. There's a wonderful little French bistro I'd love to take you to.'

Valerie was prompting wildly, urging me to say yes. 'Sure, I guess that would work.'

'Great. All I need is your address. I'll pick you up at eight.'

The Grad You Date

As it turned out, Dr Ben and I had an astonishing amount in common. We'd grown up in adjacent towns, and we'd graduated two years apart from Cornell. Even spookier, it turned out that our fathers, both now deceased, had gone to high school together. My birthday was March ninth and his was on the seventh. Like me, he had an older daughter and younger son who sounded remarkably like Ali and Brian. We both loved mussels and shamelessly sopped up the garlic-laden broth with chunks of bread. We talked and laughed for hours and hours, as if we were dear old friends.

I was glad that I'd refused to succumb to a Janine and Daphne makeover, though Janine had conducted a mighty hard sell. Strangely, it felt way better to come as myself.

The time flew. When I looked around, I realized that everyone else, except the staff, had left. I caught a loaded look from one of the waiters. 'I think we'd better clear out before they put us up on the table and lock the doors.'

'I guess so,' he said. 'But I do hate for the evening to end, Maggie. It's been wonderful. I've enjoyed every minute.'

'I've enjoyed it too. Thanks for dinner.'

'My pleasure. Completely. How about doing it again tomorrow?'

'I can't tomorrow.'

'Sunday?'

'Maybe next week.'

He must have read the doubt in my expression. 'You're right. It's good to take things slowly, get to know each other.'

'I'll be completely honest with you, Ben. My most important job right now is getting to know myself.'

'You should. Your self is wonderful.'

'I don't feel ready to even think about getting into another relationship. Maybe I never will. It's going to take me some time to figure out who I am and where I'm headed.'

He nodded. 'Sounds fine to me. I'm all for living a step at a time, seeing where things go. But in the meantime, if you're up for it, let's have another dinner together sometime soon. I've really enjoyed your company.'

'And I've enjoyed yours. Sure, let's do that. Dinner sometime soon sounds just right.'

The Runt for Mid-October

Delia's second birthday celebration was at the Central Park Zoo. The day was glorious, and Delia was beside herself with joy.

'Ammuls!' she kept exulting. 'Ammuls!'

'You love the animals, don't you, cutes?' Valerie cleverly deduced.

My mother held her nose. 'Don't encourage her. Animals stink and go potty on the floor. Pee-you.'

'Ammuls nink! Wook a tie-guh. Tie-guh woah.'

'Yes, the tiger roars, boobly boo,' Brian crooned. 'And what does the lemur say?'

Delia looked puzzled. 'Meemuh?'

Brian flushed. 'Anyone know what sound a lemur makes?'

Harold did his classic contemptuous sniff, as if Brian had raised the dumbest issue in the world. 'Heh heh.'

'Actually, lemurs make an eerie, otherworldly sound, like ghosts, which is why the word lemur takes its name from the word for ghost in Malagasy, the language of Madagascar,' said Dr Ben.

Valerie's eyes bugged. 'Wow, Ben. You know everything.'

'Not at all. We all learn the things that

interest us. I think you and Brian are amazing for knowing so much about delicious desserts, Maggie is amazing for knowing so much about speech and language, Ali and Jon have an astonishing grasp of finance, and Pearl has it over all of us when it comes to expressing her feelings without reservation, don't you, Pearl?'

My mother beamed, despite the fact that the compliment was not exactly a compliment. Ben was the first person in recorded history to be able to wrap that crusty old bitch around his little finger. I admired him mightily for that, and so much more.

Harold harrumphed, outraged at being left out. 'And I'll claim the intellectual sphere, especially philosophy.'

'Sphere shmear,' my mother said. 'Let's face it, Harold, you're a big, obnoxious know-it-all like me.'

A wide grin bloomed on Brian's face. 'Heh heh.'

We stopped at the Leaping Frog Café, where Valerie had arranged for an organic lunch, followed by one of her company's cakes. The custom confection was a bright red Elmo in a chef's hat, holding a birthday cake. So it was a birthday cake within a birthday cake. Very profound, if you ask me.

Delia was manic with delight. 'Ew-mo! Ew-mo wook!' But then, when Brian started to cut the cake, she went wild. 'No cut Ew-mo. No!'

Valerie tried to soothe her while Brian set

off to arrange an alternative dessert. But she was still screaming when Janine showed up.

Janine held her ears and got in Delia's face. 'Cut out that mother ducking noise NOW!'

As if she'd hit the off switch, the baby went still. She stared at Janine in fascination as if she was yet another exotic zoo creature, which of course, she was.

'That's better. Where's the booze?'

'There is no booze, Janine. This is a two-year-old's birthday.'

'Jiminy Christ, Maggie. Won't you ever learn? Birthday equals party, and party equals drinks. Lucky I came prepared.' She dipped into her giant tote bag and pulled out a bottle of Cristal champagne and a sleeve of plastic flutes. 'We have to toast the little rug rat after all.'

Jon popped the cork and Harold poured. When he got to Ali, she set a hand over her glass.

'Not celebrating?' Harold said.

Ali smiled shyly, and Jon took her hand. 'Actually, we are. We're celebrating Delia's birthday and her new cousin's, which will be on or about next October 15th.'

I felt the sting of happy tears. 'Oh, sweetie. You mean it? How wonderful!'

'Isn't it? We're so excited,' Ali said.

Jon kissed her hand. 'We're over the moon.'

'What's that Jewish thing, Bri? Model tub?' Valerie asked.

'*Mazel tov*. It means good luck.'

'So a big, hearty model tub,' Valerie said.

318

'That's so great!'

'Another baby,' said my mother. 'Oy.'

'Come on, Granny Pearl,' Valerie coaxed. 'I can see you're excited too.'

'Excited, my *tuchas*. And don't get any smart ideas. I won't sit and I won't knit, no matter how many babies you kids crank out.'

'That goes double for me,' Janine said. 'I'm with you, Pearl. Babies, yuck.'

'I'll sit and knit all you like,' said Valerie. 'It'll be such fun to have our kids grow up together. I bet they'll be wonderful friends.'

Ben raised his glass with a meaningful look toward me. 'To wonderful friends and joyous occasions.'

I raised mine as well. 'Amen. I must say, right now I feel like the luckiest woman in the world.'

My mother sniffed. 'Don't talk like that, Maggie, for heaven's sake. You talk like that you'll get the evil eye.'

'I'm happy, Mom. Happy is good.'

'Don't be ridiculous. And look how you're sitting. How many times do I have to tell you: don't shlump!'